I love God.
I love words.
I love God's words.

Come with me on a journey of faith and imagination.
See you at the end. ~Lori

Visit our website at:
www.SinclairInkSpot.com
www.Sinclair-Publishing.com
www.prizinofzin.com

Sinclair, 2014, 2016

The PriZin of Zin

What is *your* prison?
Can you set yourself free?
How far would you go,
to help free another?

Sinclair, 2014, 2016

Hebrews 13:2, NIV
Do not forget to show hospitality to strangers,
for in doing so,
some have shown hospitality to angels
without knowing it.
†

<u>Zin</u>: *A Biblical middle-eastern desert, a wilderness,*
a barren wasteland, an unsettled area
thought to be uninhabitable by humankind.

Loretta Sinclair
Sinclair Publishing

Sinclair, 2014, 2016

Clan Sinclair motto, origins to 1068 a.d.

ISBN 13: 978-0-9916159-7-1
ISBN 10: 0-9916159-7-1
Library of Congress Catalog Card Number: pending
Sinclair Publishing
P.O. Box 2052
Rancho Cordova, CA 95741-2052

Sinclair, 2014, 2016

Chapter 1: Hunter
hunt·er - *noun* \ˈhən-tər\: One that searches for something.

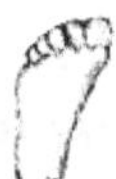

His finger twitched on the trigger, but didn't pull. Morgan stared through the scope mounted on his rifle and into the brush at his prey standing on the other side. There he was. The biggest eight-point buck he'd ever seen. The animal stood in the glen, tall and proud. It had no idea its head would end up as a trophy on some human's wall, stuffed and staring through glass eyes for all eternity; a testament to one man's hunting ability.

"Quick! Hide! Maybe we can lose the little pain-in-the-butt." Ian burst into the thick brush and crouched behind a large bush. He peered through the dark green leaves back at Hunter. Raising his index finger to his lips, he motioned for his friend to be quiet.

"No," Hunter said. "We can't leave her."

"Why?"

"Because she's my little sister— she's only ten."

"So?" Ian shrugged at Hunter's lack of response. "I don't know why she had to come along anyway. She'll just ruin everything. Girls always do."

"Hunter! Ian! Where are you?"

"See." Ian jumped back out. "Shut up, stupid! You'll scare all the animals away."

"I am not stupid!" Aeryn turned to face her brother's best friend. "And if you had any intelligence whatsoever you would know that, if you hadn't run away from me, I wouldn't have to call you to stop, therefore *not* scaring the animals away." She stood her ground, feet firmly planted, unmoving, face upwards toward her taller opponent. "It's all *your* fault."

"And if *you*," Ian loomed over her, "had any intelligence whatsoever, you would know when you are out in the woods hunting, you have to be *quiet. Stop screaming*!" Ian inched closer to her, bulking up his height as much as he could.

"Don't leave me again," Aeryn demanded. "Or else."

"Or else what?"

"Or else, Ian. I mean it. I will not play your childish games. And if you think - - -"

"Stop it!" Hunter snapped. "You're both making too much noise."

"Shut up Hunter. You're not in charge." Ian turned on his friend now. "You don't even know what you're doing."

"Yes, I do." His face flushed.

"Oh, really? Then where's your dad?"

Hunter squirmed. His eyes darted from the trees to the ground and back again, searching for any sign of his father. His palms began to sweat, but he dared not wipe them. Ian and Aeryn could not know they were lost. Hunter could feel his heart racing. Dizzy, head spinning, he staggered, but just one step. What had he gotten them into?

"You're no big game hunter, you just think you are," Ian laughed. "Just 'cause your dad can hunt deer and elk doesn't mean you can."

"Yes, I can."

"Yeah? Then do it."

"I will."

"Go ahead and find one— just one. I dare ya."

Hunter looked around, trying to decide which way to go. He hesitated just a split second, but it was too late.

"Go ahead," Ian taunted. "I'll just wait here with the little sissy."

"I am not a sissy! I'm warning you, Ian."

Sinclair, 2014, 2016

"Shut up!"

Morgan blinked hard, trying to focus his blurred vision through the thick morning mist. *Wait. He's gone.* He shifted slightly from his hiding place in the low brush. *Was that real? Did I really see— Yes, there he is.* He took aim again.   Morgan kept his gun trained on his trophy, his finger still twitching on the trigger.

It was unseasonably warm. His nose filled with misty morning dew with each breath, making it run. He dared not move to wipe it. There was a slight rustle in the bushes to his side, but Morgan remained taut. He kept his gun trained on his eight-point prize.

The deer heard the rustle, too, and froze. It raised its head, huge rack hoisting in the air, and turned toward the noise. Nervous eyes darted from one spot to another in the dense brush, then settled on the spot where Morgan lay, staring straight at him, unmoving. Morgan stared back, stunned. He couldn't believe his eyes. He released the trigger, pulled back from the scope on the rifle, wiping his nose and rubbing his face. He put his eye back up against the scope again, and stared back into the impossible;

purple eyes. It was a deer with dark, royal purple eyes. What kind of genetic mutation was this, he wondered, taking a firm grip on the trigger again. Bracing the barrel against his shoulder, Morgan tried to contain his excitement. The crosshairs of the gun scope trained on the chest of the large deer, centering near its heart. It's one of a kind, he thought, a purple-eyed, eight-point buck; one of a kind. He squared his shoulder and seated the rifle hard against himself.

One deep breath, and hold—

The rustle to his side turned into a crash. Morgan swung the gun to his left and tried to take aim at the noise, but saw nothing clearly.

"Stop," someone squealed— a female voice; a small female voice.

"Shhhh," shot the harsh reply, but it was too late. The buck bolted from its feeding spot and disappeared in a flash into the dense underbrush.

Morgan turned in his fury toward the intruders who took from his grasp his once-in-a-lifetime prize. "Who's there?" he demanded.

There was no reply.

"Come out!" The brush rustled and parted as three young figures emerged.

Sinclair, 2014, 2016

Morgan looked down into the faces of his two children, and their friend.

"You said you were going to get a Bigfoot," Hunter said. "I've never seen one, Dad."

"That's because there's no such thing. Bigfoot isn't real." Morgan clicked the safety on his weapon and lowered it.

"They do so exist," Ian huffed. "I saw one once. He was watching me through my bedroom window."

Morgan glared at Ian, but said nothing.

"Then why did you say you were going to get one?" Hunter turned away.

"Why do you have to shoot animals, Dad?" Aeryn looked up at her father. He hated those pleading eyes. She didn't even need to say what was on her mind. He could see her disappointment written all over her face.

"I hunt for meat, Aeryn. You know that."

"Can you eat a Bigfoot?" she asked.

"Yeah, sure. I hear they taste like chicken," Ian snickered. "Hey, if there's more than one do they call them Bigfeet?"

"There's no such thing as a Bigfoot." Morgan shot a sharp glare at his son's close friend. "Does your father know you're out here?"

"He knows I spent the night at your house."

"And you don't think he would be upset about you wandering around the forest with hunters shooting all around you?"

"Oh, not at all, Mr. Welch," Ian smiled. "He trusts you to always take good care of me." The lilt of sarcasm and glint in Ian's eye was unmistakable.

Morgan turned back to his own two children, Hunter and Aeryn. "You three should not be out here. It's dangerous."

"Then why are you here, Dad?" Aeryn was pouting now.

"Because, I'm a trained outdoorsman." Morgan sat down and beckoned his daughter to his side. He put his arms around her. "I'm perfectly safe out here because I know how to take care of myself in the wild. You and your brother don't. You shouldn't be out here unless you're with an experienced hunter."

"I do so know how to take care of myself. I took the hunter's safety class last summer."

"That's for gun safety, Hunter, not safety in the wild. You still have a lot to learn."

Sinclair, 2014, 2016

Hunter clenched his jaw and turned away, eyes flaring. Morgan could see he was incensed. He would have to deal with this later. "Come on," he motioned to the kids. "Let's get back home. The sun's almost up. It'll be breakfast time soon."

Morgan turned back to the clearing where the buck had stood only minutes before. "I'll be back later," he whispered. "I'll see you again."

"Did you see that big buck, Mr. Welch?"

"Yes, Ian, I did."

"It had *huge* antlers. How many points were there?"

"Eight," he sighed. "It was an eight-point buck." Morgan looked back at the kids. "It's starting to rain. Let's get back before we're all soaked."

"I like the rain, Daddy," Aeryn smiled. She threw her arms straight out to her sides and twirled in the drizzle, batting the droplets away like tiny baseballs. Morgan kept walking. He didn't want them to see his disappointment about missing his prize. The small cloudburst in the distance began to turn dark. Lightning broke free and tore open the sky, but it was still way off. There was time to get home before the storm got too bad.

"Did you see its eyes, though?" Ian pressed. "There was something strange about them."

"This slope is very slick," Morgan said, reaching back to help his daughter. "Be careful, those leaves are wet."

"What do you think spooked it, Dad?" Hunter asked.

Morgan turned and looked into his son's face. "I don't know, son," he lied, trying to spare Hunter's feelings. He started to inch his feet down the slope, then stopped. Reaching out, Morgan put his arm around Hunter's squared shoulder. "Let's come back for him later, together." Hunter smiled and nodded. Seeing his only son's smile somehow lessened the blow of losing the prize. There would be another day.

Morgan planted his feet firm on the ground, then turned back to help the kids. "I want you all holding on to each other going down the side of this mountain. It's very slick."

The three kids all looked at each other. Aeryn reached out to take her brother's hand. He batted it away. At his father's sharp glare, Hunter grabbed the back of her jacket left-handed and held tight instead. Ian grabbed Aeryn's jacket, and Hunter, right-handed, grabbed Morgan's. Morgan took the lead.

Sinclair, 2014, 2016

He stepped out. Lightning tore open the sky once again, directly overhead. Thunder roared on its heels, shaking the ground below. The flash of light was so bright it stunned his eyes. Morgan blinked to focus. The rain pelted them harder now, running in a torrent beneath their feet and down the mountainside like a small river. The earth rumbled beneath their feet, but this time there was no lightning or thunder to accompany it. The rumbling continued, rolling the mountaintop, first one direction then another.

"Earthquake!" Ian screamed as another violent wave of the ground hit beneath him.

"Look out!" Morgan yelled jerking his son toward him as a tree fell behind them. Hunter lurched forward, pulling the other two along with him toward the edge of the mountaintop. Hunter teetered on the edge, staring down at the world giving way beneath him, but Morgan's strong grip held him tight. More trees toppled and crashed around them, some of them slipping over the edge and sliding, like a swift toboggan, out of sight down the steep embankment.

"Nobody move!" Morgan yelled through the driving rain. "Stay tight."

"Is it over now?" Aeryn asked. "Daddy, I'm scared."

Sinclair, 2014, 2016

"I don't know," Morgan answered. "Everyone stay close." The four huddled together in the rain. Morgan felt his son's hard grip against the back of his jacket. He held the rifle tight against his body. Lightning and thunder ripped the sky open as the four clung together in the storm perched atop the cliff's edge. The earth shook again with the booming force of the thunder. Aeryn squealed and pressed closer to the others, inching them toward the precarious edge. Morgan dug his heels in, keeping the group on safe ground.

The earth gave another ear-shattering roar accompanied by a violent roll, causing the group to teeter on the edge again. Clinging to each other, they held fast. When the roar of the earth stopped, the roll beneath their feet continued. Morgan looked down to see the edge of the cliff where they stood give way beneath their feet. "Hold on!" he screamed as they all barreled forward, down the side of the mountain.

The four slid faster and faster, rolling over and over down the steep mountain trail in the rush of the whitewater, brush, and rocks slapping and biting at them every inch of the way. Morgan somehow managed to maneuver his body so that his feet were forward, as though he were on a water slide. Rifle lost somewhere along the path, he held tight to Hunter, with the others all clinging in tow like a human chain. The earth continued to quake beneath them violently. Through the rain and mud, Morgan saw the earth tear a giant crevasse directly ahead. They reached the bottom of the mountain and launched forward into the giant canyon.

With one final roar, the earth closed the hole, sealing the four in their dark, wet, doom.

Sinclair, 2014, 2016

Chapter 2: Lost
Lost *adj* \ˈlȯst\: no longer known

The absolute black of the cavern surrounded them as father and children all fell spinning around and around in the giant hole. With no sense of gravity and no light to see, Morgan only knew down by the direction they were falling. His only reference for himself and the others was the sound of their screams echoing off the slick slate walls of the crater they were now engulfed in. Swallowed whole... eaten alive... the four plunged downward for what seemed an eternity, until they finally crashed through a thin, brittle landing, splashing down hard into a rapid underground stream.

Swept away in a roller coaster ride of white water rapids, Morgan barely had a chance to breathe before being sucked under water and dragged downstream. Kicking and flailing his arms, he tried to swim against the raging tide, but it was useless. Both he and the children were all swept away in the powerful current. Unable to scream any longer, he fought against the rage of nature

Sinclair, 2014, 2016

just to keep his head above water and stay alive, each breath a small battle won in this war for their very lives.

Off in the distance, through the splash of the water and the echoes from the mammoth rock walls, he caught a faint flicker of light. It came from the direction they were headed. Wanting to call out to the others but unable to, he clung to the anticipation there might be a way out of this doom. Trying to relax and let the water carry him and the others toward the possibility of safety, Morgan hung with desperation on to the only thing he had left... hope.

Reaching what appeared to be the source of light, any false security Morgan had was once again shattered as the stream of rapids abruptly ended. The four now burst forward, first into thin air, then again plunging downward over an enormous waterfall. Dropping through hundreds of feet of water and air in mere seconds, Aeryn let out a deafening scream that echoed throughout the entire cavern. Reaching the bottom, the group splashed with tremendous force into the warm, soothing waters of a peaceful and tranquil pool in this underworld realm.

Coming up for air, the four gasped and choked until they were able to catch their breath. Clinging to each other for support, they floated in this new serene and picturesque land.

"Where are we?" Aeryn whispered.

Sinclair, 2014, 2016

One by one, Morgan dragged the children from the water and over to the sandy shore. Exhausted and scared, the kids all floated in the warm comfort of the underground hot spring, letting Morgan carry them to safety. He carefully checked each child for scrapes and broken bones as they were extricated from the water.

Dripping wet, sand clinging to her bare legs below her shorts, Aeryn stood and surveyed this strange new world, while the others sat motionless on the shore. It took a few minutes for them to speak.

"Where are we?" Aeryn asked for the second time.

Ian and Hunter shook their heads.

"It's beautiful." She looked at the thick, lush vegetation and a multitude of brightly colored flowers. "Wow. And where is the light coming from?" She turned around, looking for the source of the reddish glow illuminating the entire cavern.

"There," Morgan said. He pointed back across the water from where they'd come.

There across the lake was a bubbling, boiling mound of molten lava flowing down from its source higher up. It hissed and spit while churning its contents over and over again in the huge pit.

"It's a volcano," Ian said.

"Close," Morgan jumped in. "It's the bottom of a volcano. The top is up there," his finger extended upward toward their homeland, "where we were hunting. That's why the water is so warm. It's like a hot spring down here." He sniffed the air, taking in the heavy smell of sulfur. "This is an underground river."

"And how do we get back up there?" Hunter asked, pointing upward like his father had done.

"Good question."

"Maybe we could ask someone," Aeryn said.

"Ask someone?" Ian shot at her. "Ask someone? Who do you want to ask? Look around! There's no one here, in case you didn't notice!"

"Don't yell at her," Hunter jumped in. "Besides, you don't know. *We're* down here, aren't we?"

Ian snorted and jerked his head around.

"Just look," Aeryn kept going, unfazed. "There's vegetation, a whole forest over there, and a lake." She looked up toward what should be the sky. A rock ceiling and slick, gray, slate walls locked them away from their own world above. Floating as high as it could without escaping through the makeshift roof, was a fine mist rising

Sinclair, 2014, 2016

from the warm water of the hot spring. It glistened from the light of the volcano, illuminating the entire sky like clouds in sunshine. "There's oxygen, water, light, heat, and shelter. What else do people need to survive?"

"Um, food," Hunter said dryly.

"I'll bet there's food in the forest." She turned and walked toward the thick vegetation.

"Be careful," Hunter blurted out. "Don't go in there."

"I'm not going in, I'm just going to look and see- - - EEEEHHHH!" Her scream jolted the others. It was followed by another of equal intensity, but not from her.

Ian bounded to his feet and was at her side in an instant. Hunter and Morgan followed suit.

Looking around for the source of the second scream, Ian peered through the bushes and there he saw a little pair of frightened green eyes looking back at him. Gently, he pulled some of the underbrush back to reveal a tiny creature, man-like in stature and characteristics, but very, very small. It stood only two feet tall.

"What is it?" Aeryn asked, pulling more brush back so she could see better.

"EEEEHHHH!" came the shrieking reply from the little thing.

"I don't know," Ian answered. "But I think- - -"

"EEEEHHHH!"

"I think it's a- - -"

"EEEEHHHH!"

"- - -Troll."

"I am not a Troll ye eedjit," the creature snapped back, openly irritated. "I'm a Leprechaun. Learn the difference."

"You can speak?" Aeryn stared, eyes mesmerized by the tiny creature.

"O' course, I can speak. Can't ye?" it sighed.

Taken aback by the question, Aeryn stared back into the severely aged face of this tiny person. Dressed in a dark green suit and floppy, pointed hat, the creature looked like it could be a hundred years old. Skin like leather hung loose and wrinkled over his sagging face with two tired little eyes peering out from under its slouched hat.

"Why did you scream?" Hunter asked.

"'Cause the wee lassie did, when ye flew down from the world above, and nobody better call me a Troll!" it snapped. "Trolls 're mean. Gnomes 're stupid. I am a Leprechaun. Don't ferget it."

"I won't. I'm sorry," Hunter said.

"I am Alastair."

"I didn't mean to hurt your feelings. I was just—"

Sinclair, 2014, 2016

"I know what ye were doin'," it snapped again. "Ye're jus' like all the others."

"Others?" Morgan jumped, grasping at the tiny glimmer of hope. "There are others? Like us?"

Alistair nodded. "Happens sometimes. When the sun gets angry."

"The sun?"

A crooked little finger extended and pointed at the volcano bottom. "When mother sun becomes angry and shakes, beings from the above-world fall through."

"Do they ever find their way back home?" Hunter asked from behind the group.

Alistair nodded. "Some."

Hunter waited for Alastair to continue. The two watched each other in a long, deafening silence, looking each other up and down. "How?" Hunter asked when no answer came.

Alistair shook his little head and shrugged. "Evil knows. The serpents and shadows go up there often, but cannot ask them. Too dangerous. Should not know ye are here."

"Is there any other way?" Morgan pushed.

"Yup," the leprechaun answered again.

Silence again.

"How?"

Alistair shrugged. "Need to ask another."

"Another? There are others?" Hunter sighed.

He nodded.

"Is there any food around?" Aeryn asked.

Alastair grimaced. "There," he pointed.

"What on earth is that?" Aeryn asked. She ran toward the forest.

"STOP HER!" the leprechaun screamed. "She must know!"

Aeryn stopped in her tracks and looked back.

"Must know what?" Ian was by her side.

"Danger. Near." Alistair's beady little eyes darted around frantically.

"Where?" Morgan's eyes followed suit. Alistair's prickly little finger spun around in a circle, and pointed directly at the four standing in front of him. "What?" Morgan was incensed. "What are you talking about?" The finger came straight at Morgan's nose.

"Sometimes the closest danger lives inside."

"You're crazy!"

"Spirit knows." Alistair twitched, but kept scanning the grounds.

"What spirit?"

"Both. Yours and His." He lowered his little leprechaun hand.

"His? Whose? And what does that have to do with us finding food?"

"Choices. Good choices bring good favor. Bad choice…" Alistair shuddered. "Purple is for Him. Ye must never, ever take it."

"Who is him?" Ian asked.

"Him, not him. The One. But not just one. He is them."

"What does that mean?" Ian sighed and looked to Morgan for clarification.

Morgan shrugged.

"Ye understand 'leader'?"

"You have a leader?" Aeryn asked.

"Yup," Alastair said. "The three are the One. They are Them. Ask Him, not him. Only Them."

"They?" Morgan asked, confused. "That doesn't make any sense."

"What's he like?" Hunter pressed. "I mean They?"

"He is good," the leprechaun went on. "They will care for ye. Protect ye from the other one."

"There's another one?"

"Evil." The leprechaun shook in fear at the mention of his name. "Must never venture into the forbidden forest without a guide. Danger inside might be let out. Choices to make. Will be hard. Understand?"

Sinclair, 2014, 2016

The three younger travelers all looked to Morgan. He shrugged and struck out toward the forest after Aeryn.

"I won't go in," he said. "I just want to look, from the edge."

"Promise," the leprechaun demanded. "Bad things will happen if ye do not obey."

"I promise," he said grudgingly. "Only looking. Never purple. Got it."

"About the others of our kind," Ian asked, "you don't know how they got out of here?"

"No, mus' find out. Wait here. I be return." Without waiting for a reply, the tiny creature turned toward the underbrush and vanished, leaving the four alone again on the shore.

"What's in there, Dad?" Hunter tried to peer over the edge of the forest.

"It looks like a garden. I see strawberries, and greens. I think there's celery, lettuce, and watermelons.

"I'm hungry, Daddy."

"I know, sweetie. Just hold on till I make sure it's safe in there."

Sinclair, 2014, 2016

"We're going in?" Ian jumped. "Awesome!"

"But, Dad, Alistair said not to go in."

Morgan looked at his daughter. "I know, honey, but we won't touch anything. There's a path that goes right through the middle. We should be okay if we stay on it."

"Where does the path lead?" Hunter asked, still leaning forward.

"Looks like a giant tree right in the middle. I'm not really sure, Hunter. It looks a little odd."

"Odd, how?"

"Can't really tell. Everybody stay close to me."

"That's not a tree," Ian said.

"It's got branches like a tree." Hunter reached out to touch the bark, but Ian batted his hand away.

"Careful, man. I don't want to lose my best friend."

"You're not going to lose me. I just want to know what it is."

"What kind of tree has a mirror in the middle of the trunk?" Aeryn was mesmerized.

Sinclair, 2014, 2016

"It didn't grow like that. Someone, or something, created that." Morgan stared at his reflection. "Something intelligent, and very, very creative."

"Do not leave the path," a velvety smooth voice cautioned.

"Ok, Dad." The three kids all looked at Morgan.

"What?" Morgan turned around.

"We heard you," Hunter answered.

"I didn't say anything," Morgan whispered, turning back to the tree.

Aeryn squeezed in front of her father and looked into the mirror. The sky twinkled and the mirror lit up, reflecting her beautiful, smiling face.

"Do you trust me?" It was the same calm, soothing voice as before.

"I don't know who you are," she answered.

"That is very true. I am here to help you, if you choose it. What do you need?"

"I'm hungry. Can I please have some food?"

The tree shook, flapping its branches almost like a bird. When it settled, the limbs were laden with food. Not just fruit, but food from home: granola bars, candy, apple pie, roast chicken platters. There were bottled drinks of every size and flavor, and a water spout flowing at the other end. A rainbow of fruits and nuts covered every vacant spot in the tree. In the middle was a giant prime rib roast with all the fixings.

Aeryn's eyes lit up. "How can I get it if I can't leave the path?" The tree bowed low, and the branches came within her reach. She and the boys all helped themselves. When she uttered her 'thank you' the tree returned to its original height, shuddered, and the food disappeared. "You have done well, young Aeryn."

The tree turned on its roots and looked at Hunter. "Do you believe in yourself?"

Hunter froze, unable to answer. He opened his mouth to speak, but nothing came out. Palms sweaty and fingers shaking, he nodded unsteadily.

"You don't have to go through life alone. There are others out there who can assist you, if you will only let them. The choice is yours. Have faith in what you cannot see."

Hunter nodded again, seeing a tear at the corner of his eye forming in his mirrored reflection.

"What about me?" Ian jumped in, shoving Hunter to the side. "My turn now."

"Ah yes, young man. Are you having fun?"

Ian nodded. "What's next?"

"That depends on you." Ian's reflection in the mirror wavered and two paths appeared. "Two roads will show you two different possibilities. Learn to control what flares up inside, and the right path will make itself known.

"What's that supposed to mean?" Ian's face flushed and his fists balled.

The tree spun back around and faced Morgan again.

"I can't believe this," he whispered.

"Open your mind, and your heart to see all that life is truly about, Master Morgan."

"How do you know my name - our names?"

"Look into your soul, Morgan. What do you see?"

In front of him, on the glass embedded in the impossible tree, Morgan saw scenes from his life flash by. School as a child, playing, homework, graduating, college, getting married, holding his children. One memory flashed by, replaced by another, strung together with him as the center.

"What do you see?"

"Just me," Morgan answered. "My life."

"And so you shall remain. Until you can learn to see life as these young ones do, you will forever be a prisoner inside yourself, Master Morgan. Learn to see the impossibilities around you. Look outside of yourself." The tree shook again, and the mirror disappeared. It blossomed one more time with a rainbow of fruit; peaches, grapes, apples, strawberries. Low-hanging

Sinclair, 2014, 2016

branches offered fruit of every kind, albeit strangely colored for its type. Reds, blues, greens, yellows, purples, and oranges of all shades adorned the branches.

"Let's go, kids. This was no help at all." Morgan turned to leave, guiding the kids up in front of him. "He's useless." Stomach rumbling, Morgan turned back. He dashed from the path and circled the tree, grabbing fruit of every kind for his trip. "Who knows how long we'll be down here, with help like that."

"That was the most delicious apple I have ever eaten. I didn't realize how hungry I was," Aeryn said. She tossed the core off into the brush a few feet from the shore. Startled by a rustling and flapping sound, she turned back to see another small creature with long, slender wings swoop down and take off with the apple core in its mouth. "Look!" she squealed. "It's a bird."

"That's not a bird," Morgan said. "It's got the body of a squirrel, but with wings."

"It's a squird," Ian added, chuckling.

They smiled, watching the small thing fly away with its prize between its teeth.

Ian was next to try. Tossing his apple core off a short distance away, another squird swooped down from the treetops, scooped up the leftovers, and flew back up to its perch.

Morgan tossed his away and waited. No animals came. "I guess they didn't see it," he said.

"Maybe you need to toss it again." Aeryn ran to the discarded core, bent over to pick it up, and froze. Standing straight up, she spun around and stared back at him, eyes wide and in shock.

"What is it?" Hunter asked, running to his sister's side. "What's wrong?"

"It's purple," she whispered.

"What?"

"It's purple," she said louder, her voice cracking and shaking. "Dad ate a purple apple."

"What?" Hunter yelled. "Why?" he demanded spinning to face him. "You heard what the leprechaun said!"

"Relax," Morgan said. "I wanted to taste it. I've never had a purple apple before." He smiled, "and look, nothing bad has happened to me. The little runt didn't know what he was talking about. I didn't die."

Morgan looked down into his daughter's tearful glare. She grabbed the arm of her big brother for support.

Ian backed away as well, standing next to the other two. Huddled together in a tight group, they scanned the area, eyes darting every direction. Seeing their rising panic, Morgan tried to talk to them.

"Oh, come on, you guys. Look. It's just an apple—and a very good one, at that. I've never tasted anything like it before. I might just have another one. You guys should try one, too."

"I don't think it's a good idea, Dad," Hunter cautioned. "We don't know anything about this world."

"Well, I do know one thing," he said, "apples are just as juicy and sticky down here as they are up there." Morgan strolled back a few yards down to the water line and bent to wash his hands and face. Splashing the warm water on himself, he rinsed off the remnants of the snack, then stood and looked back at the others. "Don't be such chickens. I told you nothing bad—"

A giant sea serpent burst through the water's surface and hovered over him, showering Morgan with a sudden spray of saliva mixed with warm water. He looked straight up to see a long snout with giant nostrils breathing smoke and flame looming above him. A wicked snarl was wrapped across its ugly face, razor-like teeth protruding from under loose floppy jowls. The enormous snake had a red, diamond-shaped head with horns, and knife-like

Sinclair, 2014, 2016

scales covering the length of its back all the way along the spine, disappearing into the warm tranquil water. It growled at Morgan, a low vibrating rumble that shook both the water and the sand on the beach where they stood.

Morgan opened his mouth to scream, but nothing came out. Wanting to run, but unable to move, Morgan, locked in time and fear, stared straight into the face of horror.

Striking like the wind, the serpent swooped down, snatching Morgan in its mouth and slithered back down into the water in the blink of an eye. The three friends stood terrified and alone on the shore.

The only sign that evil had even been there were the lapping waves on the beach and, in its wake, two empty footprints.

Sinclair, 2014, 2016

Chapter 3: Search

Search *verb* \ˈsərch\ transitive verb: to examine in seeking
something

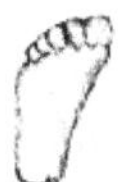

Thunder boomed once again through the new world, and the sky went as dark as night. There was no lightning, but again and again the thunder roared around them. In the distance, the faint light from the volcano bottom shone. Rather than the crimson glow it offered just moments before, this was a dark foreboding phosphorescent light. Below the volcano, in the once tranquil pool, water caught in the raging turbulence of a violent boil, steam rising with urgent fervor, locked in by the stone ceiling above. Thunder boomed again, shaking the ground under their feet with all the force of the earthquake that landed them here just a short time before.

"How dare you!" the thunder roared. "You were warned!"

Hunter, Ian, and Aeryn all looked around for the source of the voice. They saw no one.

"Does your kind never learn?"

"Who are you?" Hunter asked, eyes darting back and forth for some signs of life.

"I Am."

"You are what?"

"Silence!" the voice boomed back even more loudly, and more menacing than before. "I speak!"

Ian spun around. "There," he whispered, "the food tree."

"I am dead. Nevermore shall I bear fruit because of you," the tree said.

Ian, Hunter, and Aeryn all looked up at the massive wooden monolith before them. It had grown four times in size, and now a giant green eye glared at them from the center of its trunk. The eye blinked at them, pupil moving from one child to another, and back again, splinters dropping to the ground with each motion. Its branches now dry and brittle, leaves dead and falling.

"Please," Aeryn cried. "Where is my father?"

"Gone. You have foolishly unleashed the powers of those who will devour your essence; the ones who seek to extinguish your spark for all eternity. Only you now have the power to leash them again."

"Where? Please tell me where?"

The eye crackled and blinked again. "Nowhere."

Sinclair, 2014, 2016

All three stared in silence as the tree continued to grow and die at the same time.

"Your father is neither here nor there," the tree said. "He is not lost, but neither is he found. He is nowhere."

"Nowhere?" Ian asked. "Where is nowhere?"

"A place of nothingness. A barren wasteland with no future. He has gone to the wilderness."

"Can we find him?" Aeryn pleaded.

"You can find him," the tree thundered, "but escape is his and his alone. You can only lead. He alone must choose his path."

"How can I lead if I don't know the way?" Hunter tried to ask.

"Silence!" the tree boomed again. "Listen, and you will know. Hear, and you will understand. Seek, and you will find. You must all choose wisely from this moment on. To not choose wisely will mean certain death. You will all be sent to the place of no return. You will be thrown forever into the darkness of the Pit of Despair. It will then be too late. For now, there is still time. Knock and the door will open."

Snapping sounds crackled and popped around them. Branches began to break off and fall to the ground like monstrous spears. The giant tree listed dangerously to one side. The more it leaned, the more the trunk broke, the fibers of wood giving way under the enormous weight. It slowly began to fall in one painful, final, death throe.

"Please! Please," Aeryn cried, running toward the tree. "Where is my father? Where is the wilderness?"

"The prison," the tree echoed as it fell. "Beware of the Spark Eaters!" it wailed, timbers snapping in two.

"What is this place called?" Hunter screamed.

Seconds before it hit the ground with an earthshaking roar, the tree uttered one single word.

"Zin."

"I don't think he's coming back."

"He said he'd come back," Aeryn turned to Hunter. "We just need to be patient."

"He's not coming back." Hunter snapped. "The little green monster left us here."

"He's not a monster. He said he was a leprechaun." Aeryn looked around.

"I know," Ian shot back from the dark shore. "He's Alastair." The sarcasm in his voice was unmistakable.

"Maybe we should look for him."

"Where?" Ian screamed at Aeryn. "The bushes he disappeared into are gone, thanks to your father. That tree killed everything. There's nothing here now. Everything's dead here, including him."

Aeryn burst into tears. She tried to speak, but couldn't.

"Stop it, Ian, or else." Hunter was at his sister's side.

"Or else, what?" Ian squared off against his long-time friend. "What are you gonna do?"

Hunter turned and put his arm around his crying sister.

"Oh, you gonna be a chicken now? Gonna hide like a little girl?" Ian's anger flared. "Come on, rich boy, don't turn your back on me." Ian shoved Hunter's shoulder. At the lack of any response, he shoved again, harder.

"Stop it, Ian!" Hunter screamed. He wheeled around to face his friend head-on, and froze.

It was faint, but he heard it. The others looked around too. Hunter paused, waiting to see if he could hear it again.

Nothing.

"Push me again," Hunter whispered. He looked at Aeryn. "Cry."

Ian reared back and shoved Hunter so hard he fell to the ground. Aeryn wailed and threw her hands up to her

Sinclair, 2014, 2016

face. Ian dove on top of Hunter and the two rolled around in the wet sand for a moment, while Aeryn, ever the drama queen, sobbed on the sidelines. Then, they all stopped.

There it was again.

Laughter! Someone was watching them. Watching, and laughing.

All three bolted toward the dead food tree where the noise was coming from. They split up to surround the trunk from all sides. Hunter was the first to clear the limbs. As they rounded the backside, there was the little green leprechaun, rolling in hysterics on the ground. Hunter grabbed the tiny creature, making sure he did not get away.

"Nnnnooooo!" he screamed, his merry little mirth changing to fear. "Ye can't have me treasure." He fought against Hunter's tight grip. "Ye can't have it, I sayz!"

Ian caught up and threw himself into the mix, pinning the old man to the earth.

"Nnnnooooo!" it wailed again. "I will not give it to ye! I will not!"

"Calm down!" Hunter yelled. "What are you talking about?"

"Treasure. The gold is mine. Ye can have the other, but not the gold. NOT THE GOLD, I SAY!"

"CALM DOWN!" Ian shook the little man to get his attention.

"Ye don't have to get violent, laddie," Alastair snapped back. "I didn't hurt ye."

"No, you just left us out here alone, that's all."

Alastair giggled again.

"You promised to come back," Aeryn snapped. "What happened?"

"Never said when," Alastair giggled again.

Ian threw the little creature to the dirt again and pounced on him. Alastair screamed and wailed until Hunter pulled him off.

"Stop!" Hunter screamed. "Everybody stop!"

They all froze and turned to look at the eldest boy.

"What is 'the other'?"

Alastair looked stumped, aged little head cocked sideways. He did not answer.

"You said, 'you can have the other, but not the gold'," Hunter demanded. "What does that mean?"

"Oh," Alastair said, standing and brushing the dust off his tattered green suit. "The legend," he said, "and the wishes."

"Wishes?" The children all looked at one another. "What wishes?" Aeryn asked.

Alastair sighed, arms dropping to his sides. "Everybody knows when ye catch a leprechaun ye get three wishes. Everybody but ye three dunces, apparently. Ye can have yer wishes, and the legend, but no more! Ye hear me? No more. Then ye're on your way. The lot of ya... pain in my arse, I tell ye."

"What's the legend?" Ian asked, still holding Alastair by the coat tails.

"The rainbow. Do ye not know of the legend of the rainbow?"

"Rainbow?" Aeryn asked. She turned her head toward the sky.

"Yes, the rainbow, lassie. Ye do know what a rainbow is, do ye not?"

"Yes, I know what a rainbow is," she snapped. "Do you get them down here?"

"Oh, aye, we do. Beautiful they are. Especially when He is there."

"He?"

"Yes, He. The One."

"He lives on the rainbow?" She looked upwards again.

"Aye, there, and other places at times."

"Is that how we find Him?"

"'Tis one way. There are others."

"How do we know when He's there?"

"Look for that which is forbidden, and you will see."

"What does that mean?"

"Have ye forgotten so quickly? Dense, yer kind. No sense. No sense at all!" Alastair huffed and pulled away. "I just told ye."

"I wish you would just speak English," Ian said.

Alastair smiled. "Aye, laddie. That I will. And that be one of yer wishes."

"No, wait," Ian protested. "I didn't mean- - -"

"Too late, lad. One be gone and two to go. Use them wisely."

"Everyone be quiet," Hunter yelled. The group calmed down and stared at one another, then all three turned to look at Alastair. He stood smiling at them. Raising his little hand, he wiggled two tiny crooked fingers.

"We need some help," Aeryn said. "We can't do this alone." The boys nodded.

"Would it be an official wish, then?"

"Yes," Aeryn said. "I wish for help for us."

"So be it. Ye shall each have a helper on yer journey." One finger went down, and one wrinkled digit wiggled in the air.

"I wish I could understand what you're talking about," Hunter whispered.

"No!" Ian screamed and shoved Hunter again. "Now you've wasted the last wish!"

Alastair smiled. "Wisdom," he said, impressed, "a fine choice, lad. And so ye shall have it, but only you. Now for yer warnin'."

"Warning?" Ian asked. "Is he kidding?"

"Heed it well, child, or suffer all eternity because if it." Alastair stepped back from the group. His voice took on a serious note. "The road is long and fraught with danger. Seek the one who will stand and fight, not he who will run and hide. Ye must each journey separately, but find the same road. What ye seek is the same, though a different path."

"Why do we have to go separately?" Aeryn asked.

"Silence," the leprechaun said, "time is short. Ye must complete yer journey by the time the sun rises on the third day. For then, it will be too late."

"What sun?" Ian asked.

Alistair shook his head. One tiny aged digit pointed toward the bottom of the bubbling volcano. "Each time mother sun boils with anger is one morn. Aye? And each time she settles herself calm-like is what ye call night. Can ye grasp that, laddie?"

"Aye," Ian snapped. "And what if I refuse to leave them?" he asked, feet planted hard, pointing at the Welch siblings. "They're my friends."

"Stubbornness will get ye nothing, if not killed, lad. Learn to work with the world, and not fight against it." He turned back to the group. "Seek the great warrior, for only he can save ye when evil closes in. Listen to him. Fear the warrior. Flee when he tells you, and don't look back. It will take the essence of all of ye together to defeat the evil one. Don't hide yer spark. Let the world see it. It will be the only thing to save ye. If ye fail, then the lot of ye will be damned to die the living death – fer'ever."

"You shall each have a gift for yer journey." Alastair began backing away, almost looking as though he was afraid, eyes darting around, wringing his hands nervously. "Use it wisely. Ye shall find yer destination by land, sea, and air. Hold fast to the strings in the mist, for they alone will sustain ye when all hope is gone. There are those to guard ye, those to fight ye, and those to challenge ye. Ye must learn to know the difference."

"Only trust beyond a shadow of a doubt." Alastair was at a decent distance now. "Never forget, especially in the castle. Fear the one who can extinguish yer spark for all eternity. Flee from him."

Sinclair, 2014, 2016

Without warning, a small feather floated down from the sky and landed at Aeryn's feet. She reached down and picked it up. In front of Ian landed a small flask of clear liquid, and at Hunter's feet, a quartz rock.

"Seek the truth which will light your path. Evil must always give way to the truth, and darkness to the light. Wash away all that holds ye back. Ye can only lead your father back home. He alone must choose. Put out your hands."

Each of the three extended their open hands, palms turned upwards. Into each, floated down a single tiny yellow seed from the sky. "This is all you will need."

"What is it?" Ian asked.

"Now go!" the tiny creature boomed. He turned and disappeared once again into the rocks. The earth jerked and shook. The ground beneath their feet lurched, sending them all hurtling through time and space.

The light of the volcano went out, and the temperature plunged.

Their screams became muffled and faint as they flew through absolute darkness, swallowed up in the pitch black hole of this new world. Slamming into the dark, hard ground, three separate aftershocks rocked the earth beneath them, and then, nothing.

Hunter or Hunted?

Chapter 4: Scared
Scared/adj/: thrown into or being in a state of fear, fright, or panic

Day 1:

Hunter slammed down hard on his back, air exploding from his lungs. Rolling to his side, he gasped and choked, grabbing at his chest. The wind knocked completely out of him from the fall, Hunter's lungs fought again and again with each new breath to replace the precious air that had been forced from his body only seconds before. After several attempts, his breathing managed to stabilize, coughing subsided, and his heart rate slowed.

Hunter lay on the ground for a long moment, trying to get his bearings in the pitch blackness of the cavern. He felt around him in the dark. His hand touched fine dirt, but not much else. Then it brushed something hard. He drew it close and felt it with both hands. It felt like— oh yes. It was the rock that ridiculous little elf had given him. No directions, and no light, nothing but dirt. Hunter felt lost.

"Ian?" he ventured. "Aeryn?"

There was no answer.

On the horizon, a faint bluish glow was just beginning to rise where the crimson sun had been earlier. It resembled a moon. As it took shape, so did the world around him. Darkened by the dusky glow, everything was cast in a bluish-gray hue.

Hunter was surrounded by trees. The lake was gone, as was the fruit tree and the thick brush they had been near earlier. Wherever he'd been thrown, it was a long way from the others. Hunter was now in a dense forest. Giant redwood trees, hundreds of feet tall sat a short distance away and towered above him. The branches of the trees bore soft green needles so thick nothing could be seen between them. Around his feet a few rocks were scattered. As he surveyed them, another sailed past his head and landed with a thud at his feet.

Hunter froze, eyes scanning the dense forest cover. A light breeze rustled the branches, making them all sway. Another rock sailed out from the darkness. This time, Hunter was able to see the direction it came from.

"Hey!" he yelled.

No response.

"Help!" he tried again.

Again a rock sailed out, this one almost striking his head.

Sinclair, 2014, 2016

"Hey!" he screamed back. "Stop!"

A barrage of large rocks began to pelt Hunter from the shadows. He tried to take cover, running for a large outcropping of rocks near where he had landed. He cowered behind it while more rocks pelted his open position, bouncing off the shelter above his head. Unable to move, Hunter weighed all of the options his mind could render.

How can I escape?

I can't. I'm not good enough. I don't know what I am doing.

Why is this happening?

I don't know. I am powerless to stop it. Not good enough.

What should I do?

I'm too scared. I can't. I can't - - -

Over and over again the questions tore through his mind, as the rocks landed nearer and nearer to his hiding place.

A large rock bounced off the boulder sheltering Hunter and smashed into the side of his head. Fighting back tears and the rising fears that he had battled his whole life, Hunter heard the words of his father echo in his head.

Sinclair, 2014, 2016

Face your fears head-on, son. That is the only way you can conquer them.

He swallowed hard and looked at his trembling hands. Reaching down inside himself to depths he did not know he could reach, he summoned the courage to stand and fight. Hunter grabbed a stick that lay on the ground at his feet and leapt from his hiding place. He ran straight toward the spot in the forest where the rocks had been coming from, screaming and waving the stick over his head like a club. Bursting through the thick forest cover and into a clearing, he wailed at the top of his lungs, only to be met with a scream of equal intensity— and fear. Hunter froze and looked across the clearing at the source of his attack.

Cowering in the clearing was a huge dark brown animal. With every move of Hunter's, it cowered and yelped more, like a frightened dog.

When Hunter froze, so did the creature. When he moved, so did it. It took only a second or two to realize that this thing was just as afraid as Hunter was. Every time Hunter twitched, so did the creature. Hunter tried to move a little to one side to get a better view. It screamed again, the sound resembling something like a bear, or a gorilla, but not really. The tone of the wail almost sounded like a dog, or maybe a wolf. It had almost a howling quality, but not quite those either. After a long moment, Hunter decided that this thing would not hurt him. He bent to the ground and gently laid down the stick that he carried, then backed away a full step, and showed the creature his own shaking hands. It was a peace offering, the only thing that Hunter knew to do.

The creature stood. From its cowering position, it unfurled the entire length of its furry body until it towered over Hunter. Much taller than his father's six feet, this thing had to be at least nine feet tall, and had enormous feet. It shifted slightly on its thick hairy legs, completely comfortable walking on two giant feet, like a human, and yet it was clearly not. Dark brown fur covered its entire body, and a flat dark-skinned face with a flat nose and big brown eyes watched Hunter's every move. Hanging down at its sides were two shaking hands.

Could it be? Could this possibly be Bigfoot? Dad said that there was no such thing, but here we are, face-to-face.

It had a face that was almost human, and there was a haunting intelligence in its two sunken eyes. Hunter had half expected them to be wild creatures, attacking and eating young men alive, then tossing their leftovers to the wolves to finish. But then, they were supposed to be deathly afraid of humans, too. Deathly afraid of almost everything, he had heard. That's why no one had ever

Sinclair, 2014, 2016

seen one before. Other reports of the mythical creatures had them roasting children for breakfast and picking their teeth with the bones. That was not what this creature seemed at all. He was just as scared as Hunter.

After staring at each other, motionless, for what seemed like an eternity, it was obvious one of them had to make the first move. Hunter, growing tired and needing to sit down, took the chance. His feet hurt, his head throbbed, and his back still ached from the hard landing. He slowly moved to the center of the clearing, and sat down. He gestured for the Bigfoot to join him. Much to his surprise, it did. Hunter squatted down, crossed his legs Indian-style, and watched in amazement as the Bigfoot did the same.

Great. Now what?

They sat across from each other for what seemed quite a long time. The sun was rising and rays of light now filtered through the canopy of leaves and needles above. Hunter did not have a watch, but he felt his head grow heavy with exhaustion and his stomach growl. He was hungry. Or at least he had been until that horrid smell wafted his way. Hunter looked at the Bigfoot and winced. Did the creature know that he stank so horribly?

Bigfoot winced back.

Hunter scratched his head.

Bigfoot did the same.

Hunter smiled. *Intelligent.* That could work. "If only you could talk," he whispered.

"Why?" it whispered back.

"What?" Hunter sat stunned for a second, then regained his senses. "You can talk?"

"Can't you?" it answered back.

"Why didn't you say something earlier?"

Bigfoot shrugged. "Nothin' to say."

Hunter's stomach growled loudly.

Bigfoot smiled, growling back at his mid-section and nodding.

"Is there any food here? I'm starving."

Bigfoot looked toward the dark sky. He raised an enormous finger and pointed to the sky. "You? Fall?" he asked.

Hunter nodded.

"More?"

Hunter nodded again. "Yes, there were four of us that fell through. My father was taken by a serpent to a place called Zin. I need to find him."

Bigfoot grimaced.

"Can you help me?"

There was no response. Bigfoot moved to the edge of the clearing and turned his ear to the opening in the woods. After a second, he shifted positions and did the same thing again in a new spot. This happened several more times as he moved around the clearing from one side to the other.

"Hey, ah- - -, please," Hunter hesitated. "What is your name?"

Bigfoot shrugged, still listening into the night.

"Okay, I'm going to call you Mikey, then. Is that okay?"

Bigfoot nodded and straightened. "We go now."

"Can't we rest first?" Hunter sat down again. "I'm exhausted."

Mikey ran to the center of the clearing, hoisted Hunter up, threw him over his shoulder, and barreled through the clearing and into the darkness. "Quick. Danger. Near!"

Sinclair, 2014, 2016

Chapter 5: Journey
jour-ney *Noun* \ˈjər-nē\: passage from one place to another

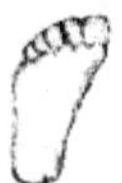

"Stop. Please stop."

"Have to move. Coming."

"Please," Hunter begged. "I'm gonna be sick."

"Evil smells."

That's for sure, Hunter thought, trying not to breathe through his nose. He opened his mouth instead to keep nausea at bay.

Mikey stopped, but did not immediately set Hunter down. His big body slowly swung around in a complete circle, scanning the forest for any signs of life, making Hunter feel even more nauseated. Extending his large muscular neck, he put his nose straight up into the air and sniffed each direction. Clearly not detecting any other signs of life, Mikey clumsily let Hunter slide off his shoulder and plop to the ground. Hunter hit with a thud, jarring his already queasy stomach. His hand instinctively went to his mid-section. He tried to stay perfectly still for a moment to quell the motion sickness brewing inside of him.

Mikey looked down. He bent down to Hunter's level and stuck a huge brown finger into Hunter's middle, pushing in an uncomfortable gesture, he asked "wrong?"

"I feel sick."

"Sick?"

"Dizzy." Hunter tried to swallow down the rising bile in his stomach. "Throw up," he said back to Mikey. At the blank stare that met him, Hunter leaned forward in a mock vomiting gesture and said "blahhhhh," gagging toward the ground. A move he instantly wished he hadn't made.

Bigfoot winced and backed away, grimacing.

Well, at least I get a break from the smell.

"I really need to get something to eat." Hungry, but at the same time afraid to eat, Hunter looked at Bigfoot. At his lack of response, he added "food," and pointed at his stomach.

Bigfoot nodded and turned, running into the forest, leaving Hunter alone - again.

Sinclair, 2014, 2016

He sat alone in the forest. The sky was bright and glowing. The sun was at high noon. The first day was here and he hadn't yet found his father. He had only three days. Only three days if he could believe that little green creature, Alistair. But then he had left them all alone when he had promised to come back. The same as this Bigfoot had done now. Hunter was beginning to wonder if this was some sort of game down here.

The last thing he remembered was the look of terror in his father's eyes as the serpent snatched him from the shore. Hunter choked back tears and the bile rising from his stomach. He wanted to cry and vomit at the same time. Was his father as scared as Hunter was right now? Where was he? What was happening? Was he really dead? And what did *'to die the living death'* mean anyway? They said it was a prison. What had he done wrong, other than just make a bad choice? Was that enough to punish someone over? Hunter replayed the scene over and over again in his mind until his head throbbed.

Stop. Just find him. Lead him back to freedom.

Hunter looked around; trees, dense brush, rocks, bushes moving – bushes moving? His heart lurched. If the bushes are moving, then what is behind them is moving, too. As gently as he could, Hunter rose to his feet and began to scan the underbrush. He wanted sight on where this moving thing was, and more importantly, *what* it was.

The bushes rustled to his left. Turning his head, Hunter tried to get a fix on it. The bushes rustled to his right, and then straight ahead. Glancing from one direction to the other, he tried to get a good look at what was stalking him. Squinting through the bushes, his eyes tried to focus on what was behind the leaves, but whatever it was eluded his sight. All he could see were branches. Again, the bushes moved in all three directions, and then large jagged antlers broke free from their cover. Across the small clearing, three deer were staring at him.

Oh, thank goodness. Hunter sighed and started to relax. He remembered little of what his father had taught him about hunting, but one thing that he did remember was that deer have a natural fear of humans. They were no threat to him. It was very unlikely that they would approach him. As Hunter sat back, contemplating his foes, the deer began to move again.

One by one, they stepped free from the cover of the underbrush to stare at Hunter, then retracted back into the cover of the forest, careful to always stay in the shadows. It was only then he noticed they all had glowing red eyes. Not a pretty red either, like when the flash of a camera is on and the people in the picture end up with red eyes. This was a deeper, blood red color, almost dripping from the sockets. Their glare was an angry one, eyes fixed, necks taut, fangs bared and snarling.

Fangs? Hunter was now being hunted.

The biggest of the three stepped out into the filtering sunlight, and then recoiled in pain, pulling back into the shadows. Sparks of electricity shot from the points of its antlers, cascading fireworks into the air. Throwing its head back to howl in agony, it bared fangs dripping with saliva tinged in blood, and glared at him again through its glowing red eyes. The other two reacted to their partner's agony, throwing their heads into the air to howl at the sky. They, too, paced back and forth, sparks shooting skyward, careful to stay in the shade of the trees. Fangs dripping, they began to snarl and drool at Hunter, nostrils flaring as they detected his scent on each pass. As the sunlight continued to move, and the shadows encroached on Hunter's position, the enemy moved forward with the shade, inching ever closer.

Evil is close, he remembered Mikey saying. Is this what he meant? They sure looked evil to him. More than evil, they looked hungry, and they were looking right at him! Hunter started to back away.

A loud crash behind him broke the silence. Hunter lurched forward away from the noise, then stopped before

Sinclair, 2014, 2016

he hit the zombie-like deer straight ahead. Spinning around to see what new evil was behind him, Hunter ducked as a large rock sailed over him, slamming into the head of one howling deer. Bigfoot broke through the forest, hurling two more stones at the other two deer, nailing them right between the eyes, silencing their howls. While they were still stunned, he grabbed Hunter, threw him over his shoulder once again, and barreled off through the trees.

"Climb," Mikey pointed up a large pine tree.

"Do we have to?"

"Climb," Mikey pointed again.

Hunter eyed the tree. The lowest branch was far out of his reach. "I don't think I can—"

A large brown hand grabbed his shirt and hoisted him up well beyond the lowest branch. Hunter wrapped his arms around the giant tree trunk, holding on for dear life.

"Climb," the command came again. He tried to move, but the giant on his tail was much faster than he was. At his lack of progress, an enormous hand grabbed his bottom and shoved, raising him like an elevator up through the tree branches. Higher and higher, deeper into the thick pine needle covering of the tree they ascended, until it was nearly impossible to see the ground. To Hunter's surprise, there at the top, was a small landing. Not a full tree house, but a sheltered platform made from several pieces of wood stretched between two branches. It was enough to sit on, and lay down to rest. Hunter was shoved onto the platform, and Bigfoot followed, hoisting his enormous bulk from the branches below. He sat opposite Hunter and reached behind him. From around his waist, Mikey pulled several long stringy vines covered with berries.

Blackberries. Hunter's heart and stomach jumped. He was so hungry. Mikey placed the vines on the platform floor between them. Nodding at Hunter to go ahead, Bigfoot reached his giant hands out into the pine tree and pulled off several pine cones. With a fine motor dexterity amazing for such colossal fingers, he pulled off each of the woody scales of the pine cone, and taking each one, placed them gently between his teeth to crush. After biting down, he pulled the crushed scale from his mouth, parting the hard outer shell, revealing a tiny pine nut inside. Laying the one small piece of treasure in the palm of his hand, Bigfoot extended it and offered the first little golden nugget to Hunter. He graciously accepted, and tossed the tiny kernel into his mouth.

Hunter's taste buds exploded. This little treasure of the forest was the tastiest thing he had eaten since he'd landed here. Almost creamy, and incredibly soft, it tasted nothing like an ordinary nut. He held out his hand and waited for another. Continuing for some time, Mikey managed to get a small pile of nuts to go with their blackberries. As they ate, Hunter's growling stomach began to settle. The two sat in silence for a long time, enjoying their meal.

"How could you run all that way?" Hunter asked. "Carrying me, too?"

Mikey shrugged, and continued his extraction of the pine nuts without a sound.

"But we ran all day."

Nothing.

"How did you get here?" Hunter asked.

Mikey cocked his head sideways, as if he didn't understand the question. "Home," he said.

"You have always lived here?"

Mikey nodded, reaching for another berry.

"Are there more of you?"

Again the head cocked as Mikey contemplated his answer. He nodded.

"What were those things back there?"

"Evil."

"I've never seen any deer that looked like that before. They looked like zombies."

"Shadows." Bigfoot took the last pine nut and offered it to Hunter.

Hunter shook his head. "They had fangs. Deer don't have fangs."

"Danger. Evil. Teeth can steal your spark."

Fear the one that can extinguish yer spark for all eternity, Alastair had warned.

"Evil can't bear light," Bigfoot continued. "Light reveals shadows. Shadows of evil have no shadows of their own. They are the shadows, and they are the evil."

"So that's why they have to stay in the dark?"

Mikey nodded.

"So I am safe so long as I am in the light?"

Bigfoot nodded again, "from them." He stretched and yawned, laying his enormous hairy bulk across the planks on the platform. Stretching out, his feet hung completely off one side, and his head dangled very near the edge of the other. Hunter sat and watched this gentle giant as he rested on their perch atop this strange new land. "How far is Zin?"

"Not far." Mikey patted his hand on the platform next to him. "Need rest."

"Can we get there soon?"

Bigfoot shook his head. "Not ready. Need protection."

"Protection from what?"

"Evil," Bigfoot said. Again patting the platform, he said, "need rest".

"What kind of protection?" Hunter pressed.

"Rocks."

"Rocks?" Hunter looked at his new friend, confused. "Like the ones that you threw at the deer?"

Bigfoot nodded.

"And at me?"

Bigfoot nodded again.

"Why did you throw those rocks at me?"

"Scared."

"I scared you?" *Some protector. You're just as scared as I am.*

"Flew down from the sky," a big finger pointed upwards. "Evil can, too."

"You thought I was evil?"

Bigfoot shrugged. "Need rest." He patted the platform again.

Hunter sat silent for a long minute, taking in his new surroundings. Looking off into the distance, he could see the mountainous area that was his destination, volcano bubbling and hissing steam into the sky. Bigfoot belched and smacked his lips to get rid of the taste, eyes never opening from his slumber. Hunter lay down next to his Bigfoot, and tried to get comfortable. He covered his nose to hide the horrid smell of his companion.

"Mikey?" Hunter asked after a long silence. "How will I get this protection?"

"Friends."

Chapter 6: Warrior

war·rior *noun, often attributive* \\\'wȯr-yər, \'wȯr-ē-ər, \'wär-ē- *also* \'wär-yər\

a person engaged in some struggle or conflict

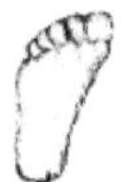

Day 2

The sun was warm on his skin. There was a slight breeze in the air, cooling his face. The motion of the tree branches was an ever so small sway with the movement of the air, the scent in the sky was – horrid. Hunter gagged and tried to cover his nose. His arms were pinned down and he couldn't move. He wiggled and tried to break his arms free with a loud groan.

Bigfoot woke up. Snuggled up against Hunter, giant arms wrapped around him and his head nestled against Hunter's shoulder, Mikey yawned, released his young friend and threw his arms over his head in a giant stretch. Hunter rolled away to the edge of the platform and retched. Clearing his nostrils, he gasped for fresh air, hoping not to throw up. Glancing down from the top of the tree, branches gently swaying in the breeze below, another wave of nausea hit him, and he held down a another retch that climbed up the back of this throat. Closing his eyes from the height and the moving branches, Hunter's stomach slowly settled back down. He heard Mikey still yawning and moving behind him. He cracked open one eye and peered across the platform.

His Bigfoot yawned, baring enormous teeth and jaws. With his mouth open, he let out a rumbling sound that resembled a purring cat. At the same moment, Hunter heard some rumbling coming from the other end, and then a waft of yet another horrid and even more offensive smell. *Great*, Hunter thought. *A Bigfoot that farts. Didn't think this could get any worse.*

Mikey sat up straight and looked around at his behind. He sniffed the air, winced, and turned back to Hunter. He pointed at Hunter's stomach. "Eat?"

Hunter shook his head. *Not with this smell.*

"Down," Mikey said, and turned to descend the tree. Disappearing below the platform, Hunter crawled over to the spot where Mikey had just been. He looked down and another wave of nausea overtook him. He pulled back and took a deep breath. Sitting there on the platform, he tried to decide what he was going to do next.

"Down," he heard Mikey command from below.

Hunter tried again to inch toward the edge of the platform, but the mere thought of looking down again made his stomach somersault. "I can't," he called down.

The branches rustled and jerked to the side, and a large brown head popped back up into view. "Down?" he said again.

"I can't," Hunter said. "It's too high."

Mikey hoisted his great bulk back up onto the platform. Standing, he towered over Hunter. With one hand, he hoisted the young man up, and once again threw him over his shoulder, then scooted down from the tree in less than a minute. Hunter felt as though he were on a water slide as Mikey shifted and twisted to avoid all of the branches and obstacles. Once on solid ground, Hunter was again unceremoniously dropped to the ground hard, his feet jarring and his stomach near revolt. He stood for a moment, holding on to Mikey, the only thing within reaching distance until his nerves and nausea settled. Mikey stood still as long as Hunter was holding him. When Hunter released his grip and stood tall, Mikey started off back through the forest. "We go," was all he said.

"Where?" Hunter asked.

"Friends."

"What's that?" Hunter inched closer to the strange object hanging from the tree. He noticed another, and another in the other nearby trees. There were dozens of these strange little objects on the low-hanging branches of nearly all the trees that Hunter could see.

They were circular in the middle, with woven strings. Some had beading, and some not. Most were colored brightly, and all had feathers hanging down from the bottom.

"Dream catchers."

"Dream catchers?" Hunter walked close to one and reached his hand out.

"No touch!" Mikey snapped. "Evil there."

"Evil?" Hunter inspected the object closely, without touching it. "How can these catch evil?"

"Friends believe. Must respect."

Lingering in the forest to see how these mystical charms worked, Hunter was filled with a foreboding sense of doom. Stepping close to a large and particularly colorful one, Hunter heard a faint sound. He put his ear up next to the catcher. There it was again, as faint as a whisper.

"Hunter."

His heart raced.

"Hunter, can you hear me?"

Sinclair, 2014, 2016

"Dad?"

"Help me, Hunter."

"Where are you, Dad?"

"Help me. I'm lost."

"I'm coming, Dad. Hold on," Hunter told the tree. "Mikey!" he screamed. "Mikey! Help me!" Hunter spun around in circles, nerves on edge, looking for his helper. "Mikey!"

"Here," the voice came from behind.

"My father. He's stuck in one of those things. We have to get him out."

Bigfoot lowered his head. "Evil has him."

"We have to get him out. It was this one—" Hunter's hand reached out to grab it, but was batted away by Mikey's large brown mitt.

"Not touch," he warned. "Father not there," he pointed at the woven piece of string and feathers hanging from the tree. "Father lost with evil. Must rescue."

"But I heard him. He's in there." Tears perched on the corners of Hunter's eyelids, threatening to erupt at any second.

"No." Mikey stepped in close. "Comm-un-i-ca-tion." A large hairy finger pointed to the dream-catcher again. "Not there. Lost. Must find."

"How?" Hunter cried.

Sinclair, 2014, 2016

"Friends," Mikey said again and turned back on the trail leading through the dangling charms. "Friends know."

Up and over the top of the rise, Hunter began to see pointy-shaped, triangular structures. Even from their great distance, he recognized them as teepees. *Indians*, he thought. *No, not just Indians - warriors.*

'Seek the warrior' Alistair had said. Mikey had called them friends. He sighed with relief. They would help him rescue his father.

Hunter ran ahead. "Come on!" He beckoned Mikey to catch up. The two picked up their pace, Mikey taking longer strides with his great height, and Hunter running alongside to keep up.

After what seemed like forever, they were within meters of the tribe.

People, Hunter thought, *human contact again.* He was so excited to meet and greet others of his own kind, he recklessly turned off the main path to take a shortcut through some brush, down a hill, and out into the meadow where the teepees were. Running downhill he began to barrel forward, unable to control his speed. Once on a fast-paced rate down the hill, he could not stop, bursting forth into the clearing at the bottom. Out in the open again, he ran for the first being that he saw, but stopped dead in his tracks.

Between Hunter and the Indians stood a tribe of Bigfeet.

Friends, he thought. *Of course.*

Sinclair, 2014, 2016

Chapter 7: Training
train·ing *noun* *noun* \ˈtrā-niŋ\
the skill, knowledge, or experience acquired by one that
trains

Hunter and Mikey stood in the middle of several dozen Bigfeet. The moment the two appeared, the large creatures stopped their games, and huddled around the two newcomers, inching close, sniffing at them like a dog would sniff at its food. Mikey's face broke into a huge smile. "Hey, brother."

A resounding slap on the back from several of his cousins was Mikey's welcome back to the group. He looked down into Hunter's widened eyes.

"Ok. Friends." Mikey gestured to the group.

"What are they going to do for us?"

"More helpers," Mikey said. "Friends there." He pointed to the small Indian village on the other side of the meadow. Teepees grouped in a small cluster along the side of a creek were surrounded by a number of dark, tanned inhabitants looking toward them.

Before he could ask any more questions, Hunter was hoisted onto the shoulders of one of the other Bigfeet and paraded around the open meadow. He looked back at Mikey, still on the edge of the forest. Mikey could see the look of uncertainty on Hunter's face. He gave the universal 'thumbs up' sign to his young friend, and settled back against a tall tree. Scanning the meadow, he counted six other Bigfeet standing guard at the edge of the tree line, all alert and watching the area as Mikey now was. Behind him, Mikey still heard scuffling and rustling in the bushes. Electricity snapped and buzzed in his ears. His hair stood on end down his spine. Standing guard, he stayed at his post while the other Bigfeet carried Hunter forward to meet his new friends in the village.

Seven large Bigfeet stood on alert at their posts.

Hunter stood in the middle of the tribe. Fingers poked at him and pulled both his hair and his clothes from every direction. They seemed especially interested in the belt loops on his blue jeans. He was nervous, but not so frightened that he had to run. They seemed to be fascinated more than anything by his blue eyes and his

Sinclair, 2014, 2016

short blond hair. His colorful t-shirt with a wolf's image imprinted on it also intrigued them. Tanned brown fingers tugged at the longer strands of his hair at the top, while they pointed to their own long dark brown locks. Their clothing resembled loincloths or very rough woven tweeds. Their hair was adorned with leather thongs tied and beaded, some with beautiful feathers tied to the ends.

All of the Indians and Bigfeet had darkened brown skin, brown eyes, and dark brown hair. Hunter looked around. The teepees were animal hides, hand-sewn together and stretched over long poles tied together at the top. They were huge hides, all of the same type. They looked to be some sort of buffalo or moose hide. Each was slick and shiny, oiled for protection against the rain and mist. There was a smoke hole at the top, and a fire pit in the center of each for warmth in the winter time. Nobody needed a fire now. The weather was warm enough to live without. A flap of hide sufficed as the door for each.

Hunter waited to see what Mikey and the other Bigfeet would do, but they all remained out in the field, playing with rocks and sticks. It looked to him like they were play-fighting using the sticks as swords, and throwing the rocks at targets. As they finished each encounter, the Bigfeet all made a half-purring, half-gargling noise, sounding almost like an eerie laughter. *Wookies!*

Sinclair, 2014, 2016

Left alone in the midst of the natives, Hunter would have to go it alone.

"Who is your chief?" he asked.

The girls closest to him giggled and shied away.

"Do you have a leader?"

More giggling. When the giggling stopped, the small sea of children parted and an older man walked through to greet Hunter. He stopped directly in front of Hunter, looking him up and down. The newcomer smiled and nodded for him to follow. Turning, the older man walked away and entered the largest teepee in the tribe.

Hunter followed.

Inside the tent, sitting in a circle around an empty fire pit, were what appeared to be all of the tribal elders. Eight older men, wrinkled and sun-worn with age, sat circled around the exterior of the tent. They all smiled in greeting, and motioned for Hunter to sit with them. Glancing back over his shoulder one last time, Mikey was nowhere to be seen. Hunter stepped forward and sat down with the tribal council.

They sat in silence for a moment, passing something around the group. When it got to Hunter, he recognized a basket of pine nuts, the same as he'd eaten for supper the night before. It wasn't until this moment that Hunter realized how hungry he was again. He reached into the basket and took out a small handful. Tossing them into his mouth, he waited for the flask to come around next.

Ahhh, cool water. Hunter drank to wash down the nuts, and to wash away his parched throat. Water never tasted so good.

Without realizing it, he drained the flask, leaving nothing for the remainder of the elders to his right.

"Oh," he said, realizing his mistake. "I'm sorry. Let me get some more." He started to stand, but was motioned back down by an extended hand from the man in charge, the eldest of the group, who'd eyed Hunter since he entered the teepee. He nodded at Hunter to sit, and clapped his hands.

Three of the young girls, who'd ogled Hunter's blond hair outside, came to the call. Still giggling, they took the empty flask and handed the elders several full ones, then disappeared outside. The basket of pine nuts was offered to Hunter a second time, and he gratefully took another handful, and an entire flask of water to himself.

"How did you come here?" the oldest of the elders asked.

"We fell through the earthquake."

"We? There are more of you?"

"Yes," Hunter answered, "my best friend, my little sister, and my father."

"Where are the others?"

"I don't know about my friend or my sister," Hunter said, "but my father was taken by a serpent."

"A large serpent?"

Hunter nodded.

"With a red diamond head and razor-sharp teeth?"

Hunter nodded again.

"So he has been taken to the prison of the lost. Did you meet Alistair?"

Hunter nodded. "He told me to seek out the warriors to help me. Mikey brought me here."

"Mikey?" the leader asked.

"Oh," Hunter smiled. "I named the Bigfoot 'Mikey'. He brought me here."

For the first time, the tribal elders broke into large smiles. "Mikey is an appropriate name for the creature. And what do you want from us?"

"Can you help me rescue my father?"

"We can equip you for your journey, and teach you the ways of the warrior, but the journey is yours to travel, and so you must do it alone."

It wasn't the answer that Hunter was waiting to hear. "No, I can't," he protested. "There is danger, Alistair said. I don't know how to fight it."

"We will teach you."

"I don't know if I can do it."

"Then your father will perish."

The words jolted Hunter like a slap in the face. "Please," he said, fighting to keep his voice from cracking. "I don't know how."

"First, you must become a man."

Oh, ho, ho, hey, ya, ya, ho, ho, yo, yo…

Hunter wasn't sure if the ritual had started yet or not. There were already dancers around the campfire, chanting, but he was not yet prepared. He still wasn't sure what all of the preparations would entail, but so far he'd stripped off his clothes to don a loincloth. Short as it was, he had feathers tied in his hair, and now was being painted. Not just face paint, either. His entire body was being covered. He wasn't sure, but he'd swear at one point he heard the words "war paint" from Mikey, but then he disappeared and left Hunter alone with his new 'friends' again.

Bright blue, red, green, and yellow stripes now adorned his arms, legs, chest, back, and face. He was attended to by four large, scary-looking men similarly painted. He barely recognized the elders from their meeting in the teepee earlier. They were now covered in paint, as well. Their faces showed no emotion whatsoever, their expressions solemn, stoic, and hard. Two men held Hunter's arms out straight inside the teepee, while the other two chanted in circles, painting his body as they moved. Twirling around, arms outstretched like giant birds, the two dancers alternately hopped from foot to foot, crouching then rising as they spun. With each turn, they would swipe another color. When they finished, the chanting and painting stopped. The four stood tall, admiring their handiwork. The teepee was crowded with all five of them.

"Are we done?" Hunter asked.

"Almost," the elder of the group said. Hunter heard Mikey call him Raging Bull. Stepping out of the teepee, followed by the other three, he returned a moment later with a large animal skull. It was the head of a very large deer, antlers and all. The elder Indian reached forward to place it on Hunter's head.

"Oh, whoa! No, no, no," he protested.

"Must," Raging Bull said. "The Rite of Manhood will not be complete without it."

"But why do I need to wear it?"

"You must become one with nature... one with the animal. Must learn to see good from evil. Must see what the animal sees. See how evil sees." Raging Bull approached again and lifted the huge head over the top of Hunter's.

And smell what the animal smells, too, he thought, holding back his gag reflex. *And I thought Mikey stank.*

Raging Bull and the others stepped back to admire their handiwork. Nodding their approval, they turned to step out of the teepee and into the camp with their tribesmen.

Hunter followed. He felt like a complete idiot but, if this would help him find his father, then he would do it.

Sinclair, 2014, 2016

Chapter 8: Victory

vic·to·ry *noun* \ˈvik-t(ə-)rē\ *plural* vic·to·ries
achievement of mastery or success in a struggle or
endeavor against odds or difficulties

Hunter emerged from the teepee, antlers and all, into the bright mid-afternoon light. The giant buck head shielded his eyes from the sun, but also blocked his view. He could see a lot of people around, but couldn't tell how many or who they were. The only sound he recognized was the giggling from the girls. From the view that he caught through the droopy eye sockets in the skull he was wearing, it seemed as though the entire tribe was here. Hunter wasn't sure if it was to support him or to condemn him, but he had no choice. He had to move on. Young girls giggled on all sides of him. He felt his skin turn red inside the mask, glad for the first time that he was wearing it. Hunter focused his vision straight ahead.

"Come," Raging Bull commanded. Hunter spun his head around to see where the elder was. Catching a glimpse of the elder's back as he headed out of the encampment and into the meadow, Hunter followed. Up ahead he saw Mikey and several other bigfeet with him, as well as the other warriors who had prepared him for this task. They all walked ahead, leaving Hunter to trail behind.

Out into the meadow they trudged. Hunter was tired by the time they got out there. It was a warm day again. He felt the sun hot on his painted shoulders. The scent of wildflowers drifted up through his animal mask and gave him some relief from the tanned-hide smell that was its nature.

"Here." Raging Bull turned to welcome Hunter.

Where? Hunter thought, but knew enough not to ask aloud. He tried to look around. Tall grass, trees with war paint, and a large pile of small rocks on the ground.

"Throw," Raging Bull commanded.

"What?"

Raging Bull pointed to the pile of stones at Hunter's feet.

Hunter bent down to pick one up. The deer head nearly toppled off. Grabbing it by one antler, he managed to slide it back, skinning the side of his head on the bones scraping against his face. Back upright with one single stone in his hand, Hunter looked at Raging Bull. "What should I throw it at?"

A long slender, yet tanned, finger pointed to one of the painted trees. There, about fifty feet away, was a red circle painted on one of the trunks, looking very much like a target. Raging Bull commanded, "Throw!" with his finger pointed directly at the center.

Hunter raised the rock and threw.

The rock fell short by several yards, to the snickers of his companions. Shame welled up inside him. Tears started to flow inside the mask, and trailed down his neck in blue, red, green, and yellow streaks as they cascaded through the paint covering him.

"I can't," he said, hanging his head in shame. "I'm not good enough."

Hunter's head was snapped back up and he was pulled eye-to-eye with a large, brown, hairy face. "Learn," Mikey commanded. Hunter felt his hand being pulled out straight, and another rock slapped in his palm. Giant hairy fingers closed around his hand, securing the rock inside. From behind, he felt another set of muscular arms drawing his arm up over his head, at a different angle than he had thrown from before. One or two practice arcs guided Hunter's arm in the technique that was needed to throw the rock.

"Throw." Raging Bull stood off to the side, gauging the distance.

Hunter drew his arm back and tried to mimic the movement he'd practiced. Throwing over his head, he released the rock, scraping his forearm against the antlers he wore on his head. Recoiling in pain, he brought his arm up to see the bloody slash on his forearm. Covering it with his other hand, he looked up to see Raging Bull searching for the rock he had just thrown. Stepping closer to the tree than his last shot, the elder smiled and came back to the group.

"Throw," he said again.

Hunter's hand was extended out again, with another rock placed in his palm. Again, the strong muscular arms from behind guided him in his throw, avoiding the antlers, but reaching the arc necessary to hurl the rock at the right trajectory to make the strike.

Again and again, Hunter tried to hit the tree, and every time he missed, the tears flowed from under his mask of shame. Hunter was so glad his father was not here to see him. Wiping away the tears blurring his vision, he raised his aching arm over and over again for hours. Each time the rock fell short. Hunter was ready to give up, but the others did not budge. Never once showing any signs that they were ready to quit, they pressed him on and on until his eyes burned, his arm ached, and his stomach churned with the turmoil he felt inside. If there was anything inside his stomach, Hunter would have thrown up long ago. As it was, his insides burned with a combination of hunger and shame. He wanted to leave, but a tiny burning in his heart told him that if he gave up now, his father would be lost forever. *Don't give up*, something in his heart whispered. He must battle through his insecurity and shame. Maybe he didn't always have to be a failure at everything.

Maybe, just maybe…

Hours passed by, or did it only seem like hours? Shadows grew long, and the day was much cooler now. The breeze on his sweaty shoulders was refreshing against the burning muscles inside. Shadows grew long in the distance.

Another rock.

And another.

And another.

Raging Bull smiled bigger. Mikey smiled, too. Hunter had given up watching where the rocks fell long ago. Glancing around, he saw them all standing at the base of the tree pointing down right at the root. Charging back to the group, the two planted yet another rock in his hand.

"Throw."

The stirring in his heart outweighed the pain in his arm and his head. Wiping away the tears and smeared paint, Hunter reared back and threw as hard as he could.

Crack.

They all stood motionless. Hunter was so stunned to hear any sound at all, he didn't realize at first what happened. Mikey and Raging Bull ran to the tree to examine the spot where the rock hit. There, in the center of the red circle, was a chip in the paint showing the tree bark underneath. A perfect hit, right in the center.

Bulls eye.

Mikey ran, covering the fifty yards back to Hunter in a matter of seconds. He thrust another rock into Hunter's hand. "Throw," he commanded.

Hunter looked back at the target, making sure that Raging Bull backed away. He stood a few feet away. Earlier in the day that would have been the danger zone, but now —

"Throw," Raging Bull commanded.

Hunter reared back and threw with all of his might.

Crack.

A perfect strike again. Raging Bull bent back in to see the second divot in the red circle of paint.

"Throw." Mikey handed him yet another rock. Again and again they kept this up. Hunter's confidence began to grow, as did the stirrings of his heart.

I did it.

I can do it!

Crack!

Sinclair, 2014, 2016

This is no fluke.
I am a hunter now.
Crack!
I can rescue my father.
I can do it.

With each throw, and each crack of the tree, Hunter's tears began to flow again. These were no longer tears of shame. These were tears that flowed, washing away all of the years of hurt and pain that he had carried with him. They were tears of newfound confidence.

They were tears of victory.

"Now, you are ready to begin the Rite of Manhood." Raging Bull and the others turned back toward the camp, but this time Mikey and Hunter lead the way. Utterly exhausted, covered in sweat and smeared paint, and in pain, Hunter stood tall and held his head high walking in front of the others.

Chapter 9: Touch
Touch [tuhch] *verb (used with object)*
to come into contact with and **perceive** (something), as a
hand or the like does.

The campfire burned warm on his skin, the air unusually moist. A light fog rolled in when the sun set. Hunter could barely see across the roaring campfire to the warriors seated on split logs on the other side, or the fire dancers circling behind them, each twirling a long-handled flaming torch.

Ho, Ho, he, ha, ho, ho, hey, hmmmmm.

It was the same chant from this afternoon in the teepee. Hunter looked back down at his bare arms and legs. They had been repainted, as had his chest. He now sported new war paint in varying degrees of what he thought looked like racing stripes. Raging Bull sat next to him, smiling. The warriors one by one retold the story of this afternoon and Hunter's failed attempts to hit the target for most of the day. Laughter floated around the campfire.

It felt good to sit down after the long day.

Sinclair, 2014, 2016

"*My* arms ached by the time we were done," Quiet River blurted. The campfire erupted in laughter and Hunter's ribs were jabbed from the side by yet another warrior. Without a second thought, Hunter grabbed a pebble and hurled it, nailing Quiet River right between the eyes. This was met with even more raucous laughter, and rib jabbing, but this time it was the young native across the fire that was the laughers' target, not Hunter. He laughed. The good-natured teasing made him feel accepted by these people. He felt at home.

Roasting meat on the spit in the fire sizzled and hissed as it turned over and over again above the coals. The sweet aroma drifted up and over the group like a welcome rain cloud. The nuts and berries Hunter survived on before barely managed to curb his hunger. This was a feast meant for royalty. Hunter could feel his mouth watering. He swallowed, hardly able to contain his hunger.

Raging Bull stood. The group quieted and turned to their elder.

"We are grateful for the bounty that the Great One has provided." He raised both hands over his head and turned his face toward the sky. "We do not take what we do not need, and do not waste what we have been given." The younger natives began to chant.

Hey, hey, ho, ho, ya, wa, oh, ha…

Raging Bull pulled his knife from its sheath against his leg and, reaching over the fire, he sliced off the best portion of the meat. This piece was set aside for their special guest, who as yet had not arrived. The spit was then lifted from the fire and passed around the campfire, each warrior taking a bite, and passing it along. When the roasted meat reached Hunter, he took the deer head and set it down at his feet.

"Do not release the mask." Raging Bull held out the spit for Hunter to bite from. "It must remain in your possession." Hunter wanted to ask why, but was too hungry to stop chewing. After taking two bites of the meat offered to him, the spit was passed on. He kept his legs protectively over the mask on the ground.

Around the fire came roasted corn, fish, and some fruit. A bite from a juicy red apple was offered to Hunter. He choked back tears, taking the bite offered by his neighbor. Swallowing the fruit, Hunter fought back thoughts of his father and held on to the deer head even tighter.

When the meal was over, they all sat back against the rocks, leaning back and lounging. Hunter thought he might fall asleep, except the heavy deer head he held tight in his hands kept him wide awake. Extremely grateful that he did not have it strapped to his head any longer, Hunter couldn't understand why he couldn't put it down. Now that the meal was over, the storytelling and the laughter long since finished, all of them sitting quietly as though they were ready for bed, Hunter still held the heavy deer skull.

The dancers stopped.

"Rise." Raging Bull was the first to his feet. The others jumped to attention, and turned toward the forest. Hunter struggled to his tired, aching feet, and looked in the direction the others were facing.

There, in the darkest part of the forest, Hunter saw a slight movement, a rustle here and there, but nothing definitive. He tried to focus his eyes on the motion. It couldn't be a threat. The Indians all stood at near-military attention looking into the forest, waiting for whatever moved their way.

There. Hunter saw something. *It's a …*

No, wait. It can't be.

Is it a Bigfoot? No too small. It walks upright, like a man, but it's not a human head. Long snout, big ears.

Sinclair, 2014, 2016

Cow? No. Pig? No. Closer and closer it came. There. It's a goat. No, a horse, with a horn.

A horse with a horn? Hunter tried to make sense of it. *A unicorn?*

There's no such thing, he chided himself.

But then, there's no such thing as a Bigfoot, either. Maybe it's just a mask.

Mikey smiled at him across the fire, and winked.

The creature emerged from the forest and walked over to the campfire. It was no mask. The Indians all bowed in respect and honor. At a gentle nudging from Raging Bull and the others, Hunter bowed as well, still holding the giant skull.

"Our healer," Rain Cloud whispered.

"Healer?" Hunter looked around. "Who's hurt?"

"You."

Hunter sat mesmerized, watching Abornazine circle around the campfire, opposite the rest of the dancers behind them. Drums beat in the distance, but he could not tell from where. From the tips of his fingers, fire danced as though each appendage was a candle lit on its own.

Moving around the circle, he chanted, waving his burning hands.

"Oh, ho, ya, wee, yaa, oooh,la, da, ba, ba, oh ya hee. I ask the Great One, Vaive Atoish, to come!"

"Who?" Hunter whispered through the mask.

Raging Bull bent close. "It means The One Who Alights in the Clouds. He calls the Maker."

"Is he really a Unicorn?"

"Shhh. Put the deer head on."

Abornazine's pace quickened. Bursts of flame now shot out from his fingers toward the darkness, flaming projectiles lighting the darkness for a split second, the sputtering out. Hunter peered through the mask. He blinked hard, and stared again.

Circling faster and faster, flame bursts shooting out. Beyond the circle of the campfire, along the tree line of the forest, Hunter saw glowing red eyes. A panic began to rise inside of him. Raging Bull's hand settled on his shoulder to keep him seated.

"It's the zombie deer," Hunter said. "We have to run."

"No run. We do not flee the rite of passage." Mikey moved to block Hunter's way.

Hunter felt an enormous hand land on his shoulder. He turned the deer head to see Mikey standing by his side,

Sinclair, 2014, 2016

tall and taut. Behind each person, as Abornazine danced past them, a dream-catcher floated down from the sky and hovered near them. Behind them, stepping quietly out from the woods, the circle was surrounded by the tribe of Bigfeet, shoulder to shoulder, all facing outward, backs to the campfire. They were standing guard around the group.

They catch evil, he remembered Mikey saying of the woven ornaments. *Can they keep evil at bay now?*

The fire dancers were at a near-frantic pace, chanting, torches spinning like windmills, fanning the flames from Abornazine's finger tips, yet the flames did not go out.

"He is keeper of the flame," Raging Bull told him. "They dare not go out until He is gone."

"Who?"

"He from the clouds. The Maker."

"Why is He coming?"

"Shhhh. Watch. Learn."

Hunter tried to soak it all in, but it was hard. There was so much going on. The drums in the background pounded out an entrancing rhythmic beat. Hunter was hypnotized by the floating dream-catchers, the spinning flames, and the beating drums.

Leaping over the back of one young Indian in the crowd, Abornazine landed in the middle of the group. All motion and noise stopped. The healer stood tall, arms outstretched toward the heavens and spoke in a voice so small the others could barely hear.

Raging Bull leaned back over to Hunter. "You cannot complete your journey until you and the Maker touch."

"How do I do that?" Hunter asked.

"You do not touch Him, He touches you. Abornazine asks Him to do that now."

Hunter's heart raced. He broke out in a cold sweat, and tried as hard as he could to keep down the rising tide of panic fighting to control him.

What am I doing here? His first instinct was to run, but where? *I can't do this,* he told himself. *I'm too scared.*

Scanning what he could see of the horizon through the thick mist, there was nowhere to run. Past the dream-catchers, through the line of Bigfeet and into the forest, Hunter counted dozens of red glaring eyes trained on him. *Run,* the voice inside him urged again.

"Do not run!" Abornazine yelled. Turning and thrusting a burning fingertip at the end of Hunter's deer snout, "Him!" he yelled.

From over Abornazine's head, a single thread descended from above. Silver in color, sleek and thin, it made a slow path down from the sky toward Hunter. Standing, Hunter backed away from the thread, fear churning up inside of him. "No," he cried, unable to wipe the tears of fear from his eyes through the deer skull. Turning to run, he tripped over Mikey's gigantic feet and landed face down in the dirt, antlers stuck in the ground. Rolling over to try and free his head, Hunter struggled with the mask. Sliding it off, he rolled over to see that he was completely surrounded by the tribe of Indians and Bigfeet. Lying on the ground, the string still hovered over his head. It wiggled for a second over his face, seeming to sniff him, then moved ever so slightly and touched the very tip of the thread on Hunter's chest, over his heart.

At once, the panic and fear that Hunter had known his whole life were gone. A calming peace that he had never thought possible washed over him. He felt washed clean. From the inside he felt white as snow. He closed his eyes and relished the feeling of complete serenity for the first time in his life.

Filled with a joy and an indescribable peace, Hunter smiled and opened his eyes.

He was alone.

Chapter 10: Focus

fo·cus: *noun* \ˈfō-kəs\a state or condition permitting clear perception
or understanding

The sky was gray and the ground cold and hard. Hunter felt as though he was in a dream— neither here nor there. Not really anywhere. He could not tell up from down through the thick fog surrounding him. The feelings of peace and comfort were still with him, although all sense of time and place were gone. Still lying on the ground, the only frame of reference he had for his location was the cold campfire surrounded by the log benches, now empty and devoid of all heat and flame, and the silvery string that still attached itself to Hunter's heart.

He tried to touch it, but his hand went right through, as though the string wasn't even there. Almost like a ghost, but not. He could see it, and he could feel it, yet he could not grab it.

You cannot touch the Maker; He must touch you. The words echoed in his head. Again he tried to grasp the silver attachment, and again his hand passed through the string in the mist as though it was water.

Hunter stood. As he moved, the string moved with him. It passed through his body as he turned around to survey his surroundings. Turning a complete circle he saw the same thing. With a visual field of about ten feet in any single direction, beyond that, all was gray. Turning back to the fire, the buck skull was still at his feet, antlers stuck in the dirt. He bent forward and wrestled it loose. Lifting it from the ground, the mist revealed a pile of stones underneath. Hunter felt a chill. These were the very stones he'd used this afternoon to train on the tree. Recognizing the color and the size, he bent to grab one. It was the same smooth finish that fit perfectly into his small hand. Keeping it close, he took a step out into the mist. Walking only a few feet one direction, and then back again, Hunter was afraid to leave the fire pit. Stepping out into the mist, he changed his mind and turned back, panicked.

Next to the fire where he'd just been was a large brown shape. A mound, low to the ground and very blurred, it moved slightly. It had not been there just a second before. Hunter tried to run. He turned back the opposite way, and was met with multiple sets of red glaring eyes. Frozen, he turned back to the fire. Clenching his hands in fear, he gripped the stone harder. With the instinct of a trained huntsman, he raised his arm over his head ready to strike.

The large brown mound made a sound. It wasn't really a growl, more like a purr, then it moved again.

"Mikey!"

Hunter leapt through the mist and threw himself onto the mound on the ground, hugging his friend. He didn't even bother to cover his nose this time.

Mikey raised a finger to his lips in a quieting gesture. Hunter nodded and settled back down on the ground at his feet. Together, the two surveyed the multiple sets of glowing red eyes trained on them from every possible angle.

"What are they?' Hunter whispered. In his heart he already knew the answer.

"Evil."

Hunter looked up into the air; the circle of dream catchers was gone. Around him, from every angle, was the dingy, thick, gray fog.

"What do we do now?" he asked Mikey.

"Be ready," was the quick reply. Mikey was in the starter's position to run. Hunter assumed the same crouching body position Mikey had. Low to the ground, hands out, buck head tucked under his arm, fingers spread as though he were on the starting block of a race.

I wonder what we would have to —

"Run!" came the command. Mikey sprinted through the darkened mist with Hunter on his heels. In their void, the eyes pounced, snarling and snapping at the spot that had once been the safety of the campfire only seconds before.

Sprinting into the darkened forest, Mikey, Hunter on his enormous heels, searched the darkened forest for shelter and safety.

Finding a small cave, the two ducked inside. It went back only a few feet, more like an indentation into the mountainside rather than a full-fledged cave. Hunter realized in a flash that this was a mistake. Now they were trapped. He turned back to the entrance to see dozens of red glaring eyes on them. Moisture dripped from the brush where they hid. Hunter's stomach sickened at a thought, it might be drool, not rain.

Mikey busied himself pushing a huge boulder toward the opening of the cave to give them shelter. Taking his place behind it, Mikey cowered low to the ground, hiding. From his position, he was able to reach further into some close-by brush, gathering small stones making a pile at Hunter's feet. Mikey grabbed Hunter's hand and placed a small smooth stone into his palm.

"Throw."

Sinclair, 2014, 2016

Hunter reared back and threw the stone, missing his target altogether. He could hear them moving around, but the thick gray cloud moved with them. Swirling mist and dense brush kept Hunter from seeing his targets clearly. All he could see was the red flash of their eyes as they moved, and the dripping of their sharpened fangs.

Hunter started to cry. There were so many of them. His eyes darted from one to the other. He tried to take aim at one, when another started to charge. He turned to throw, and another snarled at his side. They ducked and turned all around him, confusing his senses and shaking his new-found confidence. All Hunter and Mikey could hear was the scuffling of feet, rustling of branches, and the unearthly growl of these demonic creatures. Hunter's hand shook. He looked to Mikey for help. The enormous creature crouched behind the rock, as far as he could be from the vicious fight that lay ahead. He tossed another stone at Hunter. "Throw," he said again in a weak and shaking voice.

Hunter wanted to run. There was no escape. He spun around again to look for an escape. As he flipped around he caught sight of the thin silvery thread, still attached to his heart. He had forgotten. The Maker was still touching him.

"Why is this happening?" he screamed upwards. "Help me!" Again crying, the old feelings of hurt and pain crept back into his soul. *I can't do this. I'm not good enough.*

The string stirred. Hunter's heart tickled, but he did not laugh. *I can't*, he thought again.

The string stirred once again. Hunter's heart stirred with it. A second thread from the string unraveled and hovered over the top of the deer skull that he had worn earlier in the day. Hunter stared, trying to figure out what it meant. The rustling and snarling continued, moving closer with every second. Now he could see the fangs and their elongated, snarling snouts clearly through the brush. Their nostrils flared each time they caught wind of their prey, making them drool more with each breath.

The string wiggled again, like a finger pointing the way.

Hunter dropped the rock he was holding and reached for the mask. Lifting the heavy animal head over his shoulders, he seated it back onto his head and rested it against his shoulders. Hunter felt as though he had the weight of the world on his shoulders. Blinking hard through the tears, his heart stirred again. String still visible through the mask, Hunter felt the Maker's touch deep inside.

His focus narrowed through the eyes of the deer mask. His neck muscles rippled from the weight of the skull, the antlers keeping his head steady and straight. Neck taught and head steady, Hunter's focus narrowed to what the deer would have seen— to see what evil sees. He now saw only one set of glowing eyes in front of him. Kneeling down to grab a stone, Hunter, perched on one knee, reared back and threw, hitting the zombie right between the eyes with a single throw. It fell to the ground in front of him. A haunting wail emerged from the brush to his right. Hunter grabbed another stone from the pile at his feet. Turning his head, he focused his gaze on the one single threat. Lunging from the brush at him, Hunter reared back and threw again. A second shadowless target hit the ground.

Again and again, as the scuffling and wailing zombies in the brush attacked, Hunter zeroed in on them one by one, picking them off as though they were bottles on a fence. Slowly the rustling lessened. Hunter looked around the forest. From his vantage point in the cave, he could see nothing. Still, his heart stirred uneasily. He sensed a trap.

Removing the deer head, he scanned the brush. He saw nothing, but his heart told him he was not finished. Hunter looked at his feet. The rocks were gone. Mikey still hid as far from the fray as he could. Wedged into a ball in the corner of the rock formation, he didn't even look Hunter's direction any longer. He merely cowered.

Hunter looked back to the dense brush, eyes centering between two large redwood trees directly in front of him. Still seeing nothing, he sensed that evil was still there, lurking, waiting for a chance to pounce.

Slowly, the branches of the trees began to rustle, but not low to the ground. The branches moving were higher up on the tree, taller than Hunter. The eyes were the first things he saw. Glowing red orbs, they were the size of the dream catchers that had hung over them at the campfire. Antlers the size of small trees came into view, mounted on a head bigger than his bike back home. Jolts of electricity sparked in the air and arced between the points above the giant head. Snarling, dripping teeth the size of Hunter's arm were bared as the creature inched its way closer and closer, making no attempt to hide. Hunter could feel the weight of its stare bearing down on him. The sense of evil permeated the entire cave and forest.

Hunter's heart stirred yet again. He could still feel the Maker. He did not need to look for the silvery string, for somehow he knew it was still there. Instinct told him to reach into his pocket. From there, he pulled out his gift, the quartz rock that was given to him, and the tiny yellow

Sinclair, 2014, 2016

seed. Holding the seed in his hand, it jumped as his heart did.

This is all you will need. Believe just this much, and you can move mountains.

Hunter tightened his grip on the rock and focused on the enormous presence of evil lurking right before him. Rearing back, he felt the rock tingling in his hand. The closer the giant source of evil came, the hotter the rock in his fist became. The growling of the creature corresponded to the burning of the quartz. Narrowing his focus, eyes dead-center, hand steady, heart confident, Hunter drew back and hurled the rock forward with every ounce of his strength.

Instead of him releasing the rock, the rock released him. Hunter was sucked back through the mist and forest. In the blink of an eye, he was seated back at the campfire. The fire dancers whooped and hollered, Bigfeet cheering, Hunter was back among friends. Abornazine still stood in the center of the circle, head high with the unicorn horn pointing upwards, arms raised, fingers no longer burning, praising the Maker for delivering their young friend back to them. He raised the fatted portion of the meat that had been set aside as an offering of thanks. High up over his head, tears of joy pouring down his jowls and around the

Sinclair, 2014, 2016

single horn in the center of his head, Abornazine smiled at Hunter.

Hunter looked down at the quartz rock still in his hand. It glowed a bright glistening white. Closing his hand, he spotted the tiny yellow seed.

If you can believe just this much...

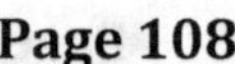

Sinclair, 2014, 2016

Chapter 11: Rest

Rest: /rest/ Noun; refreshing ease or inactivity after exertion or labor; relief or freedom, especially from anything that wearies, troubles, or disturbs; mental or spiritual calm; tranquility.

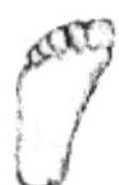

"Welcome home, Pahana." Quiet Cloud was the first to reach Hunter. "The Great One smiles on you today."

Hunter opened his mouth to speak, but was assaulted by many more congratulations. He was slapped on the back so many times the deer skull slid sideways on his head.

Feeling it being lifted off, Hunter came face-to-face with a smiling Mikey.

"What happened to you out there?"

"Must learn when to fight," Mikey said. "Not my battle."

"You could have helped me," Hunter's voice began to rise slightly as he tried to swallow his anger.

"Stop whining," Mikey slapped him on the shoulder. "You did it!"

Sinclair, 2014, 2016

Pride at his accomplishment won out as more and more congratulations came at him.

The sea of bigfeet and Indians soon parted and Hunter was face-to-face with the tribal elder, Raging Bull, once again.

"You are a man now, Pahana. The Spirit in the sky showers His blessings down on you." He turned to face the small crowd around the burning campfire. The mist cleared and Hunter could see everyone and everything clearly. "You are one of us!" Raging Bull's voice boomed. "Warrior!" Over and over the crowd cheered. Hunter was hoisted up and thrust on the shoulders of one of the elders, and paraded around the campfire as though he were a trophy. After a quick trip around once, he was lowered back down at the feet of Raging Bull.

"What does it mean, 'Pahana'?" he asked.

"Lost White Brother," Raging Bull smiled. "Come." Raging Bull and the other elders stretched their welcoming arms back toward the village. Hunter led the way.

"Now I can find my father?"

"Now you rest."

"No, I have to find my father."

"Rest." It sounded more like a command than a statement.

"No," Hunter protested. "I had only three days. It might be too late already."

"Not too late," Quiet Cloud said. "Still time."

"But I need to go," Hunter continued. "I only had three days."

Mikey placed his hands squarely on Hunter's shoulders and turned his body to face him. "Still time. Need rest."

Raging Bull was there, too. "You cannot help your father, or any other, if not ready to fight. Must rest now. Journey on tomorrow." Not waiting for a reply, the tribal elders turned and began walking back to the village. Hunter and Mikey followed.

"You still could have helped me," Hunter snapped.

Hunter's face burned bright red. He felt heat emanating from his entire chest. Looking down he saw that his chest and arms were bright red, too. He was so embarrassed he thought his entire body would turn purple.

"Why do I have to do this?"

Raging Bull laughed out loud. "It is part of the Rite of Manhood. You are a man now, Pahana. It is your right."

"But I don't want to."

"To not choose will be an insult. You will shame them all, and us. You will shame me."

Hunter felt horrible. He didn't want to do this, but he also didn't want to insult his teachers, or shame anyone. He knew all too well what that felt like.

The line of young girls in front of him giggled again, as they had done throughout the day. "Who are they?" he asked, pointing to a row of older women lined up behind the younger ones.

"Mothers. Teachers. Squaw elders. As you became a man today, so they are eager to learn the ways of their mothers. It is their destiny. They have waited for this moment."

"But I don't need anyone to tend to me. Really, I can take care of myself." Hunter looked to Mikey for help. Once again, Mikey turned his back and crouched in the corner, shoulders shaking slightly. This time it was not from fear. It was from suppressed laughter. "Coward," he whispered. Hunter turned back to the line of pretty young maidens in front of him. He would have to go it alone, again.

Sinclair, 2014, 2016

Scanning the gathering of young girls, he spied young women of all sizes and shapes. Most of them were about his own age, he guessed. They looked similar, all having long brown hair, most braided and tied in the back. Some had beads and feathers tied to their silken tresses; others wore their locks loose and flowing. All were dressed in tanned animal hides, stitched together into dresses or skirts with vests. Beading and paint adorned their clothing, making each outfit individual. Tanned skin, hands rough from work, they all smiled at Hunter, eager to take on the next task that life had to offer. Dark brown eyes followed his every move. Hunter felt as though he were being hunted again. Scanning the crowd, his gaze froze on one maiden. There in the back. His finger raised and he pointed at a tall young girl in the back row. She peered back at him through brilliant blue eyes.

"Dyani," Raging Bull said. "Interesting choice."

"Why?"

"Her name means Deer."

The Indian girl stepped forward and nodded in respect to her charge for the evening. Alongside her, stepped one of the elder women. Angry, her teeth clenched, fists balled, and eyes shooting fire his direction, Hunter tried not to run. "Your mother?" he whispered to Dyani.

She nodded, and extended her arm toward a teepee down by the river.

Hunter started forward following Dyani, his maiden's mother right on their heels.

"Why does she hate me?" Hunter whispered.

"Does not hate Pahana," Dyani answered.

"She's staring at me."

"Job is to protect me. What you call - - - chap-a-one."

"Chaperone? How do you know that word?"

"My father is not of this place." Dyani motioned for Hunter to sit on a rock in the river. Once there, she took some loose animal skins and began washing off the war paint that had been applied earlier in the day. Each wipe was a cool relief from the scorching heat that he had felt. As the paint washed away, Hunter realized that part of his redness was also sunburn. The paint had protected his skin where it was applied, but he had sunburned in the unpainted areas. He now sported bright white racing stripes against the red backdrop of his sun damaged skin. Dyani giggled as she washed off the paint from his shoulders. Oh, well, he thought. This is better than before.

Sinclair, 2014, 2016

He smiled at her, but quickly wiped the smile from his face at the glare of her mother.

"Tell me about your father."

"He fell from above when the earth shook one day."

"Your father came from above?" Hunter's heart leapt.

"When he returned, she followed him up to his world."

"What happened?" Hunter was mesmerized by not only her story, but by her gentle ministrations on his burning skin. The cool water and her light touch in the light evening breeze felt as soothing as her soft voice.

"They, as you say, married, but family could not accept her, so she returned."

"She came back down here alone?" Hunter was confused. "How did she get back down here?"

"Warriors brought her."

"The warriors can get up there?"

Dyani nodded. "This is why you seek them."

Hunter stared into the deep blue eyes of his new maiden friend. "I can't believe he let her go. I would never - - -," he broke off at her knowing smile, shades of red creeping back up his neck.

"Ran away," Dyani said. "He knew not where."

Hunter felt a sadness for her.

Sinclair, 2014, 2016

"So you never knew your father?"

"He knows not of me." Dyani bent low, ringing out the animal hides in the river. Walking to the side of the bank, she laid them out on the branches of some brush to dry. Pulling a knife from her belt, she walked over to a plant and sliced off some spiky leaves. Taking three or four back into the river, she laid all but one into Hunter's wet lap.

"Looks like cactus," he said.

"Aloe," she said. "Healing plant."

Slicing open the leaves, she laid the slimy, oozy inside against his burned skin.

Hunter felt instant relief from the burn. "Oh," he muttered as Dyani slid the leaf across his shoulders and upper body. Every spot on his bare skin where the slimy leaf touched was numbed against the searing pain. Dyani followed the aloe with more soothing cool water, making Hunter feel almost normal again. He smiled at her tending to his aching limbs, but wiped the smile away when he caught another glimpse of her mother.

"Is your father why she hates me?"

"Does not hate," Dyani said. "Protects me."

"What is your mother's name?" Hunter asked.

"Mahala. Means mother."

"Mahala?" Hunter called to her on the side of the river bank a few feet away.

"What will you do?" Dyani asked.

Face your enemies head on. Focus. Do not run.

"Make friends." Hunter stood in the river and turned to his adversary. "I'm very hungry. I can't remember the last time I've had anything to eat. Can you bring me some food?"

Mahala grimaced and pointed to her daughter, behind him in the river. Hunter looked back and winked at Dyani. "Stay here," he whispered, then struck out toward her mother.

Reaching the riverbank, he lowered his head toward the elder woman and whispered. "Please. I am far from home and I miss my mother above. No one can cook better than my mahala. Dyani tells me that you are a great preparer of food for her and for the tribe. Please," he whispered close to her. "I need a meal from a mother."

A great smile cracked on the face of the elder woman, changing her appearance immediately. The glow that emanated from her face transformed her from a creature of anger and fear, to one of joy and pride. She stood, waving at her daughter. Shouting something in a language that Hunter did not understand, she turned and ran back toward the village. Hunter started back toward the river when he heard snickering from the bushes. Reaching out and parting the branches, he saw a large brown mound shaking and rolling on the ground out of view from the main path.

"Shut up, Mikey."

Dropping the branches, he walked back to the river.

Sinclair, 2014, 2016

Chapter 12: Leave
Leave [leev] *verb,* **left, leav·ing.**
to go out of or away from, as a place: to let remain or have
remaining behind after **going**

Dyani and Hunter sat together at the fire, Mahala making trip after trip to bring them food. She bustled around the two young people, tending to their every need with a smile as big as theirs. Raging Bull wandered by at one point, shaking his head and smiling at the glowing mother. He winked at Hunter, then left the young party to themselves again.

"How will you rescue your father?" Dyani asked.

Hunter shook his head. "I don't know." He shifted on his log seat. "I don't know anything about where he's being held, or how to get to him."

"He is lucky to have a son like you." Dyani blushed, looking away so Hunter wouldn't see her. "And the others?" she asked. "Your friend, and your sister? What of them?"

Hunter shook his head, unable to answer.

"You will find them," she said. "You are a warrior now. You can fight the evil that holds them. Rescue their spark."

Mahala came back around with another fish. Hunter took the plank of wood used to char it, still hot and smoldering, and balanced it on the log between them. They both picked at it with their fingers.

"And what will be when you find and rescue your father?" she asked looking down to the ground.

"I don't know."

"Will you return to the world above?"

Mahala froze behind them, the grimace on her face returning for a split second, then turning to a saddened remembrance. She set down the grilled corn, and disappeared completely from the young couple, tears falling from her eyes.

"I don't know how to get there."

"There are ways," she whispered.

Hunter nodded. Now torn for the first time between his own family and the world he was thrust into, he had no words for the situation. The two were silent for the remainder of their dinner.

Dyani knelt at Hunter's feet. Inside the teepee the air was warm. There was no fire, but still it felt humid – or was he just sweating? His skin tingled wherever she touched it. Hunter had never felt like this before. He didn't know what was happening to him. He just knew he liked it.

Looking through the open flap of the teepee were the ever-present stares of Mahala and Mikey, Raging Bull ever watchful from behind. All standing guard at the entrance to the living quarters, they were far enough away to give a little privacy, yet close enough to keep an ever watchful eye on the two young ones.

"That's a beautiful necklace." Hunter admired the charm around her neck. "It looks like a dream catcher."

"It is." She smiled and raised a finger to a larger version of the same design that hung over their heads. "Keeps evil away." She continued massaging Hunter's feet, pouring fragrant oil over them and then rubbing it in.

"So it will keep the deer away?" he asked.

"Well, some at least."

"Oh, no," Hunter interrupted. "I didn't mean you."

Dyani smiled. "On the day that I was born, the first thing that my mother saw was a deer. It was very unusual. She said it had eyes of royalty. And so I was named."

Hunter smiled, entranced by her speech.

Sinclair, 2014, 2016

"There are both good and evil in this world," Dyani told him. "We must learn to know the difference. Some good is bad, and some bad can be good."

Hunter's feet wiggled slightly as she continued to rub the oils in. His parched skin soaked up the moisture like a dry cloth.

"With the dream catchers, we have a glimpse of what the eyes cannot see. Do you understand?"

There was no reply. Dyani looked up to see Hunter stretched out flat on his back, mouth wide open, sound asleep. A loud grumbling snore followed.

Dyani smiled. Her job tonight was done. She covered his prone body and lowered the teepee flap as she left.

Day 3

"Luck and prosperity to you on your journey, Pahana. The Great Spirit guide you as you travel." Raging Bull stepped forward from the crowd to congratulate Hunter once again. "You are a feared warrior now, and you are welcome with this tribe always." He smiled and extended his hand to Hunter. Hunter grabbed it, not by the hand in a traditional handshake, but hands grasped near the other's

Sinclair, 2014, 2016

elbow in the arm-to-arm bonding traditional to their native Indian culture. He smiled his thanks, all the while scanning the crowd.

One by one, the remaining tribal elders stepped forward to congratulate him, and shake his arm. Then the crowd followed. Young girls giggled all around, but Hunter's gaze could never seem to find Dyani.

After everyone in the tribe wished him luck, Mikey stepped forward to greet his young friend.

"What is that?" Hunter couldn't contain his laughter.

"Disguise," Mikey said. "Good?"

"Yeah," he laughed again, "it's good." Hunter reached out and touched some of the leaves and twigs stuck in Mikey's thick fur. He was covered with them from head to foot, looking like a giant walking bush, but still not smelling like one. *Camouflage*, Hunter thought. *I guess the idea had to come from somewhere.*

"Come," Mikey said. "We go now."

Hunter did not move.

"Come," he said again, touching Hunter's shoulder. Saddened beyond words, Hunter turned to face Mikey, and saw Dyani behind him. His face lit up. Stepping past the walking bush, Hunter went to her side. In her hands was wrapped a leather strap, with a woven object on the end, and a very small piece of leather, also on a strap.

"This is for you, to bring safety on your journey." She held out a dream catcher identical to the one that she wore around her neck.

"It will help you decipher evil." She smiled. Reaching up, she placed the object around Hunter's neck.

He nodded his thanks and pointed to the second object, a small leather circle, no bigger than a quarter with a leather strap on it as well. "What is that?"

Dyani held the circle up to cover her nose, and held the straps around her head. Lowering her eyes, she gestured toward Mikey. "To keep bad smells away. We call it 'Bigfoot buddy'."

Hunter laughed out loud. "So this wards off evil, too. Evil smells, at least."

She giggled and handed the leather buddy to Hunter.

He mumbled a thank you, trying not to let the entire tribe behind him hear.

"Thank you for helping me last night," Hunter managed to mumble.

"And you helped me as well. I have passed the Rite of Womanhood now."

"What does that mean?"

"In the tribe it means that I am able to be pledged to another."

Hunter's heart lurched.

Sinclair, 2014, 2016

"Are there any here who would want to be with you?"

She nodded. At his hurt look she smiled. "Worry not, Pahana. I can run faster than they."

They both laughed.

"Come," Mikey said again, softly this time. He walked a few feet away and waited.

"I will try to come back and visit," Hunter said, not knowing if he really could.

"I will wait for that moment," she smiled. "Peace on your journey, Pahana."

"Thank you, Dyani."

Hunter turned to walk toward Mikey. His feet felt like lead, and his heart was just as heavy. Reaching the edge of the clearing, he turned to wave at the tribe and to look upon his new friend one last time. Stepping back into the forest, he looked over at a snickering Bigfoot.

"Shut up, Mikey!" he snapped and headed back into the forest.

Their screams became muffled and faint as they flew through absolute darkness, swallowed up in the pitch black hole of this new world. Slamming into the dark, hard ground, three separate aftershocks rocked the earth beneath them, and then, nothing.

Land Ho, Matey!

Sinclair, 2014, 2016

Chapter 13: Voyage

voy·age pronunciation *noun, verb,* -aged, -ag·ing,
a course of travel or passage, especially a long journey by
water to a distant place.

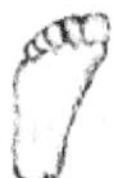

Day 1

Ian slammed down hard, face-first into the soft sand. He laid still for a moment, face buried up to his ears. He could feel the coolness of the moist sand under him. Slowly, he pushed himself up and looked around. He tried, anyway. Sand clung to his face and eyelashes, dropping into his mouth and eyes with each move. Ian spat and slapped at his face and eyes until some semblance of normal vision returned.

He was back on the beach. The water lapped gently against the tranquil shore just a few yards away. Off in the distance, across the lake, was a dense forest. Ian scanned the tree line in search of his friends. Focusing hard off into the distance, he saw movement. Narrowing his gaze, he blinked hard, and shook his head. Ian rubbed his eyes.

I'm hallucinating.

It looked as though the trees were moving. Not just swaying, but running, their large brown trunks shifting from one position to another. One even looked as though it had arms and legs.

There's no such thing as a bigfoot, Mr. Welch said. There's no such thing.

Ian dismissed it and turned back to face the water.

He sat alone on the beach. There was no one in sight. Around him were a few large boulders, and some small rocks. There was driftwood, sea shells, and seaweed, but mostly lots and lots of sand. Off to his left side, the water extended as far as his eye could see. Once in a while, a fish would jump up and splash back down into the water. They seemed to be playing with each other. There were dozens of them stretching from the coastline, far out into the water. Ian couldn't even see how far out they went. He stood and tried to stretch up on the tips of his toes, but wasn't able to get a much better view. He decided to climb up on one of the large boulders near him.

The second he stepped up, the rock unfurled itself and whipped its huge tail around in anger. Giant jaws with razor-sharp teeth swung back and snapped at him, missing his leg by mere inches. Ian lurched forward, launching his body from the rock and ran waist-deep into the water. Swimming out until he felt a safe distance, he tread water and turned back to the shore. When he did, he nearly fainted.

The giant crocodile on the shore just a dozen or so yards away lifted its enormous head and snapped again, this time catching a seabird in its jaws. Swallowing the thing whole, it lay back down and re-curled into a ball. Waiting for more prey, Ian watched as its eyes scanned the shoreline in rapid movements. Glancing around at the other rocks on the shore, he saw eyes blinking on the rest of them, too. Occasionally a tail would whip out in a lethal jab, then tuck back under its owner again in a tight ball. There were hundreds of them.

Ian floated in the warm inlet, trying to figure out what to do next. He clearly could not return to the shore and the dangers that awaited him there. Off to either side were the thick forests with the running trees, and behind him lay the open expanse of water as big as any ocean he had ever seen. Ian was dumbfounded. He had no options. Not knowing what to do or where to go, he floated out to a tiny island that lay off the shore and climbed up on it to think and dry out.

Ian took off his boots and dumped out the water. He removed his shirt and wrung out as much as he could before putting it back on. Sitting on the highest mound on the small island, he closed his tired, burning eyes.

Sinclair, 2014, 2016

What on earth was happening? First thing this morning he was hunting with his friends, then a nasty storm hit, catapulting him into a scary new world. Not to mention the odd little leprechaun giving advice. Now that was just weird. Now he was alone and didn't know which way to go. Mr. Welch was a prisoner of some evil serpent. Hunter and Aeryn were who-knows-where, and a giant crocodile nearly ate him alive. Ian took a deep breath and opened his eyes. Blinking hard, he looked back at the shoreline. It seemed farther away, but that couldn't be right. He was on an island. Ian knew he was tired, and had been through a lot. He was just imagining things now.

With a deep sigh, he tried to re-group. *What am I going to do? How am I going to get out of this mess and back to the world above? What had that little green thing said about finding a road somewhere? I have to make my own path to something.* Ian looked around again. Was there a path somewhere? Was there a road?

"Oh no." His stomach tied into knots. He felt like he would throw up. He squinted hard through the rising sun. Ian could barely see the shore now. His island was floating. He was drifting out to sea. Ian stood and scurried down to the shore. For a moment he toyed with the idea of jumping in and swimming back to the main beach, but one thought of the giant crocs squashed that idea.

Sinclair, 2014, 2016

"Great," he said. "Could this get any worse?"

The island lifted its enormous head and twisted back to face him.
"Why?"

Chapter 14: Ian
I·an [ee-*uh*n, ee-ahn, ahy-*uh*n] *noun*
a male given-<u>name</u>, Scottish form of <u>John</u>; meaning: God is
gracious.

Ian gasped at the giant head leaning down at him. The long, craning neck hovered high in the air, looking a lot like the serpent that had snatched Morgan from the shore just a short time ago. He screamed and backed up on the tiny island, realizing it was no island at all. Turning, he dashed down the creature's back heading for the water and flung himself in.

Ian swam as hard as he could. With no sense of direction or time, he knew he just had to get out of there, and fast. A few feet into the water, the serpent's giant tail skimmed the surface and dragged him back up onto its back.

"Stop," it called to him, but Ian launched back into the water again, swimming harder and faster.

Again the tail swung across the top of the water and hurled Ian back onto itself. "You can't—" the creature tried to speak, but again Ian leapt into the warm water.

Over and over again they followed this routine, with Ian growing more angry with each new try at freedom. Harder and harder he stomped back into the water, fear gone and rage taking its place, only to be flung back onto the serpent's back one more time.

"Let me explain," the serpent tried again, but Ian's closed mind would have no part in it.

"Let me go!" Ian swung his boot back and kicked the thing as hard as he could.

"Fine!" it sputtered, then submerged, leaving him floating in the water once again.

Ian gasped and choked from the sudden splash of water against his face. When he relaxed, he looked around all directions, spying nothing but water as far as his eye could see. Somewhat bewildered, he struck out toward nothing.

When the giant head popped up in front of him, he gasped, again taking in a mouthful of water. Choking, he stopped swimming to catch his breath. Without a word, he turned to swim another direction.

"Don't you want some help?"

"I don't need your help," Ian snapped. "You, or anybody – anything – else."

"Oh, come on," the thing prompted. "Let's be friends. My name is Nestor."

Ian kept swimming.

"And you might be…?" it trailed off.

"None of your business."

"You know, for a human, you're pretty angry."

Ian spun around in the water to face Nestor and tread water. "You dumped me in the water."

"You kicked me."

"You made me mad."

"You made me mad first," Nestor quipped. "And now that we're through with all this nonsense, can't we just be friends?"

"I don't need any friends."

"What about the ones you are trying to find?"

Ian slowed again, still floating, with Nestor following closely behind.

"Do you know where they've gone?"

Ian was silent.

"Because, I do." Nestor stopped.

Ian spun to face it again. "Why didn't you tell me?" Ian screamed back through the rippling surf.

"You never asked."

The answer seemed so simple, yet it enraged Ian again. He swam back toward the creature with hatred shooting from his eyes.

Sinclair, 2014, 2016

Nestor bobbed and weaved his long neck both in and out of the water, dodging Ian's attempted blows. The more Ian missed, the angrier he became. Turning to swim away, Nestor's great tail swung in front of him and dragged Ian up onto his back, again protruding from the water like a tiny island. Ian screamed and flung himself back into the water. Again and again they followed this same routine. Ian finally collapsed near the waterline of Nestor's back, exhausted. He lay still, barely breathing, not sure what to do next.

Nestor's giant head hovered over him just like it did when this whole nightmare began. He snorted, but Ian swore it was more of a snicker. The head dipped down to his prone body and sniffed. Ian reached out a balled fist and slugged the snout as hard as he could.

"Ouch!" It reared back, ready to strike, then settled down. "Ok, I guess we're even. Now can we be friends?"

"Why do you want to be friends with me?"

"Because we can help each other."

"Help each other? How?" Ian asked.

"I can help you find your friends."

"Yeah," Ian ventured. "What do I have to do?"

"Nothing," Nestor said with a grin. "Just let me tag along."

It's a trick, Ian's insides churned a warning. *It's too simple*. He eyed the serpent, an uneasiness rising in the back of his throat.

"What do I get out of it?" he demanded.

Nestor's grin disappeared and his head descended down to Ian's level. Squinting eyes narrowed down until tiny slits peered at him. He was so close his exhaled breath blew Ian's wet hair back. "You get to find your friends, and you don't drown." Raising back up, Nestor glared down at his new companion.

"Deal," Ian said, then curled up to go to sleep. "I need a nap."

Sinclair, 2014, 2016

Chapter 15: Sail

Sail [seyl] verb/to move along or travel over water

Ian stretched and yawned on his make-shift floating shore. The warm ocean breeze felt good against his cool skin, baking in the late sun's warmth. The wind came in spurts, like small bursts of the earth's energy. He stirred, and slowly opened one eye.

In front of him was a giant blue sphere with a big jet black globe in the middle. The warm breeze washed over him again. The sphere blinked. Ian bolted up straight, nose-to-nose with Nestor, curled up into a tight, floating ball.

"What are you doing?"

"Just catching a few zzz's." Nestor stretched his giant neck skyward and yawned, unrolling his tail into the water.

"How could you be sleeping? You were supposed to be taking me to land."

"I never said I would take you to land." Nestor laid his head back down on his back, and curled back into a ball. "I said I would take you to your friends."

"Yes, but my-friends-are-on-the-land," Ian snapped.

Sinclair, 2014, 2016

"I know where they are. Don't worry. We will be there soon."

Ian stood on the back of the enormous sea creature. He climbed to the top of the hump protruding from the water. Looking around, he saw nothing but sea.

"We're not even close to land."

"That's not true," Nestor smiled. "What you call Scotland is right up there." A fin stuck skyward.

"No, California is up there," Ian snapped. "That's where I came from. Scotland would be down there."

"Indeed," Nestor said, "but the world has turned since you've been here. California is now down there, and Scotland above. Likewise, your friends are not back there, but ahead."

Ian looked around and tried to make some sense of what was happening. He couldn't tell one way from another. "Well, we can't just sit here."

"We're not sitting, we're swimming."

The softer, female sounding voice startled him. Ian looked beside Nestor in the water to see an identical creature, only smaller in size.

"May I introduce you to my cousin? You may know her as Nessie. Your kind has dubbed her that."

"Nessie? As in, the Loch Ness Monster?"

"I am not a monster! Why is it that anything that is different from a human is dubbed a monster?"

"Ummm. I dunno."

"Well, I do not like that name. Nessie is okay, but not the monster-thing. Deal?"

"Um, sure. Deal." Ian sat down. "How do you get down here? I mean up there? Where are you guys from, anyway?"

"We go where we are needed," Nestor said. "Mostly we reside down here, but travel above when it is necessary."

"Why Scotland? Why not anywhere else?"

"What you call Scotland has the easiest passage to the world above. It has quick access to the oceans for worldwide travel."

"Oh." Ian smiled. "Kinda like a freeway."

Nessie laughed. "Kind of."

"Do you even know what a freeway is?"

Both creatures remained silent, although Ian swore he saw them smile at each other. "So what are you two anyway? What is your species called?"

"We have been named the Plesiosaur."

"Are you dinosaurs?"

"If you please. We have been around since the dawn of mankind."

"So you were part of the Big Bang then?"

"Excuse me," Nessie snapped, "but I have never squirmed around in a mud puddle. I have been beautifully and wonderfully made by the Maker. Just look at my wings."

"Um, those are fins."

"Call them what you will. With them, I can soar."

She spun around, dancing in the water like the dolphins at the water park near Ian's home. Fins stretched outward and long neck skyward, she twirled in the water like a ballerina. Nestor followed suit, spinning Ian around.

He grabbed on to Nestor's back for the ride. "Okay, okay. Sorry. That's what we learned in school."

"Yes, well. They used to teach that evil spirits could be sucked out of you by leeches, too."

"They can't?"

"Very funny," Nestor said.

Ian climbed up Nestor's neck so he could see where they were. "Which way are we going?" he asked.

"The right way."

"Is that supposed to be a joke?"

"You would prefer the wrong way?"

"I just want to get to my friends."

"I understand," Nestor said, "but you must know that the road will be long and fraught with danger."

Sinclair, 2014, 2016

"Yeah, the green gremlin said that, too."

"Ahhh, so you've met Alistair then. Good."

"Yeah, we met him. He gave me this." Ian pulled the small flask of clear liquid from his pocket. "Never told me what I need to do with it though."

"Save it," Nessie said. "You will need it later,"

"What is it? Is it magic?"

"No. There is no magic here. Only Him."

"Who?"

"Him, the Maker." She slowed her speed so she could see Ian. "That is a gift."

"What is it?" He shook the flask. Nothing happened.

"Careful," she cautioned. "It's water."

"Water? Since when do I have to be careful with water? Maybe I'll just drink it and be done with it."

"I wouldn't do that."

"Why," Ian asked. "Will I die? Is it poison? What will happen if I do?"

"Nothing."

"Nothing? You two aren't making any sense. I have to be careful with it, but I can't drink it; it's not poison; and nothing will happen if I open it; but it's mine it and I have to take care of it. Is there anything else?"

Sinclair, 2014, 2016

Nestor stopped swimming and curled his head back around onto his back again. "It's special water. Not magic as you said, but touched."

"Touched? By who?"

"By the Maker. When used the right way, it can wash away all that holds us back in life."

"There's nothing holding me down."

"Not down, Ian. Back. Before. Things like fear, hurt, rejection, —"

"I don't have any of those," he cut in.

"—anger."

"Who you calling angry?" he barked.

"No one," Nestor smiled. "It was just an example."

"So how does this stuff work anyway?" He shook the bottle again. He peered at it with a skeptical eye.

"First of all, you must believe."

"Ok. What else?"

"When the time is right, you will know. Magic comes from within and will always fail you. Miracles come from above, and will never let you down. Always thank the One who gave it to you. He alone is in control."

"Hmmm." Ian nodded. He thought about Alistair. Ian had no idea how he would be able to thank the little green thing for it, so far away. He didn't even know where he was.

Sinclair, 2014, 2016

"Tuck the flask away someplace very safe," Nestor instructed, "and lay low. We must be very quiet. We are heading into some very dangerous waters."

The smell of seaweed was pungent. The rope Ian had braided to secure the flask around his neck was strong. The strands were still moist against his hot skin. He lay flat on his stomach, on Nestor's barely protruding back. Both Nessie and Nestor were low in the water, only their nostrils and the tops of their heads floated above the waterline. The three slinked along the water's surface for some time.

Ian loved adventure. He loved the sea as well; the sand, the salt, the smell. He thrived in this environment. Well, usually he did. Right now he was bored to tears. There was no adventure. There was no action, and there certainly didn't seem to be any danger. In fact, there didn't seem to be any reason for the stealthy incognito approach at all. Yet every time he made a sound or tried to sit up, Nestor had snapped him back down, quieting him. That giant green lug was really beginning to get on Ian's last nerve.

At least they appeared to be getting closer to land. They had passed several rocks protruding up from the water. These were real rocks, too, not Plesiosaurs disguised as rocks. He had reached out his hand and touched them on their way past to make sure. Actually, 'mountain' would be a better term for them. These rocks were bigger than Ian's house, and wider than a bus. Ian thought it odd that they were sticking so close to the rocks, though. Why not just swim back out in the open sea like they had done before? But each time he tried to ask, he'd been shushed quiet. Well, he'd had about enough of this game. Ian had decided that as soon as he could spot land, he would jump on to the next rock, then swim to shore once his pals had disappeared. He could find his friends and rescue Mr. Welch without any help. Ian felt fairly sure that if he was on dry land that Nestor's tail couldn't get to him, although he wouldn't bet his freedom on it. Not yet, anyway. For now, he just laid low and watched for the perfect opportunity.

The group floated up against a particularly large rock, and settled into its shadow. The two serpents stretched their long necks out and peered around the corner in front of them. Drawing their necks back, they looked first at each other, then back to Ian. "Shhh," Nestor whispered.

"Why?"

Sinclair, 2014, 2016

"Shhh," Nessie urged. "Danger is near."

Ian tried to crane his neck to see what was on the other side of the rock. He could not get it out far enough to see what was there, but he did catch sight of some land. *Perfect. Now my plan will work.* "What are we waiting for?" Ian whispered back.

"Darkness," Nestor whispered, keeping both his voice and his head low.

"I want to see." Ian inched forward, holding Nestor's neck and slipping into the water by his head. Nestor's tail swung around at the ready, by Ian's side. "I just want to see. What is it?" He could hear chains rattling, and water slapping up against something hollow. There were many footsteps, raucous laughter, and scraping sounds that reminded Ian of when his mother would move furniture around the house. He inched forward a bit more, but was snatched back by Nestor's tail.

"That's far enough," Nestor cautioned. "It's not safe."

"But what is it?"

Nessie gasped, and began swimming backwards. Nestor followed suit, inching his way back around the rock to the other side. The noises they heard were getting louder. Ian kept trying to inch forward while the serpents paddled back. Frustrated, bored, and ready to strike out on his own, Ian put action to his plan and leapt from Nestor's back and up onto the giant rock. Trying to scurry up the wet surface, Ian lost his footing and slid down the opposite side, splashing down into a small bay.

"Man overboard!" someone screamed.

"Man overboard! Drop the anchor. Lower the sails. Set the buoys and bring the matey aboard!"

Sinclair, 2014, 2016

Chapter 16: Red

red[red]: any of various colors resembling the color of blood; *Informal.* to become very angry; become enraged:

Ian looked up at the hull of a wooden sailing vessel.

Waving in the breeze, a black and white flag. The emblem unfurling on the flag both frightened and excited him at the same time. It was an arm from elbow to fingertips showing the back of a hand, and a sword crossed in an X pattern from corner to corner. On the back of the hand was branded the letter "P" — the mark of a pirate.

Ian's heart pounded.

"Man overboard!" he heard someone yell again. A rope was thrown over the ship to him. For an instant, he thought about trying to escape, but the thrill and adventure of being on a real pirate ship took over. Eagerly, he swam to the rope dangling over the ship's rail and grabbed hold.

The first hoist jerked him from the water. Ian's heart jumped with each hoist. Halfway up the hull, the rope began to spin with his unbalanced weight. Circling around and around, he closed his eyes against the dizziness that

Sinclair, 2014, 2016

was seeping into his consciousness. When the hoisting stopped, and the spinning slowed, Ian cracked open one eye to gauge his surroundings. Arms from several owners grabbed at him, his own arms jerked up over his head. Ian felt hands grabbing at his belt, and sliding his body over the side rail. He was thrown face-down onto the splintering deck of the vessel.

Ian tried to push himself up onto all fours, but felt a large boot in the middle of his back slamming him back down. Anger surged inside him as he tried to push back up again, only to be shoved back down again and again. Raucous laughter exploded around him as he fought against the boot holding him down. Ian flailed his arms and legs at the many other pairs of boots in his line of sight, but to no avail. They kicked back at him, or shook with laughter at his futile attempts to get free. Seething inside at his failure to stand, Ian gave up and laid flat on the deck, grinding his teeth.

I'm gonna hurt someone when I get up from here! You better watch out — all of you.

"Look!" Ian heard. "He's hair like a flame." He felt hands tugging and pulling on the strands at the back of his head.

Sinclair, 2014, 2016

"Haven't you ever seen red hair before?" Ian tried to raise his head to the side, but the boot stayed firm in the middle of his back.

"What manner of pantaloons be they?" Again he felt hands tugging and pressing against the blue denim jeans he wore. "They be stiff." The voice sounded confounded. "How de ye git ye inside?"

Oh, for heaven's sake. Are you really that stupid? Before Ian had a chance to say anything, he was flipped over onto his back, and the boot again lodged into his stomach.

"Ahhh!" one pirate screamed. "He be the devil 'imself." Several pirates backed up. Fingers pointing, fear causing their entire bodies to tremble. Braver pirates moved in for a closer look.

"Nay," one toothless man said. "It be a paintin'."

"Why would ye wear a paintin'?" The raucous laughter started again, and fingers once again jabbed at his midsection. "Paintin'," he heard over and over again. "Jus' a paintin'."

Ian looked down at his soggy t-shirt, now smeared with dirt from the filthy deck. Under the smears and smudges was the once colorful picture of his favorite rock band. He thought about trying to explain it, but gave up. There was no point.

"Who sent ye?" When the voice bellowed, the deck fell silent. "Be this some manner of witchery?" The pirates surrounding Ian parted like the Red Sea. Off in the distance he could see a figure moving toward him, his face blocked by the glow of the sun behind him. The footsteps sounded odd, more like one step and one thump.

Step.

Thump.

Step.

Thump.

Silence permeated his senses as the figure came into focus. He was a giant of a man, standing with one wooden peg for a leg.

"Who sent ye to spy on us?" he growled.

"No one. I'm not a spy."

"Them be peculiar words ye use, lad. Where de ye hail from?"

Ian pointed toward the sky.

"He be a liar, Cap'n. That be an ol' sailor's tale. Folk don't jus' fall from the heav'ns."

"I did," he tried to protest.

"Shut yer mouth." The boot pushed farther into his midsection. "Ye speak only when the Cap'n says ye can. Got it, lad?"

Ian nodded, wind pushed out of his lungs. At this point he was struggling just to breathe.

"So, ye be either a spy or a liar." His jet black hair and long beard whipped around in the breeze. Ian thought he looked like a crazy man. The captain leaned down close to Ian's face. "Which is it? We hang spies on this here ship."

"What do you do to liars?"

"Feeds 'em to the sharks."

"Look," Ian tried to reason with them. "I'm not a spy. Nobody sent me. I just - - -"

"Ahhh!" The captain waved his hands in frustration. He spun on his peg leg and thumped away. "Lock 'im up."

Again, the hands grabbed him and jerked him up straight to the grizzled and weathered face of a sailor.

"Where d'ye want 'im Cap'n?" the deck mate holding him asked.

"To the brig, after ye search 'im."

"No, wait!" Ian's protests weren't even heard over the jostling and snickering of the men. Jerked up, spun around, his face slammed down onto the side rail, his hands wrenched behind his back, Ian's heart sank deeper and deeper into despair.

The last thing he saw from the bow of the ship was Nessie and Nestor submerging far out to sea.

Then, once again, there was darkness.

Sinclair, 2014, 2016

The stench hung in the air so thick Ian couldn't breathe. He tried covering his nose with his shirtsleeve and his hand, but to no avail. The dense odor of rotting fish, sea slime, and wet decaying wood was almost more than he could stomach.

He felt around the darkness, afraid of what his hands might touch. So far, he could determine that he was in a small room under the main deck. There was no porthole to the outside. Inside the room with him were a couple of wooden crates, both empty, and some oak barrels filled with something so heavy he could not move them. They also had a strong odor about them, but he could not distinguish it. Ian felt his way all around the room, past the closed door, and around all four walls. Nothing. Other than the barrels and empty crates, there was nothing else around. Nothing. Ian felt his way back across the rough-hewn walls to the door. He tried the handle. Locked. Angry and afraid, he balled his fist, slamming it on the door, shaking it on its hinges. Outside he could hear laughter from his pirate guards.

"Let me out!" he screamed.

"Oh, lets me out!" they mocked back. "I wanna go home to me mummy."

Ian screamed and slammed the door again. This time it opened. In the doorway were two toothless, filthy, smiling pirates illuminated by the candle glow in the lantern behind them.

"Cap'n request'n yer presence," one said.

"Yeah, request'n yer presence," the other echoed.

"What for?" Ian asked.

"He desires a word."

"Yeah, a word."

Ian looked back and forth between the two. When he didn't move, the closest one pulled a dagger and smiled. "Or, ye could die right here."

Ian stepped out of the tiny room and into danger.

Chapter 17: Swabby

Swabby: (swab·bie.; <u>swab</u> + <u>-y</u>[2]: A fool or simpleton; ninny

"Stop pushing me!" Ian planted his feet and pushed back, only to be shoved to the ground. His pirate guards laughed as they kicked him. Dragging him to his feet, they slid him once again across the deck toward the Captain's quarters. Reaching the closed door, the guards knocked and entered without waiting for a command.

"We brung ye the prisoner like'n ye aksed, Cap'n."

"Thank ye, mates. Man yer stations now. Leave the lad wit' me." The two nodded and left the room, closing the door behind them.

Ian stared across the small room. It didn't look anything like what he'd thought the Captain's quarters should look like. It was just a small room. No riches or gold spilling out of treasure chests. No skeletons of defeated foes hanging from the rafters; just a small room, about the size of his bedroom back home. Ian eyed his adversary just a few feet away. Up close he didn't look nearly as frightening. Of course, the last time he'd seen him, Ian was flat on the ground looking up.

Sinclair, 2014, 2016

He stood slightly taller than Ian did. Legs, or leg rather, was very short, with the rest of his body making up the remainder of his height. Wild, uncombed black hair hung past his shoulders and shot outward from his head in every direction. Rich blue eyes, wide and deep-set watched him from the very small desk on one side of the room. The peg he was perched on was carved from a solid piece of wood, rounded at the top to hold his leg severed at the knee. It tapered down to a simple peg at the ground. Ian could see the fine lines of the wood grain running the length of the wooden limb from knee to ground. The grain lines of the wood wound around in almost a circle at the top end, tapering off to a point at the bottom. It was a snake-like pattern naturally embedded in the wood grain. Mesmerizing.

"Who sent ye'?"

"Nobody."

"Aye, so ye're tellin' me that ye fell from the sky, then?"

Ian nodded.

"An' next I 'spect ye'll be tellin' me that thar's giant green sea monsters out thar that eat folk?"

"I don't think they eat people, but - - -"

The Captain burst into uproarious laughter. He fell backwards into his chair and chuckled until tears rolled

Sinclair, 2014, 2016

down his face. When he finally settled down, he faced Ian once again. "It'll go better fer ye if'n ye jus' tells the truth now. Who sent ye to be spyin' on us?"

Ian stood still, not sure how to answer. Clearly, the Captain would not believe anything he could say. He'd already made it clear that he didn't believe in Nessie or Nestor. Ian could hardly believe himself. At this moment, he truly didn't know what to believe, or do.

"It 'twer that loser, Gamblin' James, weren't it?"

Ian tried to think quickly, but his words didn't come quick enough.

"I knew it!" Peg Leg yelled. "That good fer notin' loser had done lost his soul to the Badun's in a game of chance."

"The Badun's?"

"Aye. Ain't ye never heared of the Badun's?"

Ian shook his head.

"Them so evil none can stand 'em." He eyed Ian again, his tone serious. "So how came ye to be in thar company, then?"

Ian said nothing. Again he pointed skyward.

Peg Leg laughed. "Aye, right then. Ye fell from the sky." He snorted. "Weel, ye be my prisoner now, lad. Heed yer warnin' weel sonny. Foller yer order' and it'll be weel wit' ye. Don't, and yer punish'n weel be harsh. Weel not be havin' any mutiny on this ship."

Ian nodded.

"Prove yerself and ye can join us."

Ian's heart jumped. "I can join you? Really? I've always dreamed of being a pirate."

"Yer awful eager, son. Mos' folk ain't so pleased 'bout bein' a slave. I still ain't sure you ain't a spy. I need to do some check'n firs'."

He stood from the chair and banged his peg on the floor three times. The door immediately opened and the same two guards entered. "Take 'im back to up top. He's kin swabs the deck till dark."

"Aye, Cap'n," the two muttered. Ian was again grabbed from behind and shoved back out into the darkened galley-way leading up to his punishment.

The sun was blinding after the absolute blackness of his room. Ian tried to focus his eyes, but still had to shield them with his hands until they adjusted.

"Put yer' hands down, swabby." Ian lowered his hand, but the man standing next to him did not.

Sinclair, 2014, 2016

"I cain't see," he tried to protest. Ian focused enough to see his hand slapped away from his face. Both prisoners closed their eyes waiting for more punishment to come. Ian inhaled the fresh salty sea air and tried to clear his head. A loud crash, and something hard slamming into his shin jerked his senses back. Opening his eyes, he saw a wooden bucket, a rope, and a straggly mop with barely any mop strands remaining, laying on his feet.

"One of ye pull the water from the sea, and the other swab. Cap'n likes the deck to shine like the sun. Understand?"

Both nodded.

"Weel git, then."

The other man dove for the bucket. "I fetch the water. Ye swab," he ordered. Turning his back on Ian, he tied the rope onto the bucket handle and lowered it over the rail. Ian picked up the mop and eyed the head. There weren't more than a dozen stringy pieces, some barely attached. He shook his head. Looking around at the deck of the ship he knew there was no way this would do the job. Maybe that's why his so-called partner took the easy job.

The first bucket of icy water sloshed at his feet. Ian turned to look at the aged man who was his partner. Raggedy and harsh, he truly looked like a pirate. Toothless and dirty, his eyes darted from one end of the ship to the other constantly. He looked scared, but of what Ian didn't know. Perhaps he truly was a spy. Maybe that's why old Peg Leg thought Ian was one, too. Well, he'd just have to prove otherwise. Ian saw no other options right now. His shipmates had to trust him. It was his only choice at this point.

Another splash of icy water washed over his feet. "Swab, boy," he heard his partner order. Ian ignored him. He laid the mop down and pulled off his t-shirt. Ripping the shirt in two, he tied the two pieces around the bottom of the mop handle. Then carefully, he sliced the bottom ends against a ragged piece of the deck rail, shredding it into long strips. After creating a make-shift mop he thought would work, he gave it a try. Dunking the end into a large puddle of seawater, Ian scrubbed a small area of the deck. The new mop head worked great. Looking around to find his partner, Ian found not only him, but several other crew members staring at him.

"What?" he asked.

The guard who'd brought them out this morning pointed at the mop. "Goods works, lad."

Ian smiled.

"Fetch!" he heard the guard yell at his partner. Ian put his head down and concentrated on his work.

Sinclair, 2014, 2016

Ian tried to lie down in his room, but couldn't. He hurt too much. Shoulders sunburned and hands blistered, he couldn't find a comfortable spot to rest. There was no bed. There was no window. There was no light. Ian tried to feel his way around the room again, but his hands were raw and bleeding. He wanted to cry, but dared not. He wouldn't give them the satisfaction.

The door jerked open and two guards entered with a lantern. Again, Ian's eyes took a minute to focus. They were carrying an armload of stuff, but he couldn't yet tell what it was.

"Cap'n said to give ye these." They dropped the pile at his feet. A third man came in from behind. He set his lantern on a crate and handed Ian a plate of food and a glass of something. With the room well-lit and his eyes adjusted, Ian could see a blanket on the floor. On top of it was a folded shirt and a pair of gloves. The first man spoke. "Cap'n said to tell ye good works up on the deck." He shifted his weight and pointed to the pile on the floor. "That be one of Cap'n's shirts fer ye, and 'is own blanket, too."

"Why is Cap'n givin' 'im 'is own stuff?" the second of the three men blurted out. He was quickly clouted on the back of the head by the third man. "Never question Cap'n's orders. That be treason." The same man reached into his pocket and pulled out a small jar of something. He threw it to Ian. "Put some salve on yer hands. Good fer healin'." The three turned and left.

Ian looked at the lantern they had given him, and the bedding on the floor. Satisfied he had done a good job for the day, he sat down to eat. Fish, salty beans, and stale bread had never tasted so good. Ian gulped them down, barely chewing. Falling onto the blanket, he closed his eyes and drifted off.

Chapter 18: Spy

spy [spahy],*noun,* a person who keeps close and secret watch on the actions and words of another or others.

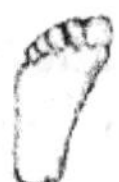

Day 2

The next morning, Ian found himself back out on the deck, hands greasy but feeling better with the salve. It amazed him how dirty the deck could become just overnight.

Without asking Ian, his prisoner-partner grabbed the bucket and threw fresh, cold seawater on Ian's feet, just as he had done yesterday. Anger bubbled up inside him at the second day of insults. Ian threw the mop back at him. "You mop today," he ordered.

"Nay!" he shot back. "I be fetcher 'gain."

"No." Ian was firm. "It's my turn on the rail."

A hand shot out and hit him on his sunburned shoulder. Ian's anger flared. He turned and swung at the other man, who wistfully dodged the blow. Ian tried again, but connected with nothing. A crowd of pirates immediately surrounded them, egging the fighters on. Unable to connect with any blows, Ian lunged forward and

Sinclair, 2014, 2016

tackled the man. The two rolled around on the deck, locked in a tangle of swinging arms and legs. Whoops and cheers surrounded them, until they heard it. The sound of a banging stump on the deck silenced the entire crew.

Again, the men parted like the famed Red Sea and there stood the wild-haired Captain. "Fight'n ain't 'lowed on my ship."

Ian opened his mouth to protest, but a hand slapped over it. A harsh warning was whispered in his ear. "Quiet! Questionin' Cap'n's orders be treason."

Ian lowered his head. He didn't know much about sailing ships, but he did know that treason meant a death sentence, and not a very nice one. Swallowing his anger, he looked down.

"You," Peg Leg pointed to Ian's partner. "Yer on the mop today." He grabbed the mop from the ground. Before handing it to the prisoner he pulled off the t-shirt strands that Ian had put on it the day before. Returning it back to its original straggly condition, Captain Peg Leg shoved the mop at the man. "You," he barked at Ian. "On the bucket, man." Without another word, he spun on his peg and left.

Ian turned to the man who'd stopped him from speaking. It was one of his toothless guards. "Cap'n likes ye. Don't be mess'n up." He grabbed Ian and pulled him to the rail. Handing him the bucket, he gave another stern warning. "No matter what, ye cain't be fight'n. He be watchin' now." He handed the bucket to Ian. "Best be fetchin'."

Bucket after bucket of fresh seawater Ian hoisted over the rail and threw in front of the mop. Even though he initially tried to be kind to the man, throwing the water in front of him rather than on him, Ian still felt the other prisoner's hostility toward him. At every opportunity, the man hit Ian with the mop. All morning he repeatedly slammed it into his feet and cracked the handle against his shins. Each time Ian turned to retaliate, he caught a glimpse of Captain Peg Leg, or Toothless staring at him. Swallowing his anger again and again, Ian swore that the other man taunting him would not get the better of him. He had no idea what the man's plan was, but inciting Ian certainly seemed to be part of it. When the physical attacks didn't work, the verbal assault started.

"Gimme them gloves, boy," he ordered.

Ian looked at the man's rough calloused hands. Clearly he was used to this type of grueling work. Ian rubbed his hands together. They were just starting to feel better. Between the salve and the gloves, they appeared to be healing. A rope burn on top of the blisters would certainly do his hands in.

"You don't need them," he said.

"Gimme them gloves, boy," he barked again. His tone was more menacing, although he still kept his distance. Ian looked around. Toothless and the Captain both kept a stern eye on the situation.

"No."

Anger flared in the man's eyes, but he dared not lash out. Not yet anyway. "Trade wit' me. Yer on the mop now." It was not a question.

"No."

Again the man surged with visible anger. His eyes flared and his hands clenched. Darkened and crooked teeth ground out his words.

"I'm – on – the – rail – now, - boy."

Ian was enjoying this. His own anger unusually under control, he could see past his own feelings and could sense something bigger going on.

"Why?"

"I's needs to be on yonder rail."

"Why?"

The man started to move in close, but backed off when he saw the guards notice.

"Please, kid." His voice had a tone of urgency.

"Hey," Ian said, "whatever you're planning, tell me. Maybe I want to do it too."

"No. I does things alone."

Ian shook his head. Anger in check, he looked back at the man. "Then you stay on the mop."

"Nooooooo!" the man raged. He lunged for Ian but was intercepted by the surrounding crew. "I'll git ye fer this, kid. Ye'll be mine soon, and ye'll be sorry sure."

Ian looked back at the man, wondering what he had ever done to make him so angry – and at him, no less. Ian had never seen the man before. Why was he filled with such rage?

"Keel-haul 'im." All eyes turned to the Captain standing at the mainsail.

A long rope was fetched from below. The man began to wail pitifully. He slumped to the ground in a heap and curled into a fetal ball position. He was begging all around him not to do this. Ian's heart felt for the man, but at the same time knew he could not interfere. A Captain's power at sea was absolute. As the men surrounded the prisoner preparing to carry out the Captain's orders, a shout came from high above.

"Battle stations!"

Ian looked up. There, in the crow's nest at the top of the mainsail, the lookout shouted his warnings.

"Be Gamblin' Jim and the White Lightnin'. Battle stations!"

Sinclair, 2014, 2016

"Hoist the sail! Raise the boom! Load the cannon!" Captain Peg Leg was shouting orders one after another at his men. "Raise the anchor! Hard to port!"

Every man ran for their places, leaving Ian and the other man on the deck. Seizing the opportunity, the prisoner ran for the side rail and leapt over. Splashing into the warm water, he began to swim toward the other ship. All eyes were on Ian now. Should he follow? Would he?

Ian turned his back on the man, and climbed the stairs to stand by the Captain on the ship's bridge. "Waiting for my orders, sir," he said.

"Thar be yer spy," Toothless said to Peg Leg, pointing at the swimming man. "This'n be jus' a lost lad." They both patted Ian on the back. Peg Leg smiled at him. The three all turned to watch the other ship.

Both ships sat motionless in the water, waiting for the other to move first.

"What are they doing?" Ian asked.

"Waitin'," Peg Leg whispered.

"For what?"

"Fer us to lose our temper an' fire firs'."

"Why is firing first bad? Aren't they the enemy?"

"Don't want to go chargin' in. May be a trap. Need to stay in control so's we can see ever'thing. Keep a safe distance till we know's what's what."

Sinclair, 2014, 2016

Ian squinted and looked out over the water at the other ship. At first, he thought his eyes were playing tricks on him. He rubbed his eyes, and focused again. "Why does that ship have two main masts?"

"That ain't two masts, boy. That be two ships."

As soon as he said it, the two ships separated and turned to face theirs head-on.

"Make sail!" he shouted. "Full speed! Git us out from here! Full to port! Go, man! Go!"

The ship lurched forward and turned away from the others. Peg Leg and Ian kept an eye on the other ships, as the rest of the crew busied themselves with their orders. The first cannon blast echoed across the water, rippling the surface, and splashing down a safe distance away.

"Full speed, lads! Move this ship!"

Still swimming toward the enemy in the water was the spy.

"What about him?" Ian asked.

"He'll git 'is. Don't ye worry none, kid." Peg Leg turned to check the other side of the ship. "Know when to fight, boy - and when not to." As he turned back to watch, a giant, red diamond-shaped serpent head with wickedly sharp horns and a long neck rose up from the water. It hovered over the sole swimmer for a second, then swooped down. Snatching him from the water with its

Sinclair, 2014, 2016

razor teeth and loose floppy jowls, it dragged him down below the surface, leaving a calm ripple in its wake.

Ian stared in disbelief. *Not again.*

"I guess some do eat folk after all." Ian turned to face a smiling Peg Leg. "Spies always git their due."

Chapter 19: Message
mes·sage [mes-ij] *noun*
a communication containing some information, news, advice, request, or the like. *Idiom Informal*. to understand or comprehend, especially to infer the correct meaning from circumstances

Ian tried to shake the vision, but couldn't. The memory of the serpent dragging that prisoner under the water, as it had Morgan, was more than his brain could process right now. The chilling memory was just another reminder that this was no game he was playing. It was real and it was, without a doubt, deadly.

Ian opened the door. He no longer had any guards. They apparently were satisfied that he was no spy. He had shown his loyalty by the choices he'd made today. Ian made his way through the dark galley-way and up onto the deck.

Only a few men manned the deck after the fight. Most were below, licking their wounds and preparing the ship for the next battle. The cool breeze felt good against the last remnants of the sunburn he'd gotten the day before. Ian walked the lonely deck, trying to clear his thoughts. Stopping at the side rail, he leaned over to look at the ocean. Water churned beneath them as the ship continued to make its way through the choppy waves. Ian ignored the sounds of the ship around him, until a familiar sound found him.

Step.

Thump.

Step.

Thump.

Without turning, he asked the question that had been plaguing him all afternoon, "I thought you said you didn't believe in sea serpents."

"Aye, weel now. I kin see how he'd be think'n that. But what I said t'wer, 'is that what yer tellin' me?' I ne'er said I dinna believe ye."

Ian smiled. "Technicality."

"I know not that word, son, but it matters not. I git the jist of it."

The two stood silent for a minute, Ian still looking down at the water.

"Why does the serpent bother ye so? Ye seem a good lad. He shan't be takin' ye."

"It's not me," Ian said.

"Oh, aye. So ye be knowin' 'nother who got his'self took?"

He nodded.

"He 'twer wit' ye when ye fell from thar?" Peg Leg pointed up.

Ian was too choked up to speak. He nodded again.

"Weel, I got no words fer ye, then, son. I hear tell of some folk findin' their way out, but I know not how. It be a prison, ye know. An' not's a good 'un."

Ian nodded again. "Why do they call it Zin?"

"Zin be a wilderness."

"A wilderness? Down here?"

"Aye. Any place where thar be no hope is a wilderness. I hear tell it be a place of despa'r an' misery. Ye'll not be want'n to go thar, sure." Peg Leg turned to leave. "Git ye some rest, son. Be a big day tomoree."

Peg Leg limped away, leaving Ian at the rail. Unable to get his mind off Morgan, he stood for a long time watching the pattern of the water against the hull of the ship. As the bow sliced through the water, it churned up bubbles against the side of the great ship, splashing tiny droplets all the way up onto his face. The cool water was refreshing. Silence all around him, Ian could hear the bubbles popping as they hit the ship, each with a sound unique to itself.

Pop.

Snap.

Spit.

Ping.

Help.

Help? Now he knew he was tired. Ian shook the grogginess from his head. He leaned over a bit further. Just one blast of cold water against his face, then he'd be off to lunch with the crew.

Snap.

Pop.

Help.

Ian froze. This time he was sure he'd heard it. He looked down into the water, but saw nothing. The voices kept coming.

"Ian. Where are you? Help us."

"Hunter. I'm here!" he yelled back.

"Ian?"

"Mr. Welch! I can hear you!"

"Ian! Find the others. You can't save me but you can save them."

"Where? Where do I find them?"

Pop.

"Ian. Ian, can you hear me?"

"Yes, Mr. Welch, I'm here!"

Snap.

Glurp.

"Find them! Find them before it's too late!"

"But how? How will I know?"

Pop.

Spit.

Pop.

Silence.

All voices stopped.

Ian stood tall. He wiped the ocean and the tears away from his face and turned back to his cabin. Lining the deck behind him were several members of the crew. They said nothing, but stared blankly.

"Mermaid," he said. "I've never seen one so beautiful before." Ian had to leap out of the way as the men ran for the side to catch a glimpse. Leaving them behind, Ian stalked away, haunted by what he had just heard.

He swabbed the deck in complete silence— alone. Very few people were around, and the ones who were, did not speak. It was late and everyone was tired. He decided not to wait for someone to tell him what he had to do.

Sinclair, 2014, 2016

Perhaps if he got the deck cleaned from one end to the other, he would be so exhausted he could do nothing to fight off the sleep that had eluded him the night before.

Or could he?

Ian was still choked up about what had happened earlier today. He'd heard them. He knew he had. Hunter and Mr. Welch had called out to him through the surf. But how could that be? Ian dunked the mop back into the bucket. Empty. Picking it up, he went to the side rail and hurled it over, then slowly pulled on the rope to drag it back up.

The ship was moving and the bubbles churning still. He watched them, mesmerized by the fluid motion of the water against the wooden hull.

"A beaut', ain't she?"

Ian turned to see Captain Peg Leg standing at his side.

"Yes, sir. She is."

"What ails ye, young 'un?"

Ian shrugged his shoulders, not sure how to answer.

"Be it the spy been 'et from that serpent?"

Ian shook his head. "No. Not that."

"Then ye heared 'em. Did ye not?"

Ian looked to the elder seaman, but dared not to speak.

Sinclair, 2014, 2016

"Aye, then. It be so." Peg Leg motioned for Ian to follow. Yanking the bucket back onto the deck, he dropped it at his feet and followed the Captain to the wheel.

"I hears 'em from time to time, too." He picked up the lunar sextant and looked toward the skies, trying to set their position. "When the sea calls to ye, best be listenin', lad."

"How do I know what it's telling me?"

"Weel, then. That's when ye be 'cypher'n.'"

"'Cypher'n?'"

Peg Leg nodded. "Aye. Listen fer that that wee voice inside ye. Mos' folk it tells right from wrong. But if'n ye listen weel 'nough, it guides ye through the storm, it will."

Ian was silent while he contemplated this new thought. "What if you don't have a wee voice?"

"Got to, man. Ever'one git one from the Great Capt'n up thar. Mayhaps ye have not found yers yet."

"How do you find it?"

Peg Leg raised a finger to his lips. "Shhhh," he whispered. "Listen."

Ian lingered by the Captain's side for a few minutes more, then turned to head back to his duties.

"Make sure the deck be a'shinin'. Mayhap be celebratin' later on." Ian nodded. Still disheartened, he went back to his mop and bucket.

Sinclair, 2014, 2016

Chapter 20: Gauntlet
gaunt·let [gawnt-lit, gahnt-] *noun*
a medieval glove, as of mail or plate, worn by a knight in
armor to protect the hand; take up the gauntlet; to accept
a challenge to fight, to show one's defiance.

"Yo, ho. Yo, ho. This meetin' of the ship council hereby is called to order. Summon the yung'in."

"Come, boy," Toothless said, taking the mop away from Ian. They turned from the rail to face the entire crew.

"What's going on?" Ian's voice wavered a little as he eyed everyone from the Captain down to his fellow swabbies.

"He ain't ready, Cap'n. I says nay." Rumblings of aye and nay mumbled around the deck, with all eyes on Ian. His face flushed, feeling as red hot as his ruddy hair.

Peg Leg raised a silencing hand. "We ain't e'en done asked the boy does he wants to yet."

"Weel, boy. Does ye?"

"Do I what?"

"Aw. He ain't e'en know'd what we's doin'. How kin he be joinin' us likes that?"

"Join you? You mean," Ian's heart skipped a beat, "be a—, a—"

Peg Leg's stump slammed down, silencing the crew. Again his hand went up.

"Step forwards, boy." Ian felt hands pushing him to the front of the crowd. Here he faced the Captain straight on. "We seems to be in needs of an extr' deck mate, son. Since ye did prove ye be naught a spy, it be up to the crew here whether'n they be willin' to vote ye on board as their kin."

"I say nay! The boy ain't fit yet."

"Ain't fit how, MacKenzie?" Peg Leg eyed his ship's first mate.

"He be angry inside. Cain't be a fight'n all times."

"I'm not angry," Ian snapped. When the crew stifled their laughter, he lashed out again. "I'm not! Stop laughing!"

"Aye," Captain Peg Leg agreed. "Mayhaps ye have a point 'er two. The question be is, can ye hold it?"

All eyes turned to Ian. He felt the heat of their stares against his still flushed cheeks.

"Ain't but one way to find out, Cap'n."

"Aye," he smiled down at Ian. "The gauntlet, it is."

Ian tried to wiggle free as he was forcibly led across the deck.

"What's the gauntlet?"

"Oi, simple mate," Toothless grinned. "We takes ye to the bowels of our ship here, and ye finds yer way back up top, ye does."

"That doesn't sound too hard."

"Aye, lad. Buts ye does it without gettin' angry at nobodys, ye does."

"And if I do it, then I get to join you?"

"Aye," Captain Peg Leg said. "Do this and ye be a full-fledged member of the crew. Our spoils is yer spoils. Sails to the ends of the world and back wit' us, ye will. But ye must control that tempers of yers, or ye'll never make crew wit' us. Does ye agrees?"

"Of course!" Ian jumped at the chance. "When do we go?"

"Rights now!"

A cloak was thrown over Ian's head and he was wrestled to the ground. Muffled laughter was all he heard as he fought to free himself from the dark, dank smelling hood. "No!" he screamed, but the laughter only increased.

"Too lates, lad. Ye's already agreed." Ian recognized Peg Leg's distinctive voice. "now off to the ship's bowels with ye. And don't be long. If'n ye miss dinner, it'll be shark bait wit' ye."

Bump.
Thump.
Bang.
Bump.
Thump.
Bang.
"Ow!"
Slam.
Bump.
"Stop!"

Ian bounced down the stairs, dragged again by his captors, still tied up in the canvas cloak from the deck. They seemed to care little for his welfare as he bounced down the stairs and across the wet deck below. Again, he was hurled into a room. Behind him, the door slammed. Ian heard the distinctive click of a lock. After a struggle, he managed to wiggle free of the covering and look around.

Great. Right back where I started.

Moldy fish smell and the stink of salty air still lingered in the tiny room where he'd been sleeping. Again it was dark, as it was on his first night aboard.

Ian stood, felt his way to the door and tried the cold latch. Locked. How on earth was he supposed to make it out of here? He'd tried before. There were no loose boards, or portholes; no escape that he could find.

"Let me out!" Ian screamed.

Snickers came from the other side of the door.

He sighed. Toothless. Again.

Ian could feel the anger rising inside of him. Balling his fist, he slammed it into the door, shaking the entire wall.

"Twer that a knock?"

"Nay. Twer more likes of a bang."

"'Er, ye sure?"

"Aye."

"Mayhap he tries it 'gain. Then we's bein' sure."

Knock and the door will open, Alistair had said. *Seek and ye well find.*

Could it really be that simple?

Ian stood silent for a moment. It could be a trap. But then it could not. His only other choice was to wait, and then become shark bait. He raised his hand and rapped lightly on the door.

Click.

The lock slid and the latch turned. Swinging wide, Ian came face to face with Toothless and his partner.

"Well, I'll be a monkey's uncle," Ian smiled.

"Why would ye want to be such?" The look of pure confusion on Toothless made Ian laugh. He walked out of the darkened room, past his captors and into the passageway. One step and his feet slid out from under him. Down on his butt he went landing hard.

"Ohhh!" Ian put out his hands to try to stand, but they slid across the deck, too.

Greased.

He raised his hand to his nose. The rotting fish smell almost curled his hair. At least he knew where it was coming from. *Those barrels*, he thought. Turning his face away from the rancid odor, Ian planted his feet against the floor and pushed himself up again.

Slam! He went down hard, hammering his forehead on the deck.

The laughter of the crew echoed through the hold. "Whale blubber, lad!" One moved in for a closer look, and he, too, ended up flat on the deck. Ian watched as he tried to stand time after time, with no success. This stuff was so slick each time he tried to move, the pirate crashed back down, to the sheer delight of the remainder of the crew who were all watching.

"Help me!" Ian screamed. Scrambling up, he slid down yet again on an already sore backside. Ian yelled at

Sinclair, 2014, 2016

the top of his lungs, and punched the slick floor with all his might. "Get me out of here!" he ordered.

"Be that anger?" Toothless looked to his fellow deckmates.

"Peers te be." The crowd settled. "Fish bait, sae soon. 'Tis a sad day fer the Wayfarer, it is."

Ian fought to calm himself. He thought for a moment, then decided to stay low to the ground. Rolling over onto his stomach, he slid his hands across the deck looking for small finger holds in the wooden planking. Finding them one by one, he pulled himself, sliding across the floor. With some patience and persistence, he managed to get to the other side. He stood, looking back at the motley crew across the deck.

"So there!" he shouted back at them. "I can do it!"

Shouts of anger now rose from the crew at his taunting. One by one, they tried running across the slick deck to Ian, crashing hard, and landed one on top of the other. He laughed out loud at the sight, provoking their anger even more.

"How dares ye laugh, swaby! Waits tills I gits 'cross this deck. I tans yer hide, I's will- - -"

He was cut off by Ian's laughter. "You can't even get across the deck. How do you think you're ever going to catch me?"

"Oh, I catch ye, sure. And when I does - - -"

"When you do, nothing!" Ian yelled. "You're too stupid to get across the floor."

"*I's* not." The booming deep voice both startled and frightened Ian. He swung around to run and slammed into the chest of the biggest pirate he'd seen yet, his battered and sore face bouncing off the man's rippling chest muscles. Ian staggered backwards, stunned by the force of his stance.

"Ye kin go backs to thems," he said. "Or ye kin goes through me." He smiled broadly. His darkened, dirty teeth sickened Ian. Opening his mouth to speak, his reply was cut short by the pirate-mountain in front of him. Ian was once again grabbed, hurled high up in the air, and slammed down on to the ground, the mountain man dropping on top of him.

Ian was surprised that he wasn't hurt. He'd expected to be. It wasn't really a fight, but more like the wrestling matches he'd seen at school. Ian knew he was just pinned to the ground. He would have to find a way to wiggle to freedom.

Ian held his breath, mustered all of his strength and shoved the man as hard as he could, letting out a primal scream in the process.

Nothing. The mountain didn't budge.

He tried again, screaming louder and kicking with his legs.

The only movement that he felt was the giant chest bouncing when the man laughed.

Ian's anger flared and he flailed, kicking and screaming until he had completely worn himself out.

Nothing.

Ian felt his strength drain from him. He'd lost. He might as well just give up now. They would kill him, throw him to the sharks, and carry on as though he'd never been there. What an adventure this was turning out to be. He couldn't even become a pirate. Tears welled up in his eyes, and tickled his cheeks as they fell to the floor beneath him. Raising one hand to wipe them away before any of the pirates saw, Ian's hand brushed against the giant's mid-section. The mountain cringed and giggled, sliding part way off Ian.

"No fair," the pirate protested, moving to regain his position of superiority.

Ian tickled him again. Again, the pirate cringed and giggled like a little girl, ducking to cover his tender spots. Zeroing in on his prey, Ian laughed as the pirate laughed when both sides of his giant trunk were savagely attacked. The enormous man curled up in a ball and rocked from side to side, trying to keep Ian's wiggling fingers from touching him. When he had sufficiently incapacitated his opponent, Ian turned and bolted up the stairs toward sunlight and the upper deck of the ship. Perhaps he could join their ranks, after all. Bursting through the opening, he froze, staring at what awaited him on the other side.

Chapter 21: Matey
mate·y [mey-tee] *noun, plural* mate·ys. *Chiefly British Informal* .
comrade; chum; buddy.

Ian was met at the top of the landing by the remainder of the crew circled around the open hatch. In the middle, with him, were two fighting pirates. This was no wrestling match; this was a full-blown fist fight, one man relentlessly pummeling the other into the deck. Ian jumped back out of the way as a fist flung through the air, barely missing his own face, and slammed into an already swollen and bloodied face just inches from his own. He joined the circled ranks.

"What did he do?"

"Nothin'."

"Nothing? Why is he being beaten up then? That doesn't make any sense." Ian's rising alarm at the man's condition prompted him to step forward without thinking. "Stop!" he commanded. All eyes turned his way. A deathly silence fell over the crew as everyone awaited Ian's next move.

Ian recognized the man through his swollen and battered face. He was a member of the crew. He had been with Toothless that first night.

"'Er ye willin' to take his beatin' fer him?"

"Why are you beating him?"

"'Tis his test to join wit' us."

"What kind of test is that?" Ian could not hide the shock and surprise in his voice.

"Be he a coward. Ain't no place fer no cowards herein. We's needs to be knowin' that he kin take what's dished out fer him in a fight." The man who was inflicting the beating drew closer to Ian.

"So's, will ye be takin' his place?"

"I will," Ian said. "If you can explain to me why it takes more courage to stand there and allow yourself to get beaten, than it does to stand up for yourself and what is right."

"'Er ye mockin' me, boy?"

"Not at all." Ian maneuvered his way off to one side, drawing the attention of the entire pirate crew away from the victim. He continued, "I just don't understand the point of what you're trying to accomplish. If a life of violence is the only reason this gang exists," he winked at the beaten pirate, "then what is the attraction? Why are we all here?" As he continued walking across the deck, the surrounding mob of pirates followed. Ian turned to see the beaten man slip below deck alone. Turning back, he caught Peg Leg's eye from the bridge.

"I mean, don't you all have a higher purpose?"

"Huh?"

"A reason for being together? A brotherhood? You know, all for one, and one for all kind of thing?"

"Ye mean we all's sticks together?"

"Right," Ian said. He pointed at the pirate in the crowd who'd had that great revelation. "You protect each other." They all nodded. He heard rumblings of assent among the crew. "You stick up for each other."

"He be right," someone shouted.

"Yuppin's, we do." Nods and mumblings surrounded him.

"Like I just did."

The crew fell silent again.

"If I am to be part of this crew, and we protect our own, and we stick together like you've indicated, then no one beats one of my crew members without going through me first." Ian's heart was racing. He had visions of being hurled to the deck and savagely beaten as some ridiculous orientation into this would-be gang of pirates. He held his breath, awaiting their next move. The silence was deafening.

Clap.

Clap.

Clap.

"Weel done thar', son!" Peg Leg looked down at the crowd of confused pirates below. "Ye passed the test although, most jus' takes the beatin' instead. Ye gets the point jus' the same."

Step.

Thump.

Step.

Thump.

"All's in favor of young Ian here bein' part of the crew, votes aye." Captain Peg Leg quickly raised his hand with the first resounding, "Aye!"

The rest of the crew followed.

"Aye."

"Aye."

"Aye, Aye."

"Aye, lad."

"All opposed, nay."

The deck remained silent.

"The Wayfarer welcomes ye, laddie. She be in yer blood from this day on. There's no escapin' the hold she gits on yer soul."

Step.

Thump.
Step.
Thump.
"And all a'fore we sup, too. Weel done. Weel done, lad."

Ian watched Peg Leg thump his way below deck. One by one, the crew followed, until he was alone on the deck.

Ian took a deep breath, his head still pounding. Raising a hand, he felt his swollen lips and tender nose. He looked down at his filthy, grease-covered clothing, and the scratches on his arms and legs. He had visible bruising on his forearms, and his knees ached. Ian looked up toward the black and white pirate flag billowing in the wind over his head. "Yes!" he screamed, leaping into the air. Fists flying and legs dancing, Ian did a victory lap around the deck, before following his Captain and crewmates below deck for his first pirate victory supper.

Congratulations lasted late into the evening hours. Ian received so many welcoming slaps on the back his shoulders ached. His knees and arms still hurt from the day's events. Still, he reveled in the thought of it all.

"I'm a pirate," he repeated to his new friends.

"Aye, ye near be," they retorted.

Now he found himself back up on the deck, in the dark of the night, surrounded by all of his shipmates for the final celebration of the day. He had no idea what would transpire, but it didn't matter. Whatever it was would cement his bond into his new and wonderful life; a life of adventure and surprise. It was what he had waited his entire life for, and now the time was here. He belonged. He finally belonged somewhere.

Ian was as content as he thought he'd ever been. Just the atmosphere alone was enough to make his heart skip a beat. The night sky shone brightly with the moon above. The seas were calm and the surf quiet. He could hear the bubbles slipping to the surface from under the gently rocking hull.

Snap.

Pop.

Help.

Sinclair, 2014, 2016

"Welcome's aboard, matey!" Ian was spun around to face the man he'd helped earlier in the day. "I's be Ruben."

"Nice to meet you. Your face looks better."

"Aye, jus' a little funnin' was all, it was."

"That didn't look like much fun to me."

"Aye, weel. I's likes to see how many times I's can turn to the other cheek and stills be standin'. Ye ken?"

Ian started to nod, then shook it instead. "No. I guess I don't."

Ruben laughed at that. "Aye. It matters naught to ye. Y're kin now, an' that's all matters."

Peg Leg stomped his stump on the dimly lit deck. All noise stopped and attention turned his way.

"Young Ian, step forwards, man. Time fer yer oath-takin'."

"On this here boat, friends is thicker 'n blood." Peg Leg reached out his hand to Ian. "When ye swears in, yer in for the lot." Ian was drawn in close to the Captain. Through the lantern's dim glow he could see the whites of his new Captain's eyes. The glimmer of a new life of pillage and plunder shot bolts of excitement up his spine. Ian gladly grasped his mentor's hand and smiled. The Captain smiled back, eyes glimmering, jet-black hair waving. Funny, but there doesn't seem to be any breeze, Ian

Sinclair, 2014, 2016

thought. Yet Peg Leg's hair and beard were moving as though the ship were at full sail. No matter. He was just happy to be here. The gleam in Peg Leg's eye shone so brightly it reflected dozens of times in the tips of his beard. The ends seemed to twinkle in the moonlight. His whole face was alight with pure delight. Ian smiled.

This was gonna be good.

Peg Leg grabbed his wrist with a firm hand and held it straight up in the air. He firmly laid Ian's wrist up against Ian's. On the railing were several lengths of rope, one a fine silvery thread-like piece glowing in the moonlight as brightly as Peg Leg's eyes. His Captain's hand reached right over the top and grabbed an ordinary piece of rope lying next to it. Lashing their arms together, wrist to wrist, Peg Leg instructed "repeat whats I says. If'n ye means it, ye be ones of us forever."

Ian nodded.

"The bonds of ye brothers runs deep as the oceans."

"The bonds of your brothers runs deep as the oceans," Ian recited.

"Their bond fer ye be the same."

"Their bond for me is the same."

Peg Leg held the end of the rope in his free hand. "We ties our souls to one another, and to this ship. We swears our oath to the Cap'n, save none."

Sinclair, 2014, 2016

Ian heard the other pirates repeating the oath with him. Ruben stepped up and stood next to him.

"We lives together. We fights fer our own. We dies as one for 'er brothers and 'er Cap'n. Wayfarin' souls be we."

Ian smiled.

"No friend lef' behin'."

"No friend left behind." Ian looked across the deck at his new crewmates, swearing their loyalty to him.

"None dies alones."

"No one dies alone."

"Be's we 'gether, or be's we 'part;"

"Be us together, or be us apart."

"No'ne can tear ye from 'er brother's heart."

The entire crew repeated the last line.

Then Ian said alone, "none can tear us from our brother's heart."

Cheers went up and the dancing began. The ship rocked slightly as the men jumped, whooped, and hollered, spiriting themselves around the deck. Several members of the crew climbed part way up the mainsails and swung out from the booms. "Wooo! Hooo!" they screamed at the tops of their lungs. "Gots us 'nother brother, does we!"

The ship tilted even further as they swung like monkeys from boom to boom, Ruben leading the way.

Pop.

Plop.

"Ian."

"He be's the bestest crow on the seas, Ruben is." Peg Leg unwound the rope that had bound them together for the oath of loyalty.

"Crow, sir?"

"Now, there. Ain't bein' no 'sir' here, boy. On this here ship we's all be equals. I be yer voted-in Cap'n. We's bein' in a democer'cy, we is."

"Ok, Captain. But what does it mean to be a crow?"

"Ups thar," Peg Leg pointed. High atop the tallest mast sat a basket. "That be the crow's nest. Him which got's the bestest eyes be's the crow. Protectin' us, watches fer danger, the crows does."

Ian nodded.

"We gives ye a try up thar tomorree. Tonights," Peg Leg threw his hands up in the air and twirled around, "we celebrates." He danced off with the others, rocking the boat, and leaving Ian, smiling, in the center of the party.

Slosh.

Slop.

Plop.

Pop.
"Help."
"Ian."
Pop.
Slop.
"Help."

Chapter 22: Crow's Nest
crow's-nest [krohz-nest] *noun*
Nautical. a platform or shelter for a lookout at or near the
top of a mast.

Day 3

The musket shot rang out.

Ian scurried up the mainsail mast as fast as he could.
Faster than climbing a ladder, he tried not to be reckless,
but still he had to beat Ruben to the top.

"I's on yer tail, laddie! Hahahaha!"

Ian dared not speak or turn around. He didn't want
even the simplest movement to slow his progress. Another
test, yes, but it felt more like a game at this point. It was
no longer against his enemies, but his fellow pirates; his
brethren; his new friends.

Ian grabbed the nail pegs hammered into the sides of
the mast. They were barely wide enough for a handhold,
or a foothold, yet were staggered and spaced up the post
like the rungs of a ladder. One by one, Ian grabbed hold
and pulled himself up toward the reward at the top — the
coveted position in the crow's nest. It was the prized

position on the ship, and it had been offered by Peg Leg to Ian for his loyalty. That was, providing he could beat Ruben to the top. Loser had to hoist and secure all the sails for the day.

"Me Gran kin move faster 'en ye can, Ian. Ye climbs the likes of a girl, ye does. Move on ov'r, lad, and lets the man git up thar!"

Cheers from below floated up. The entire crew lined the decks, cheering the two on.

Ian wanted to laugh and make a snide comment back at Ruben but, at the same time, he had to prove he could do it. He had to prove it to Ruben and to the rest of the crew. More than anything, he had to prove it to himself. Rung after rung, he raced to the top. He had to win. He had to.

Almost there.

He almost had it. Ruben was just a few rungs below. Ian reached for the next peg near the top. Pulling his weight upward against it, the rung came out in his hand. Ian fell back, losing his balance, both feet slipping from the rungs they were on. He dangled by his one remaining hand, clenched in a death-grip on a single nail.

Ian panicked. His mind went blank. He screamed, but no sound came out. Gasps and moans came from the deck below. The ship spun beneath him. "Ahhhhh!"

Sinclair, 2014, 2016

A big hand grabbed his thigh and stopped him from flailing. "Grab the next peg."

Ian faltered for a brief moment, trying to get his bearings. The hand squeezed his thigh and guided his leg to the safety of a rung. "Grabs it, I say!"

His mind cleared and Ian let go of the loose peg in his hand, grabbing the next rung. He held on, trying to regain his senses.

"Holds on, lad," he heard Ruben say. "I got ye."

The peg finally crashed onto the deck. Ian mentally calculated how high up they were, based on how long it took the peg to fall. He dared not look down. Not now, when his nerves and his senses were so shaken.

"Steps up, lad."

Ian could feel Ruben's body behind him, almost sheltering him against the mast, preventing another fall.

"Reach," he commanded.

Ian couldn't move. He closed his eyes against the sun and the wind, not daring to look at anything. All he could manage was to shake his head.

"I's not's gonna stands here holding yer scrawny behind up forever. Ye got's to git up, 'er down. Sae picks one. Up's shorter."

"I can't," Ian whispered.

Sinclair, 2014, 2016

"Sure's ye kin." Ruben's words were kinder now, softer. Ian felt a gentle tap on his right elbow. "Move this 'un."

Ian cracked his eyes open and looked for the next peg above the one that had fallen out. He reached a shaky hand up and grasped the peg. The sweat on his palms made it hard to hold on, but he gripped it with all his might.

"Now, moves this 'un." There was a tap on his right leg.

"Thar's ye goes."

Ian pulled himself up a few inches against the mast.

"This 'un." His left hand was tapped.

"This 'un." His left leg.

Tap by tap. Hand over hand. Foot after foot, Ruben and Ian climbed the remainder of the mast to the crow's nest.

At the top, Ian was the first into the nest. Ruben followed. The two leaned against the relative safety of the small enclosure. Cheers rose from the deck below as the two reached safety.

"Why did you do that?" Ian asked.

"Friendship is thicker 'en blood on this here ship. The bonds of yer brothers runs deep as the oceans. Their bond fer ye be the same." The two pirates took turns, reciting their vows back to each other.

Ian smiled. "We tie our souls to one another, and to this ship. We swear our oath to the Captain, save none."

"We lives together. We fights fer our own. We dies as one for 'er brothers and 'er Cap'n." Ruben smiled back. "Wayfarin' souls be we."

"No friend left behind." Ian perked up. "No one dies alones."

"Be's we 'gether, or be's we 'part;"

"No one can tear us from our brother's heart."

"Aye," Ruben smiled, "'tis the pirate's code."

Rested somewhat, Ian stood. "So I guess I've lost, then." He made for the gateway out of the nest.

"Hold it thar, laddie. Where does ye thinks yer goin'?"

"I have to string the sails. That was the bet."

Ruben smiled. "If'n ye thinks I's gonna lets ye swing 'round outs thar after whats we jus' done, yer crazier than ye looks." He winked and smiled again. "'Sides, 'twer kinda unfair to race ye on yer firs' day likes that." Ruben stood and moved to the gateway. He turned and started to back down the ladder. "Stays here and catch the rope when I's tells ye. Ye's gits 'nother chance te beats me after ye practices up a bit."

Ian smiled back at his new friend. "Thank you, Ruben. I won't let you down."

"Ye did not yesterday, lad. Ye stepped up te helps me, so's tis the leas' I's kin do back."

Ian nodded. Yesterday was such a long time ago. He had almost forgotten about the fight he'd stepped in on, and the beating Ruben was taking for no reason at all. Ian nodded again. There was one person he could fully trust on this ship.

Sinclair, 2014, 2016

Chapter 23: Save
Save [seyv]*verb (used with object)*
to rescue from danger or possible harm, injury, or loss: *to save someone from drowning*

Ruben swung from mast to mast, guiding the ropes while the crew below hoisted the sails. He fed the lines through the rigging, and dangled as the sails raised, making sure there were no bunched lines or tangled ropes. Ian watched, mesmerized, as Ruben floated from boom to boom with a practiced ease that he staunchly admired. *Perhaps one day.* As each sail unfurled and caught wind, the ship lurched forward, swinging the boom and the masts with exaggerated motion. Ian grabbed his stomach against the queasiness rising up the back of his throat.

Sail by sail, Ruben threaded his way back up the main mast toward the crow's nest, and a waiting Ian.

"What do you want me to do?" Ian yelled down, not taking his eyes off Ruben.

"Jus' stays thar, lad."

"I want to help."

"Ye kin raise the flag, then."

Ian looked around the nest. Folded up off to the other side of the small landing was the black and white pirate flag. He gently unfolded it. Reaching up the flagpole in the center of his perch, Ian tied the bottom end of the flag on to the rivet. The top rivet was just out of his reach. He tried to stand on his toes, but didn't quite make it.

One foot perched on the top of the crow's nest, Ian stretched his arm out as high as he could, reaching for the rope to attach the top of the flag. He wavered a little as the ship pitched and rolled in the surf, but held on tight to the rope and the flag. No pirate ship was ever caught without its flag. Beneath him, Ruben swung from rigging to rigging, stringing the sails to get the ship under way.

"Wacha doin' thar laddie?"

"Raising the flag, like you said."

"Good jobs, yung'un. Raise it high and proud."

Ian stretched again, the flag unfurled and flapping in the wind directly in front of him. He fought to keep the untethered corner close to him and still reach the upper clasp.

Almost. Ian reached out with his other arm. *Just another inch. I know I can.*

I know—

The ship pitched and rolled sharply to the side. Ian hung on to the rope with one hand and the flag with the other. With one foot on the ledge and the other on the floorboards of the crow's nest, he swung back and forth with the sea. Laughing, Ian was at ease in the perch, knowing that Ruben was right below *him.*

A pirate always defends his own. No brother left behind. The pirate's code.

Ruben would protect him.

Ian was proud of where he was. He belonged now. He was part of something. He had a purpose and a direction to his life. He was a pirate.

He looked back at the flag in his hand. Again he stood, reaching, stretching for the clasp to hold the upper corner in place. He was so very close now. Ian braced against the main mast with one arm, and lifted his other leg to the rim of the crow's nest. Hoisting himself up, he stood tall against the backdrop of the ocean billowing below him. Smiling, he reached for the clasp to tether the flag. Fastening the loop securely, Ian released the flag, letting it flap in the wind. The mainsail caught the wind at the same time and the ship lurched forward. The flag whipped backward as the ship turned, slapping Ian in the face. The sting against his skin was sharp and painful. He grabbed his cheek to ease the sting. The second he released the mast, Ian toppled backward and fell from the crow's nest. He jerked hard, with his foot tangled in a rope. Ian hung precariously, upside down, peering downward toward the deck below.

"Help! Save me!"

"Hold on, lad. I's comin'." It was Ruben's distinctive drawl. Ian could see him scampering up the rigging to his aid. Others were also beginning the ascent to his side, but they were significantly farther away. Dangling by one foot, spinning in the breeze, Ian closed his eyes to keep the waves of dizziness and nausea away.

Help me, please. Anybody.

"Almos' thar, lad. Keep holdin's on."

Ian wanted to answer, but was afraid he could not hold his nausea down, or up. In his predicament, he didn't know which.

What he did know was that the rope he'd managed to get himself tangled in was firm around his ankle. It felt almost like a hand grabbing him. Funny, he thought. It's warm.

Ian cracked open one eye and dared to look back up toward the crow's nest.

The blood was rushing to his head. His temples felt like they would explode. His head throbbed, his eyes hurt, and the world sounded like it was filtered through a tunnel.

Sinclair, 2014, 2016

"Comin', kid." Ruben climbed faster. "Hold's ye on, thar, boy."

"Help! Ian." Another voice. Faint. Familiar.

Help? Is that - - - "Mr. Welch?"

Ian spun around, held by the single rope twisted around his ankle.

"Ian. Get me out! Find Hunter!"

"Hold on, Mr. Welch! I'm coming."

"Ian?" It was his best friend. He knew Hunter's voice anywhere.

"Hunter! Hunter, I hear you!"

"Believe in yourself. You can do it."

"Soar!"

"Aeryn?" Now he heard Hunter's little sister.

"Let go and soar."

"Aeryn, where are you?"

The echo in his head throbbed louder. His head was splitting. If he didn't get back upright, Ian felt like his brain would explode. Reaching both arms out, he tried to grab for the first thing to stop his world from spinning and hold his body still. He managed to grab a peg on the main mast. Holding on, he opened his eyes and tried to pull his body back upward.

Ruben scampered up underneath him and steadied Ian's body against his massive chest.

Sinclair, 2014, 2016

"I's gots ye. Yer safe, lad."

Ian breathed easy and felt the throbbing ease between his ears. Slumping against his fellow pirate, Ian took a deep breath.

"Best be gittin' ye—" Ruben's voice trailed off into nothing, then gasped.

"What?" Ian opened his eyes again and looked up. When it registered in his mind what he was seeing, Ian gasped, too.

Wound tightly around his ankle was the rope that he had felt. It was not a rope from the ship's rigging.

Descending from the clouds above was one end of a long silvery rope, with the other wound securely around Ian's ankle. The glistening threads sparkled in the sunlight from his foot, right up to where it disappeared into the clouds above.

Ruben stared, holding his little friend, unsure what to do next.

"What is it?" Ian whispered.

"I be's not sure, lad."

"Get it off." He jerked his foot around, kicking and yanking, but the rope held firm.

"Do it hurt ye?" Ruben asked.

"No." Ian stared at the anomaly, not sure what to make of it. He shook his foot again, angrily trying to get the thing off.

"Weel, it saved ye, sure. Mus' be not from evil, then."

Another kick.

Nothing.

"Aaahhhh!" Ian lashed out, jerking and kicking to release his captive foot.

"Stop, lad! We both be fallin', sure." Ruben grabbed the mast again, more securely.

"What am I supposed to do now?" Ian snapped.

"Weel, did ye ask it to be releasin' ye?"

"Ask it? Are you kidding me? It's a stupid rope."

"Aye. A rope that saved ye, and holds ye safe still. Did ye ask it to save ye?"

Ian thought for a second. "I think I said 'help'."

"Weel, then. If'n ye asked fer help and it came, then ye'd best ask to be released."

"Let me go!" Ian belted out toward the sky. The rope released him. Ian teetered backward. "No!" he screamed. The rope wound back around his ankle, securing him again.

Ian and Ruben stared at each other.

The others scaling the mast were now at their side.

"Matey, what be thar?"

Toothless smiled. "I's thinks that be the Great Cap'n hisself."

"The Great Captain?"

"Aye," Toothless smiled again. "Lookin' down on his sailors, he does."

"How do I get down?"

"Weel, first ye thanks hisself fer savin' ye."

"Thank you," Ian said to the rope, feeling more than a little stupid.

"Thens ye jus' asks hisself to brings ye down."

"That's it?"

"Aye."

Ian looked at the attachment to his leg. The warmth crept up his leg and toward his heart. "It can't be that simple," he whispered.

"Aye, lad. But it is." Toothless moved in closer. "Sometimeses things be's harder than they aught 'cause of angers. If'n we kin let's that angers go, and jus' asks hisself to helps us, we kin gets farther, sure."

The warmth turned into a tingling sensation. There was an excitement growing in his chest. "Just ask, huh?"

"Try's it, lad."

Sinclair, 2014, 2016

Ian looked at the sparkling silver thread that kept him attached to something above. "Will you please let me go?" he asked – quickly adding "after I am safe."

The rope grew taught against his leg. Pulling skyward, it jerked him back up, out of the reach of his friends.

"Aaahhhh! No!" he screamed. "Put me down!"

The rope wiggled slightly, then lowered an upside-down Ian slowly down to the deck. Ruben, Toothless, and the others descended at about the same pace, keeping an eye on their protégé as they came down. When they were down low enough, Ian put out his hands and lay down easily on the deck. The rope unwound to release him, then zipped back up into the sky, leaving the pirates surrounding a shaken Ian lying at their feet.

Step.

Thump.

Step.

Thump.

Step.

Thump.

"On yer feet, swaby. Gits to work, all of ye's." Peg Leg glared at the idle crew. "Throw's ye in the brig, I will, if I catches ye layin' 'round a'gin."

Step.

Sinclair, 2014, 2016

Thump.
Step.
Thump.
Step.
Thump.

Chapter 24: Stalactite

sta·lac·tite [st*uh*-lak-tahyt, stal-*uh* k-tahyt] *noun*
a deposit, usually of <u>calcium</u> carbonate, shaped like an
icicle, hanging from the roof of a cave.

"All hands on deck!" The call jolted Ian from a deep slumber. "Death looms ahead!" Wide awake, senses reeling, he struggled to gain control of his whirling emotions.

The ship's crew flew into action around him. Pirates bolted for the hatch leading to the deck, leaving Ian to follow behind. Desperate to keep up, yet still unable to comprehend what was going on, he followed the others, trying his best just to keep up. To Ian, it seemed as if he was the only one moving in slow motion.

"Drop the sails! Raise the boom! Head for cover, man, whilst there's still life on this here ship!"

The pirates swirled around him like a hurricane. Ian, nearly frozen in place, was unable to think. Slow to process, and even slower to move, he tried to help, but to no avail. It wasn't until he felt strong arms on his shoulders that he was snapped out of his daze.

Sinclair, 2014, 2016

"Up the mast, yung'un. To the nest, yonder." Ruben's arms guided him to the main mast. "I's rit behind ye."

The first few rungs of the mast-ladder came awkward and slow. Ian felt sluggish and bogged down. He looked around to see a thick, bluish-gray fog creeping in around them, quickly sealing the ship in its wake. He felt a foreboding sense of doom come over him.

"Git!" Ruben's order barked from below. "Git, a'fore we's all died!"

Ian managed somehow to snap out of his funk and kick himself into high gear. With Ruben on his tail, they took the rungs two at a time and scaled the mast in a matter of minutes. Both pirates entered the crow's nest within seconds of one another.

"What is it?"

"Death." Ruben spun around the small enclosure, straining to look into the dense cover. "Best watch fer 'em."

"Who is them?"

"Evil."

"But I don't—"

"Shhhhh! They be listenin'. Careful what they's hears."

Ian opened his mouth to speak again, but a sharp glare from Ruben silenced him. A long slender finger pointed outward into the thick mist. With his arm outstretched, Ruben's extended finger was barely visible in front of him.

Ian, vision strained out into the dense cover, took his place in the nest. He craned his neck every direction and tried to see, but he could not. The bluish-gray fog was thick, and it swirled around in a circle, disorienting all around them. There was an odd odor in the air, also. The stench was so thick, Ian felt as though he could grab it. Nauseated, he raised his hand to wipe away the sweat that had formed on his forehead and cheeks. His hand came away with a slimy grey mucous.

"Death," Ruben whispered. A finger came up to his lips in a hushing motion. "If'n they gits one, they be's happy and will leave. Watch fer 'em."

The Wayfarer zig-zagged back and forth between the scattered rocks. 'Rocks' didn't do these formations justice. They were more like tiny mountains sticking up through the ocean, each one an island by itself. The formations were impressive. Each one had a coloring unique to itself. Some had jagged cliff formations, and others were as smooth as glass. Many on the outer edges of the grouping had both stalactites and stalagmites growing from them. As they passed within inches, Ian and Ruben both reached out to touch the overhanging rocks, marveling at the maneuverability of both the ship and its captain. They got close enough on several occasions for Ian to reach out and touch the higher mineral formations, all covered with the same grey mucous material that hung so thick in the air. Each scaly stone piece showed layers of calcification, yet felt slick and smooth in his hand. Ian wondered at the science of it all. What caused these sharp formations to grow, and why here? They were not on every rock, just some.

Why?

The ship lurched violently to one side.

"Git the blades!" he heard screamed from below. "Chop us loose! Quick! A'fore 'tis too late!"

Ian looked down toward the deck, but could see nothing.

"What is it?" There was an urgency in his question.

"Ye should not speak, lad. They mights—"

The first strike came from nowhere. All Ian saw were the clenching jaws and razor-sharp teeth.

"Duck!" Ruben hit the floor, yanking Ian's head down with him. They huddled below the rim of the basket, shielding themselves from attack.

"Wha—?" Ian didn't finish the word before his question was answered. A skeleton of a giant shark circled the crow's nest, swimming in thin air. It cut through the thick, gray, hanging mucous like a hot knife through butter. Gray sunken eyes rolled around the boney sockets looking for their prey. Razor-sharp teeth, dripping deathly slime, and snout flaring as the creature tried to sniff out fresh prey. Ian shrunk back further into the elevated basket.

Death.

"Git us free a'fore we goes under!"

Chopping and hacking sounds, mingled with screams, billowed upwards. Ian crawled in a circle flat against the floor of the nest to the opening. Looking down, he saw thick seaweed vines slinking up the mast and the sails toward them. Moving at an incredible pace, Ian reared back to keep from being snatched by one, only to have his head butted by a skeletal tail above. A flash of anger tore through him. Ian bolted up and let out a scream at the creature that had just slapped him. The hunting remains turned in the fog and sped back toward the mast.

"No!" Ruben reached out to grab Ian. He was a split-second too late. The slimy goo on his skin made Ian impossible to hold onto. The creature, jaws open wide in a deathly smile, slammed into the main mast, hurtling Ian from the basket. With several skeletons free-falling behind him, Ian splashed down into the churning hot waters below, leaving Ruben and the rest of the crew chopping away at the mutant, spreading, seaweed.

Ian hit the water in full stride. Arms overhand and legs kicking, Ian made way toward the nearest shelter. He heard the splashes behind him, but never slowed down. Reaching the first formation of huge stalagmites, he flipped his body over them and onto the higher ground behind them. In the relative safety of a small cave, Ian let his guard down. He stood to face the intruders head-on. Seeing them through the dense fog, they circled inches away from him.

"Yeah! That's right! You can't get me, you slimy blood-suckers. You and whose army?" He was pacing. Back and forth across the rocky ridge, Ian barely noticed when the island began to move. "Come on! I'm right here, you cowards! Come on over here and get me, why don't ya?" He had to grab one of the rocks for balance. Ian looked down to see the platform under his feet shift away from the rocks in front of him. Losing his balance, Ian toppled backward and fell face up. It was then that he noticed the ridge of stalactites that so closely matched the stalagmites below. They almost looked like— *teeth*.

He tried to squirm away, but it was too late. The rows slammed together in an ear-shattering jolt.

Ian hurtled down a long, slender waterfall, and splashed down into a warm, churning pool —
Again.

Sinclair, 2014, 2016

Chapter 25: Swallow

swal·low [swol-oh] *verb (used with object)*
to take into the stomach by drawing through the throat
and esophagus with a voluntary muscular action, as food,
drink, or other substances; to accept without question or
suspicion.

"AHHHH!!!!!!"

Ian fought against the swirling tide trapped inside the creature. He struggled also to keep down his rising tide of his emotions. Anger reared up inside of him once again at the situation he found himself in.

"No!" Ian kicked out, his foot, landing against something hard. The beast recoiled, sending Ian hurtling across the pitch dark space, slamming into something equally hard on the other side. Dazed, he tried to feel his way around in the darkness.

There seemed to be rows of hard structures, with softer, pliable areas in between. Ian felt his way past several of the boney hard pieces, but once again found himself thrown back across the cavernous insides when he touched a tender spot. Every inch covered with the thick mucus ooze that had been suspended in the fog, Ian found it hard to breathe or move. Each step he took felt like he was walking in gelatin. He fought to stay standing.

Maybe I can climb up the throat.

Ian felt around until his hands were reaching more upwards than sideways.

This must be it.

He stretched his hand up as high as he could, grabbing on to a soft fleshy mound protruding from the rest of the tissue. He lifted his foot to take a step and pulled with all his might, hoisting his weight upwards.

A growl began to rumble deep in the flesh that was in Ian's grasp. Around him, tissue reverberated as the low rumble turned into a hideous scream. It swallowed hard, pulsing all of the muscles in its throat, throwing Ian backwards into the pool of mucous and water. Slamming down hard into the fluid, Ian fought to swim for the surface and a breath of stale, belched air. A split-second before he surfaced, flames shot from deep within the belly of the creature. They flew like a flamethrower straight over the top of the mucus pool Ian was submerged in, and up the throat of the beast. Lasting only a few seconds, the flames blew out quickly and the thick pool settled. Ian burst upward gasping for air.

He sat stunned for a moment, then lashed out, kicking and screaming.

"Let me out!" Ian tried to run, but slipped over and over again back into the slimy pool. "Ahhhh!" He tried to wipe the mucous away from his eyes, but it was so thick, the grayish matter just slid down from the top of his head again.

"Who are you?

Taking several steps across the warm pond, Ian slowly made his way across the cavern to the hard, ribbed structure on the other side. "What are you!"

With each step, he shouted.

"Let me out!"

Ian realized that the harder he fought, the harder his fight was. The snot just slowed him down more. He tried taming his actions, but not his tongue.

"Come on, you coward! You wanna fight me? Go ahead! Take your best shot!"

Stepping gently, he continued through the middle of the pool.

"I ain't afraid of you, whatever you are."

He wiped his eyes free of the slime again.

"Come on. Show yourself. Lousy, stinking, coward."

Ian reached the side of the thing, and stepped up on the edge, out of the slime.

"I'm ready for you. Whenever you want a piece of this, just show yourself! That is, if you ain't scared! Stupid slime ball."

Ian sat down.

There was silence. The creature seemed to have settled back down.

"And turn on some lights, would ya!"

Silence.

Ian's frustration began to surface. He felt on the verge of tears but fought them back. He could not let this thing win, no matter what it was.

"Please," he half whispered. "Just so I can see."

The rumbling growl started again from deep in the belly. Ian dove for the safety of the obnoxious liquid, no matter what it was. Just as the growl became a scream, the flames shot forth once again, illuminating everything from the bowels to the nostrils of this thing.

It's a dragon.

Ian surfaced and sat stunned in the warmth. *I've been swallowed by a fire-breathing dragon.*

There was an eerie glow in the cavern when the flames had receded. Ian looked up to see the hard boney structures that he'd felt were the ends of its ribs. Each of those ends was now on fire, glowing like a row of candles lighting the rest of the dungeonous cavern. The side opposite him had another row, lit in the same fashion.

Rib cage. A cage, and I am locked in the middle.

"Let me out!" he screamed again. The rib cage shifted slightly but, when Ian calmed down, it calmed down, too.

Ian slid down on his butt. He could no longer hold back. Here, locked up in this new prison, he let his tears have their way.

Ian woke up some time later, exhausted and in pain. His head ached. His ribs hurt. His hands were sore. His pants torn and his knees skinned. There was no sense of time. No way to tell if minutes, hours, or days had passed. It was all just time.

He looked around. Still in the belly of the beast, he was still covered in gray ooze. And he was still unable to get out. The only bright thing that he saw was the rib candles still burning, giving him some measure of light to see by. He tried to sit up, but when the waves of pain hit, he gave up and slumped back down.

Ian conceded defeat. He wasn't just trying to stand, but trying to care. He'd finally gotten himself into a mess he couldn't get out of. His anger got the best of him, once again. Ian was a goner, and he knew it. It was just a matter of time. He settled in for the long haul.

Swishing the ooze with his feet, he marveled at the pattern the slime made. Not exactly a wave, but more of a highly-exaggerated ripple. Ian watched, mesmerized by the pattern the junk was making, and the light reflecting off each circle. He wiggled his foot again.

And again.

The ripples began to form a pattern of circles, one inside the other. Each circle seemed to be rotating the opposite direction. The smaller circles in the middle protruded up higher than the larger circles on the outside. It was beginning to take shape, almost like a half-submerged ball. Still the candles flickered and glowed, casting an eerie aura.

Ian scooted back. It was growing. Circles spinning faster and faster, the giant orb now took on an unearthly glow from within. It lifted itself from the surface of the pool and hovered in the center of the cage, spinning and casting a bluish-red glow against all near it.

"What on earth?" Ian muttered.

"I am not from this earth," the thing answered.

"Who, who, wha—, wha—, what are you?"

"I am your messenger."

Ian swallowed hard. "What's your name?"

"Messenger. I am also your counselor."

"What message do you have?"

"What is your question?" the spinning orb asked.

"Why am I in here?"

"You are here because you cannot control your anger."

"I can so," Ian spat out.

The orb laughed.

"Okay, maybe I get mad sometimes."

"And where has that anger gotten you?"

Ian waved his arms. "In here."

"Precisely."

"Where am I?"

"This creature is called Angor Motivus."

"What is it?"

"It is a reflection of what burns inside of you."

"How can I be inside of myself?" He sat up straight.

"You alone are what holds you back."

Ian scratched his slimy head. "Can I get out?"

"That depends on you."

"What do I have to do?"

"Remember..."

The orb began to spin faster. From its bluish-red glow, it turned crystal clear and smooth as glass. Inside the glass, Ian could see clear images. Like a crystal ball, Ian saw himself, Hunter, Aeryn, and Mr. Welch all hunting the morning of the earthquake.

"Hey, look! That's me!"

"Yes," the orb said, "you and your friends."

The picture grew cloudy, and a new picture appeared. Ian was on the pirate ship taking the oath.

> ***The bonds of your brothers run as deep as the ocean;***
> ***Their bond for me is the same;***
> ***We tie our souls to one another, and to this ship;***
> ***We swear our oath to the Captain, save none;***
> ***We live together;***
> ***We fights for our own;***
> ***We die as one for our brothers and Captain;***
> ***Wayfaring souls are we;***
> ***No friend left behind;***
> ***No one dies alone;***
> ***Be us together, or be us apart;***
> ***No one can tear us from our brother's heart.***
> ***Wayfaring souls are we.***

"Your new friends," the orb said. "You swore an oath to them but, as you swore it, you had already broken it."

"What are you talking about? I didn't break any oath."

"Remember."

The ball clouded again, and a picture of Morgan appeared, on the beach. Right behind him the serpent rose and snatched him from the shore.

"I didn't have anything to do with that. He ate that apple on his own. I didn't - - "

> **No friend left behind;**
> **No one dies alone;**

The orb shifted again. Clouds cleared and he saw Hunter in the forest. Behind him was a large brown creature.

"Hunter! Look behind you!" he screamed.

"Hunter cannot hear you now. You have left him behind."

"I didn't leave him. He - - We all - - -" he broke off. "It's kinda hard to explain."

> **The bonds of your brothers run as deep as the**
> **ocean;**
> **Their bond for me is the same;**

The cloud in the orb cleared again and Ian saw Aeryn, huddled in a tree. She looked scared. Black streaks screaming and diving toward her while she hung on. Terror showed clear as day in her eyes.

"Aeryn, hang on! Don't let go!"

No one can tear us from our brother's heart.

The orb clouded again, and the blue-red glow returned.

"You have left your friends behind. They need you and you chose not to go to them. You have broken the oath."

"But it's not my fault."

"Fault does not matter. They need you. You must go."

"How?" Ian's frustration began to rise again. "How am I supposed to get out of here?"

"You have the power within you. Just make the right choices. Do not let anger rule."

"You're not making any sense."

"Have you so quickly forgotten?"

The orb flashed again. The surface settled, the cloud disappeared, and there stood Alastair, the leprechaun.

Seek the truth which will light your path.
Evil must always give way to the truth.
Wash away all that holds ye back.
Ye can only lead him back home.
He alone must choose.

Ian felt for the flask still tied to his belt loops. He had forgotten that it was even there.

Sinclair, 2014, 2016

"Ordinary water," the orb said, "it has been touched by the Maker. Use it to wash away all that holds you back in life."

The orb flashed blue-red again.

"Tell me how to use it."

"The choice is yours, but choose wisely."

"How will I know when the right time is?"

"Set aside all anger. It is in the quiet times when the still, small voice of the Maker can be heard loudest. Listen for that. He will never steer you wrong."

The surface of the orb began to ripple again. The glow began to fade as the ball lowered itself back down into the pool below.

"No! Wait!" Ian tried to reach out and grab it, but his hand was slowed by mucous and slime. At his touch, the orb burst like a water balloon and rained back down into the pool below.

Ian sat alone on the lower end of the rib cage, in his dark, dank prison, wondering what had just happened.

Remember.

Chapter 26: Snot
Snot: [snot] *noun*
Vulgar . mucus from the nose; *Informal* . a disrespectful or
supercilious person.

Ian sat with the flask in his hands. Over and over, he turned the bottle, eyeing the clear liquid inside.

Simple water, touched by the Maker. It will wash away all that holds you back.

Ian had thought long and hard.

The only thing holding you back is you.

You need to control your anger.

Ian didn't understand a lot of what his messenger had said. He knew that there was some truth to it, but there was also a lot that he couldn't piece together.

If the dragon was part of himself that he could not control, that meant that he was now a prisoner inside of himself? How can that be? And how can you hold yourself back? That's what the food tree had told Morgan, too. "You will forever be a prisoner inside of yourself."

"What am I supposed to do?"

Sinclair, 2014, 2016

Arm reared back, he hurled the flask across the stomach of the beast. As soon as he'd let it go, Ian regretted his action. What if it was true? What if that tiny flask held the only secret to his being freed from this prison? Plugging his nose, Ian slid back down into the slimy ooze and made his way across the cage to the floating flask. Picking it up, Ian tried to wipe away some of the ooze on the silver and glass jar. When he did, the cork popped from the top and a small amount of the clear liquid spilled out into the slime. There was an instant reaction from the beast. It recoiled and shook with an intense fervor. Gagging, the musculature of its throat opened up wide enough for Ian to see daylight above. Clamping shut again, the beast gagged and coughed, splashing Ian back up against a rib cage, and blew out all of the burning candles. He fumbled with the flask, corking it again. That's when the rumbling started again. Poised at the side of the slime pool, Ian waited for the tone to intensify and change into a scream. That was when the flames would come. The rumble continued. It neither grew nor stopped. It just continuously reverberated, sloshing him around like a tiny ship on a stormy sea. Ian pictured the dragon squirming uncomfortably. He must be moving around a lot, judging by the amount he was being thrown around.

Then came the gas.

Large bubbles of putrid fumes began to boil up from beneath him. Faster and faster they came, one after another. Ian felt like he was swimming in soda. The smell was more than he could take. Just when he felt he would pass out, the throat gagged and the gas escaped. As soon as the sunlight from above disappeared, the bubbles began building up pressure again.

It's burping. I've upset myself.

Ian didn't know why this thought struck him as funny, but he chuckled out loud nonetheless.

All of this from a little water. I guess I need to meet this Maker.

Maybe this stuff did work after all. Right now the only thing holding him back was this stupid dragon. Whether it had a meaning deeper than the obvious, Ian didn't know or care. Right now he saw a means of escape.

Maneuvering over to the base of the throat, he waited for the next gagging burp, and a little sunlight to see clearly. Gauging his position, he tried to reach as high up the throat as possible. He was counting on the discomfort in the dragon's stomach to keep it off guard as to his whereabouts. With a small glimpse of sunlight, he popped the cork from the flask and dropped another single drop of the water at the base of the dragon's throat.

Sinclair, 2014, 2016

Recapping the flask, he held on as tight as he could. The slime began to churn violently beneath him. Now gas bubbled and popped around him at a fevered rate. Ian held on as the dragon writhed back and forth in its pain. With each swing of the giant neck, Ian slithered a step further up into the throat. Poised near the top, gaseous fumes churning, Ian tipped the flask again. This time, the gag reflex triggered the second the droplet touched flesh. Slamming the cork back into the flask, the giant serpent cut loose with a painful howl, and threw up. Ian hurtled forward and splashed down hard, back into the ocean where he had been a short time before. Swimming with all of his might, he tried to get out of reach of the creature before being sucked back down its throat once again. Arm over arm, he swam without looking back. With every ounce of strength he could muster, Ian swam as far as his strength would take him. A safe distance away, he grabbed on to a rock and turned back.

There, a short distance back, was the still-belching, writhing dragon. It looked horrid splashing around in the water. Then as suddenly as the entire ordeal began, the beast submerged, leaving in its wake only a foul-smelling trail of bubbles.

Ian shuddered. Releasing the rock, he struck out away from the danger zone before it happened again.

Sinclair, 2014, 2016

"Man overboard! Drop the anchor. Lower the sails. Set the buoys and bring the matey aboard!"

Ian looked back up at the giant wooden hull of the Wayfarer.

"Praise be, lad. We be lookin' all o'er creation fer ye." Peg Leg stomped his stump across the deck. He slapped Ian on the back.

"You were?"

"Weel, o' course we was, lad. 'No friend lef' behind.' Did ye ferget yer vows sae soon?"

The glowing orb still fresh in his mind, Ian shook his head. "No, I haven't, sir."

"Good man, then. Tells us then. Where's ye been hidin'? And what in blazin' skies have ye done te yer hairs?"

Ian raised his hand. He felt the side of his head. "My hair?" He could feel it. It was still there.

Peg Leg smiled. "Oh aye, it be thar, sure. But is nay red any longer. Be it silver now. Like's that of me Gran."

"Silver?" Ian looked around for a something that would show his reflection. He saw nothing.

Ruben stepped forward from the others. "Welcomes back, Ian lad. I thought ye's a goner sure when that beastie swallered ye whole."

A collective gasp from the crew silenced the ship. One by one the members of the Wayfarer backed a safe distance away from Ian.

Peg Leg, a stunned look on his face, inched his way backward also, unable to break his shocked stare away from Ian. "Ye twer in the belly of the beast, then were ye?"

Ian nodded.

"We's thought ye dead." Ruben, the only remaining crewmember to stand alongside his friend, patted Ian on the back. "What manner of beastie t'wer she, then?"

"Um. I don't really know." He shifted, feeling uncomfortable, the entire crew staring at him. "It was foul." Ian wrinkled up his face, "and thick, like mucous."

"Likes what?"

"Um. Snot." Blank stares continued. "You know, the stuff that comes out of your nose when—"

"Ewwww! Aghhh!" The crew backed up again, widening both their eyes and their distance. This time Ruben backed away, too. The look on Ruben's face told Ian everything he needed to know. He smelled disgusting.

Ruben pointed from a distance to his head. "Be that what turned yer hairs old?"

Sinclair, 2014, 2016

"I guess," Ian said. "I'm not really sure."

Peg Leg stepped forward from his crew, his face screwed up into a confused scowl. "Sae was ye, um, ye did," he stuttered. "Wer swimmin' in the beasties middle parts, then?"

"I guess I was in his stomach."

"Oh!" The crew backed away. "No! Agh!"

Ian faced them. "What's wrong with you? It all washed off."

"An' he bein' such a good lad." Toothless shook his head and turned to walk away.

"Ruben," Ian reached out to his friend. His fellow pirate jerked back just out of Ian's reach. "What's the matter?"

"Weel, laddie. When ye's touched by evil, then ye's becomes evil."

"You think I'm evil?"

"Weel, ye were swallered by such. Now," he explained, "If'n ye'd be throwed up right quick, then thar's a chance evil not to grab hold of ye."

"How long was I gone?"

"Oh, pert near to three hours now."

"Three hours!" Now Ian gasped. "No." Ian ran to the side of the ship to peer over. Nothing but open seas surrounded them on all sides. The protruding rock formations were far behind them. His heart sank.

"What ails ye, lad?"

Ian turned back to face the crew. "When I was in the dragon- - -"

More horrified gasps lurched from the crowd.

"How 'ere ye knowin' it were a dragon?"

"Because of the fire."

"Evil! Evil, I say!" Toothless screamed. "He be's sent to the fiery pits of hell and lives to tell."

"Quiet!" At Peg Leg's order, the crew fell silent. "Goes on."

Ian swallowed hard. This was not going well. Peg Leg motioned for him to continue. He wanted more.

"Well, it would cough, or sneeze or something, and fire would come up from deep inside somewhere."

"And how did ye keep from bein' burnt?"

"I dove into the slime."

Peg Leg and the rest groaned and stepped back again.

"Hey," Ian snapped. "It kept me alive, okay? You go down there and tell me what you would do instead."

Peg Leg motioned again for Ian to continue. "After a while — a long time, I guess, there was this glow."

Ruben nodded.

"It was like a ball, but it floated above the rest of the slime. It was spinning."

"Ye say it glowed?"

"Yes. And it spoke."

"Witchery!" Several of the pirates began to pace. Like rabid dogs, they eyed Ian as their prey, circling the group. Making the sign of the horns with their fingers they tried to ward off any evil that Ian brought back with him.

"No!" Ian tried to explain. "It's not witchery! I didn't summon it. The thing just came."

"What did it do?"

"It showed me some friends that I had left behind, and told me —"

"It spake!"

"Well, yes, when I asked it—"

"Sorcery! He be a conjurer now!"

"No. That's not what happened." Ian's protests were muffled by the disturbing murmurs of the crew. "It wasn't me."

"He be consortin' with evil now."

"No, no! I don't think it was evil. It felt good. Like a helper."

"Arrrgh!" Fingers shot out and pointed accusingly. "I knew he be'd a spy, from the moment I laid me eyes on the little bugger." Toothless spat on the deck and held out

Sinclair, 2014, 2016

his hand. Forming his fingers into an upside down W, he shook off the evil presence from around him. The other pirates followed suit.

"Evil on 'er ship mus' be dealt with," Peg Leg said. "Cannot be tolerated."

"That's what I'm trying to tell you," Ian said. "I have to go. I need to find my friends. They need me. If I was there for three hours it might be too late. Please."

"Weel then. Ye say ye're no' evil."

Ian shook his head.

"And ye 'er not a spy then?"

Ian shook his head again. "No, sir. I am not."

"Ye'll git yer chance to prove it. Only one way off this here ship."

Ian was afraid to ask, but saw no other way. "How's that?"

"Oh, ye'll be seein'." Ian caught a spark in Peg Leg's eye, just as the world went dark. Once again, a canvas cloak was thrown over his head and he was slammed back down on to the deck.

"Then, we's be knowin' if yer of evil or not. Lock him up!"

Sinclair, 2014, 2016

Chapter 27: Again

a·gain [*uh*-gen, *uh*-geyn] *adverb*
once more; another time; anew; in addition; to the same
place or person: *to return again.*

Ian woke up in pitch blackness— again. Feeling around the room and the walls, he soon recognized it as the same room he'd been locked in before. Going straight for the door, he fumbled around until he found the handle. Locked.

"Can you please open the door?"

Nothing.

He knocked.

Nothing.

Hey, it was worth a try.

"Ok, Messenger, where are you to help me now?" Ian felt his way back over to the barrels of stinking whale blubber and sat down. There was nothing to do but wait.

It didn't take long. The scuffs and scuffles on the deck above him slowly made their way down the hallway and to the door of his prison cell. The lock turned, and candlelight flooded the dark space. Two large shadows graced the doorway. "Come."

Sinclair, 2014, 2016

Ian rose. At the door, both of his arms were grabbed and wrenched behind him. "Hey, ease up there. Where can I run?"

A hard jerk was the response. Dragged down the darkened hallway and up the stairs, Ian was shoved through the hatch, onto the deck facing the remaining crew. Ian scanned the deck and found Ruben in the crowd. Ian got a wink from his friend, but no other outward show of support.

"Ye say that ye'er no' evil," Peg Leg surprised him from behind, "and ye shall have the chance to prove it. Ruben feels it only fair bein's ye took the oath of yer brethren."

Ian scanned the crowd again, only this time could not see his friend.

"Aye, ye'll not be seein' him here to save ye, lad. He but took his place up thar," a long finger pointed to the crow's nest high above the deck. "Thar he'll be seeing firs' hand whether ye be's evil or no." He walked across the deck. The pirates gave way, allowing Peg Leg to lead Ian across the open deck. "Thar be only one way off the Wayfarer, laddie. Ye'll be takin' it. If'n ye survives it and does not be cavortin' with evil, why then ye kin join again sure after ye saves yer friends. But, if'n ye does not survive, or if'n the evil takes ye again — weel, guess bein' wit' evil would be better fer ye than to be here on this here ship wit' us."

Ian stood motionless, insides shaking, stoic and solid outside.

Peg Leg shouted up to Ruben high above. "Ready up yonder?"

"Aye, sir. Ready."

"Ready on deck?"

The crew responded. "Aye, Cap'n."

"Steady to port?"

"Steady to port, Cap'n."

Peg Leg calmed his voice and turned to Ian. His voice took on a tender tone of gentleness, almost caring. "Ready, then, lad?"

"What do I have to do?"

"Walk the plank."

Behind Peg Leg and Toothless was a plank jutting out from the side of the ship. The railing had been taken down immediately above the board and a small step stool was placed there.

"If'n ye survives and does not cavort wit' evil, then ye's are welcome back after ye rescues yer friends," Peg Leg whispered. "Remembers that."

Ian nodded, and stepped forward. He peered out over the ocean. Off in the distance, he could see the rocky mounds. *If I can just swim that far, then I can get to some land and try to find Hunter.*

Apprehensive, but not scared, Ian stepped up. He raised a foot up to the step , but was jerked back by Toothless. "Not sae quick, thar. Ye's not ready yet."

"What do you mean?"

Peg Leg smiled. "Ye git yer hands tied first." Reaching to the side rail, Peg Leg's hand hovered over several various lengths of rope. He settled on a thin silvery strand which wiggled on its own. Ian was spun around and his hands wrenched behind him. The thin rope was strapped around his hands and secured with a knot. Shoved up on the stool and out onto the plank, Ian, for the first time in his life, felt a foreboding of death. Anger began to well up inside him at the situation he had gotten into. The anger dissolved into fear, and fear into doom.

"Where are you, Counselor?"

"Ahhh! Aye! Call yer spirits, then." Taunts and laughter stabbed him in the back as he stood on the plank.

"Walk it, boy!"

Ian looked up and saw Ruben looking down on him from above. He looked down to see large floating chunks of white, slimy stuff floating below.

"What is that?"

"Whale blubber," Peg Leg answered. "Shark bait. Draws 'em in close."

Doom descended again. The world seemed to darken around him. Ian looked back out overboard. There were, indeed, sharks circling beneath him. Out of the water, in their midst, appeared a flash of red. It would surface for a moment, then disappear. Swimming with the sharks, it seemed to be leading them. On one sweeping arc closing in on the ship, a red diamond-shaped head surfaced and glared up at Ian. Razor-sharp teeth glinted in the sun, and then submerged.

Oh, no.

"No," Ian protested. "I changed my mind. I want to stay here." He turned to go back onto the ship.

"Nay, lad. Ye must walk."

"But that's the serpent that took Mr. Welch."

"Aye. Be evil, sure."

"No, please," Ian pleaded. He tried to push back but, with no hands, he could not get very far. He pushed harder until a pistol cocked and landed against the side of his skull.

"Walk it, boy." Toothless was no longer smiling. The gun barrel pushed him back the direction he was trying so desperately to get away from. The pirate climbed up the

Sinclair, 2014, 2016

step stool and out onto the plank with Ian. Resigning himself to his fate, he turned toward the end of the plank.

With each step, Ian made a mental note of his failings.

I'm sorry, Hunter. I let you down.

The gun prodded his shoulder blade from behind.

Sorry, Mom and Dad. I won't be able to say goodbye.

His hands began to tingle from the ropes behind him.

And whatever you were inside that dragon, I'm sorry I let you down, too.

The ropes burned now against his skin. Ian could feel them moving. It wouldn't be much longer now.

Reaching the end of the plank, a hard shove hurtled Ian forward and into the waters below. Slamming into the water with a huge splash, Ian was sucked under the surface. Kicking his feet, he fought to get back to the surface. Thrashing back and forth, he wrestled to break free.

The sharks came into view just as his world began to go dark. Oxygen cut off and quickly losing consciousness, Ian felt the ropes still tingling and burning, even though he was under water. His hands slipped free from their restraints. Surging forward, he spun around and found himself face-to-face with a red diamond head. Ian kicked away and swam for the surface.

Bursting through the surface, Ian gasped and choked for air. Shattering the calm water, the serpent exploded up right in front of him. Rising up out of the water, the long neck hovered over Ian. Jaws open wide, saliva dropping from its jagged teeth, the thing looked just as it did the day they had first met.

Please, help me.

From the side, a green flash caught Ian's eye.

"Nestor!"

The word was barely out of his mouth before the creature's long tail shot out between Ian and the beast. Whipping back, it hurled Ian up onto its back and the two raced off, skeletal sharks and a red-headed beast hot on their tail.

"Godspeed, yung'un," Ruben yelled from the crow's nest, smiling. "Be safe. Off wit' ye."

"What is it?"

"That is a waterhorse," Nestor said.

"I can see through it. Looks like glass."

"Creatures of the deep, they are but a shell, holding on to that from where they come."

"It's full of water?" Ian could see what looked like waves crashing inside the rib area of the horse. It glowed a combined bluish and silvery color. The mane looked like a wave cresting, white bubbles bursting as the hair waved back and forth in the wind.

"Now listen close. There is not much time. You had only three days to find your friends, and that's nearly gone."

How did you know that?

"A waterhorse can run like the wind. There is no faster way to get you to where the others await you. But heed you this. On land it is but a horse, but if you smell water, then it is too late. The beast will drag you to the depths and you will be caught with the evil side forever."

"It's evil? I can't go, then."

"The waterhorse has an evil side and a good side. Your kind struggles with this, too. Stay on the good side and there will be no problems. Stay on land. You must dismount before you can smell the water, and before she stops. You must jump while she still runs."

"How will I know?" Ian felt the sickening feeling creep back into the pit of his stomach.

"When she smells water, she runs faster. At the instant her speed increases, you must dive off, or it will be too late. There is no time to think. You must pay close

Sinclair, 2014, 2016

attention, and jump when you feel it. If not, you shall be stuck to her forever. If you smell the water, you will be glued to the horse for all of time. You will not be able to break free no matter how hard yo try. You will belong to the evil one, then. I cannot help you."

"Why can't *you* take me? I promise I won't cause you any more trouble."

"Nessie and I are not fast enough now, lad. Time is critical, and you must travel like the wind. The waterhorse is your only hope."

Ian stared at the beautiful watery shell. It whinnied and nodded its head toward him.

"Go," Nestor urged. "Your friends await."

"Are they...?"

"They are well for now, but they need you with them. No one can break free on his own. It will take all of you to finish the race. Stay the course and you will triumph in the end. Do not stray. Fight the good fight, aye?"

Ian nodded. He walked over to the waterhorse. He reached out a hand to pet her neck.

"Nay!" Nestor yelled.

Ian turned back.

"At the moment you touch her, she will take off. Mount quickly and hold on tight. It's the only way."

Sinclair, 2014, 2016

Ian looked back at the horse. Swallowing hard, he set his jaw and backed away about twenty feet. Lowering his head, he took off at a sprint toward the animal. Leaping at the last moment, he landed on the back of the waterhorse, grabbing its mane.

Electricity surged through his veins as the animal bolted forward. Ian clenched his fists, closed his eyes, lowered his head, and held on tight.

"Godspeen, young Ian," Nessie whispered.

Their screams became muffled and faint as they flew through absolute darkness, swallowed up in the pitch-black hole of this new world. Slamming into the dark, hard ground, three separate aftershocks rocked the earth beneath them, and then, nothing.

Let go and fly!

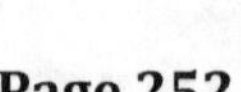

Chapter 28: Fly
Fly [flahy] *verb, (used without object)*
to move through the air using wings; to be carried through
the air by the wind or any other force.

Day 1
She hit the ground hard. Without time or warning, Aeryn got slapped over and over again from all directions — hard. Her flesh stung. She gasped for breath. Aeryn tried to fight. Swinging her arms with all her might, she connected each time with hard, flying, creatures. All she could see was black. Pitch black.

She found a split second to gasp for air, and belted out an earth-shattering scream. All motion around her stopped. The darkness parted. When light streamed in, she saw them. One by one they landed in a circle around her. Aeryn looked to see giant Black Widow spiders surrounding her. Actually 'giant' didn't describe them well enough. These wicked things were enormous — bodies the size of her head. There were hundreds of them. The pincers on their jaws clacked loudly, even though they dripped with saliva. Each was staring at her with glowing red eyes. Aeryn screamed again and backed away. Without thinking, she backed right into one that lunged at her head with its hungry jaws. She screamed again and jerked away, the spider missing her face by only millimeters.

Surrounded, the deadly creatures circled her, clacking, walking, stalking. There was no escape. When they moved, she screamed again, this time sending them back into flight. On each spider, black bat-like wings unfurled from each of the eight legs and flapped above its head. Wings spun, humming like a helicopter. One by one, they took off and hovered around her head, forcing her back to the ground. Aeryn started to cry. She knew she was going to die. They dive-bombed her again, slapping at her with their wings, keeping her crouched low, fighting them off with all her might.

The sky darkened. The hum grew louder. In the distance, Aeryn could see a dark swarm of something headed their way.

Oh, no. More.

Trees and leaves around her shook with the deep intensity of vibrating air. One by one, the bat-spiders spun around, their backs to her, hovering. They, too, were waiting for yet another unseen enemy, one of greater importance than she at this moment. Aeryn sat breathless on the hard, cold ground. Fear within shook her from head to toe. Tears streamed down her face, yet she dared not move or scream. Who knew if what was coming was worse than what was already here.

The first one hit the ground at her feet; a long slender creature, resembling an arrow. Sleek, narrow, bright green in color, legs and wings tucked underneath for better aerodynamics. It stood and turned to face the enemy. Without warning, a second green arrow slammed down from the sky, this time knocking one of the spiders from the air at her feet. The two arrows maneuvered in on the spider. Their sleek green heads covered with eyes on all sides, they could watch for enemies from every direction. Brilliant purple eyes darted from side to side, as the eyes in front remained locked on their target.

The bat-spider flinched, and the arrows pounced. Both arrows wrestled the winged creature down with their own six muscular legs. The first arrow reared back and bit the head from the spider, dropping the lifeless corpse to the ground. The remaining flying spiders scattered.

Aeryn, eyes wide with terror, scooted back as far from these terrifying things as she could. The two green arrows clacked their mandibles toward the sky, and their waiting army. Arrows rained down around her, knocking down the bat-spiders as they came. As quickly as they hit the ground, black heads were bitten off and spat to the side, rolling alongside Aeryn as she fought to stay out of the way. Lifeless, blazing red eyes gazed upon her from the discarded heads. She tried to run, but again ran into the creatures continuing to rain down around her. Fighting for her freedom, she dodged each new enemy one at a time, swinging with all her might, and running when she could. The battle raging all around her, Aeryn zigged first one direction, then zagged another to get free from the carnage surrounding her. Breaking free, she ran as fast and as hard as she could into the forest where she was dumped. The hum of the attackers grew faint in the distance, yet still she ran on without slowing.

She ran until she could run no more.

Aeryn stopped to catch her breath. She turned back to see how far she'd gotten from the fight.

Safety. She couldn't see them, and she was pretty sure they couldn't see her. Collapsing on the ground, Aeryn curled into a ball, wrapping her arms around her own shoulders, she cried.

Will I ever get out of here?

Where am I?

Will Hunter save me, like always?

Where is Daddy?

Did he get away from the monster yet?

Aeryn waited for what seemed an eternity. The sounds of battle had long since waned, as had her tears and her strength. It was clear that no one else was going to come to her. No one could save her now. Wherever Ian and Hunter were, they were not able to help her. She would have to find them, instead. She was on her own.

Standing and brushing herself off, she looked around. Looking back from where she had come, she shook her head.

Nope. Not that way.

Aeryn looked the opposite direction. The forest was so dark and dense she was not able to see through the leaves.

Nope. Not that way, either.

Off to her side, there was a slight hum. Not the hum of battle wings that she'd heard before, though. This was musical. Straining her ears to hear, Aeryn was enchanted by the melody. She took her first step that direction, then froze. There was a familiar clacking sound that locked her in place. Turning back to see, Aeryn screamed.

Two green arrows right behind her grabbed her by the arms and whisked her away toward the treetops.

Bursting though the dense leafy cover and into the blue sky above, Aeryn was flown by the two long, green, angular creatures over the tops of the trees. Kicking and screaming, squirming and wiggling, all did no good. The things held tight to each of her arms. Sweeping across the forest's roof, they slowed very close to the edge of the tree line, dove sharply down, thrusting back through the dense cover, making an abrupt landing on top of the highest tree. Her arms released, Aeryn fell against the branches, clutching them with both arms and legs to keep from falling straight through. Steadying herself, she rose to see the green arrows shoot back up to the treetops in the forest around her. There, they took their place with the others; on guard, surrounding her. Pushing up to a sitting position, Aeryn spun to see that they were all around her, hundreds of them, all high above her head. But something was odd. If they were guarding her, they should be facing her. They were all facing outward. She wasn't being guarded— she was being protected.

From what?

Sinclair, 2014, 2016

Chapter 29: Feather
feath·er [feth -er] noun
One of the horny structures forming the principal covering of birds, consisting typically of a hard, tubular portion attached to the body and tapering into a thinner, stem-like portion bearing a series of slender, barbed processes that interlock to form a flat structure on each side.

Wasting no time, Aeryn began to shinny down the tree. Sliding from one branch to another, the silky smoothness of the leaves brushed against her arms and face, tickling her chin with each touch. Still scared and angry, she batted the branches out of her way as she continued her trek down the tree. The branches were not cooperating, though. Each time she would push one out of the way, it would swing back and brush her face and neck, tickling her again. Aeryn stopped and scratched her face. Something wasn't right. She surveyed her surroundings.

Trees.

Forest.

She blinked hard.

"Is that?" Aeryn rubbed her eyes. "A tree house?"

She blinked hard again. Trying to focus through the distance, she narrowed her gaze.

Black hair, huge limbs, could it be?

"No. Not possible. They don't exist. Bigfoot isn't real."

She turned back to her own predicament.

Back down the tree she descended, and was tickled again.

Tickled? These leaves are awfully soft.

With a single finger, she reached out and stroked the closest green leaf in front of her. The silken threads separated rhythmically with her touch, and deftly slid back into place after her finger had gone.

It's not a leaf. It's a feather!

Aeryn twisted her head in all directions. Feathers covered the tree on every branch. Fluttering ever so slightly in the wind, it looked to her as though the branches were floating in the air, soaring almost.

A single green arrow descended to the neighboring tree, level with her, its many eyes staying focused on her every second. Aeryn snapped out of her amazement, and continued her downward spiral. Round and round the trunk, she descended, branch by soft fluffy branch, reaching the bottom.

Aeryn froze.

She stared at the ground under her tree, then at the ground under the other trees around her.

How?

What?

This doesn't make any sense.

Still a good five to six feet up in the air, the tree trunks did not touch the ground. They actually were floating—soaring, all on their own. The branches fluttered ever so slightly in the faint breeze; the movement so slight and so graceful, she had barely noticed.

How am I gonna get down?

She looked again at the feathery leaves apparently keeping them in the air. Aeryn reached out and plucked one.

The branch she sat on jerked, knocking her off balance. A shriek pierced the air, with the surrounding trees joining in. The entire tree began to shudder and shake like a flapping of wings. Aeryn's branch jerked up, then down, back up, and back down. The movements were so violent, that she held on for dear life, wanting only to cover her ears from the painful shrieking from the tree's trunk. The flapping branches jerked more and more angrily, flopping Aeryn around the tree bottom as though she were a feather herself.

Sinclair, 2014, 2016

She screamed. Losing grip of the branch, Aeryn slipped. The branch flapped again, and she was hurled once more through the air, landing hard on her back six feet down on the hard ground. When air found her lungs, she sucked in to bellow out a big scream, but stopped. The entire forest flapped their branches, elevating even higher, and flew away; leaving her once again facing the bat-spiders, now crawling toward her over the barren ground.

The clacking of their mandibles grew louder. Inching closer, this time the bat-spiders chose to stalk her rather than a full on frontal assault. Aeryn sucked in a deep breath. She scooted up onto all fours and faced them. The oncoming hoard split, surrounding her. Keeping their distance, their red eyes scanning the horizon for signs of their own predators, the fiends cautiously moved forward, encircling her. Keeping a conservative margin between them, the pitch black beasts circled, spinning around, watching from all directions; above, behind, and below. Moving around, but not advancing, they circled until Aeryn felt dizzy, nausea beginning to rise in the back of her throat. Wings appeared, yet they did not take flight. They simply stretched out their legs, primed and ready for any attack that may occur.

The clacking grew louder. Aeryn spun, and spun again, making sure she was not being attacked from the rear. Her mind raced and her head spun. Around and around she turned on her hands and knees, keeping an eye on all the creatures, or as many of them as she could at any one time. Still, the clacking intensified.

Under her, the ground began to shake and roll. She swallowed hard to keep her growing sobs down.

Another earthquake.

She didn't think she could take any more. Where were Hunter and Ian? Why hadn't they rescued her? Where was her father?

"Help! Someone, please!" she screamed.

The earth shook harder. Spider-bats backed away, enlarging the circle. Dirt rumbled and fell away, a large mound arising in front of her. Taller and taller it grew, bursting upwards like the beginnings of a new volcano. Reaching its peak, the top blew off in an explosion of dirt and rocks. Aeryn crouched down, covering her head, trying to deflect the debris that now showered her at the base of the mound. When the dust settled, she raised her head, staring.

The huge iron vehicle balanced precariously atop the shifting mound of dirt. Giant drill bit spinning on the front, its tip still dropped fresh bits of the earth it had just tunneled through. On the side was an emblem, a medieval metal shield with iron aircraft wings jutting out both sides.

Next to the picture, a motto. Smeared with fresh dirt, dented and scraped by the rocks beneath the earth's surface, the words were slightly marred, but still clearly readable: <u>Iron Lightning, Thunder of Doom.</u>

The door opened up and a helmet popped out. "You coming?"

Aeryn stared, fear so deep she could not move. The clacking of the bats intensified. They rushed her from all sides. A siren blared from the military machine. A loud click unlocked side panels. Two wings shot out like a switchblade, piercing the air sharply. They sounded like a sword being unsheathed.

"Now!" the helmet yelled.

Aeryn rolled up onto her feet and ran up the small hill, clacking close behind. At the top of the heap, an iron-covered hand shot out, grabbing the back of her clothing and pulling her inside the metal caged cockpit. The door slammed behind her. Spider-bats slammed into the door behind her, covering the vehicle, their mandibles tapping against the glass of the windshield. Small cracks appeared and chips of glass began to fall away.

"They're getting in!" she screamed.

"Get your seatbelt on!"

Aeryn sat down and grabbed the belt. Hands shaking badly, she was not able to click the ends together. Afraid not to have it on, she took the two pieces and tied them in a knot around her waist. Once secured, the pilot engaged the controls, lifted the vehicle, hovered over the ground, and lurched forward at lightning speed. Spider-bats flew from the winged fuselage, littering the ground below. She watched with a mix of both relief and rising panic as they ascended higher and higher into the air, above the floating trees and the volcano top.

Reaching one gloved hand to his head, the pilot clicked the latch, releasing his visor. It hissed loudly, released, and flipped up, revealing a smiling face underneath.

"Ryder, ma'am, Iron, Corporal. Pleased to meet you."

Sinclair, 2014, 2016

Chapter 30: Rescue
res·cue [res-kyoo] verb, to free or deliver from
confinement, violence, danger, or evil

"Command Base, Eagle One Rescue—over."
"Copy, Eagle One. Status?"
"Package onboard. Inbound. ETA five minutes. Over."
"Roger that. Good work, son. Base, out."
"Eagle One, out."

Aeryn sat frozen to her seat, heart racing, watching everything. The pilot's skills were more than apparent as he maneuvered the flying machinery over the trees, through the clouds, above the volcano, and off to—wherever they were off to. The thought jolted Aeryn like a lightning strike. This man is a stranger, and she had no idea where she was.

Never get in a car with strangers. But then, this isn't a car, either.

"Where are we going?" she asked.

No response.

"Excuse me, but where are you taking me?" she demanded.

Silence.

Aeryn's hands began to shake. Fear crept down her spine and grabbed hold of her stomach like a wrench. She felt like throwing up. Scanning the cockpit, she reached out, looking for anything resembling a door handle.

"What do you think you're doing?"

She froze, trapped like a caged animal. Aeryn thought her heart would explode right out of her chest.

"We're almost there. Just hold on a few more minutes."

"Almost where?" she managed to choke out.

"What?"

"Almost where?" she blurted out a second time.

The gloved hand pointed toward a button on the side of his helmet. "Turn on your mic so I can hear you." The same hand pointed underneath the seat she was strapped in. Aeryn reached down and felt under the seat. Pulling out a helmet, she slid it over her head. Trembling fingers fumbled up the side for the button. Feeling across the side, and up onto the top, she tried to find it, but could not. Ryder reached over and gently touched the button on the far side.

"There," he said, "that's better. Did you say something?"

"Where are we going?"

"Back to Rescue Base."

"There's a Rescue Base down here?"

"Yes, ma'am, there sure is." Ryder kept his eyes focused forward, hands on the controls at all times. "Every now and again, when folks fall through from above, some get into a little trouble and need help. That's what we're here for."

"You rescue others?"

"Just the ones assigned to me."

"My brother? And Dad—"

"I can't help them. I can only help you."

The fears that had eased somewhat clamped down on her insides again. "Why?"

"This is a military operation, Miss. We follow orders. And right now my orders are to—"

"I order you to stop this machine."

"I beg your pardon?" he asked.

"I want out," Aeryn demanded. "If you won't help me find them, I'll do it myself."

"I can't let you out."

"Why?"

"Because you'll get killed, that's why." His hands tightened on the controls.

Aeryn tore the helmet from her head and tried the door handle. "I will not get killed! I can handle myself."

"Like you handled yourself back there?"

Her eyes lit up with a fire that burned inside like a torch. "I was doing just fine until you came along."

"Uh-huh."

"What's that supposed to mean?"

"What about the Spatz?"

"The what?"

"Spatz. You know, the spider-bats, those evil black things with the glowing red eyes that were going to eat you alive."

"I could have gotten away."

"How? They have eight legs and eight wings. They can run faster than any human, and fly with lightning speed. And those clacking jaws weren't there just for show. They can tear you apart."

"I said I can handle myself," her angry eyes glaring.

"They start with your arms or your legs. They always go for the joints. It's the easiest place to disable you. Then they—"

"Stop trying to scare me."

"I'm not trying to scare you, Aeryn." Ryder took a deep breath. "I'm trying to get you to understand the danger down here. This is not like your world."

"What do you know about my world?" She slid as far away from Ryder as the seatbelt would allow. Eyeing him from afar, she took the defensive. "And how did you know my name?"

"I've been there. My last charge lives not far from your home."

"How do you know where I live?"

"I told you, I was assigned to take care of you."

"Assigned by who?"

"Um, that's whom, and it's not important. Right now I just have to get you back to base." Ryder clicked the mic again. "Command Base, Eagle One. Over."

"Eagle One, go ahead."

"Eagle One on approach. Two miles out."

"Roger that, Eagle One. You are cleared to land."

"Take me back," Aeryn demanded.

"What?"

"Take me back where you got me. I don't want your help."

"I can't do that."

"I'll just escape."

"Look, Aeryn. This world can be a very dangerous place. Bad decisions will get you sent to the prison. Very few, if any, ever come back out again."

"But my father's there! I have to get him out." She grabbed the door handle again and jerked.

"It's locked for your safety, Miss."

"Unlock it. I want out."

"I can't do that."

"You said you follow orders. Well, follow this one. LET ME OUT!"

"No, ma'am."

"You suck!"

"Yes, ma'am." Ryder's expression never flinched.

"And quit calling me ma'am!"

"Yes, ma'am."

Chapter 31: Recruit

re·cruit [ri-kroot] noun; a newly-enlisted or drafted
member of the armed forces.

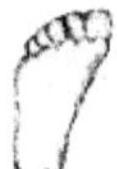

The speed and the force of the aircraft's landing pulled Aeryn down hard into her seat. The weight of her body kept her pinned down as the machine rolled to a stop. The runway appeared out of nowhere, trees parting for the plane to glide under, and quickly drifting back overhead. They were completely hidden from view.

"Where are we?"

"Command base."

"Yes, but where is it? Where are we?" A severe uneasiness took over her senses. *What was I thinking going with him?*

"You'll see." Ryder hit a button on the console in front of him, both doors shot open with a loud hiss. The rush of cold air from outside was sobering. She sat still as Ryder leapt out and ran around the vehicle. Jumping up onto the wing on her side, he held out a gloved hand to help her. She did not respond.

"Come on, Aeryn. Let's get out of this big bird."

"Not until you answer my questions."

"We have to report to the commander. He can answer any questions that you have."

"I'm not moving." She stared, eyes front, arms folded across her chest, seat belt still tied around her waist.

"Fine. Have it your way." Ryder jumped back down and strolled off to the side of the runway.

"So, what? You're gonna just leave me here?"

Ryder stopped and turned back to his charge.

"Some protector you are." Aeryn untied the seat belt and slid out of the cockpit. By the time Ryder got back to the plane, she'd jumped off the wing and stood facing him. "Well?"

"Well, what, ma'am?"

"Are we just gonna stand here?"

"No, ma'am." Ryder turned back toward the fluttering, feathered, tree line.

"And stop calling me ma'am!"

"Yes, ma'am."

Ryder was the first to emerge from the dense coverings. Aeryn charged straight past him to the first person she saw.

"Who's in charge?" Her voice squeaked out the words.

"Ten-hut!" he boomed. Behind her, she heard uniform clicking of heels, hundreds of them it seemed, together with a rhythmic marching sound. Her head swung back to Ryder, but he was gone. The panic inside her flashed again, but she fought the urge to flee. Planting her feet, she stood firm on the outside, trembling on the inside.

"Hut, two, three, four… Hut, two, three, four…"

The chanting marched closer and closer, louder and louder. With each stomp of a foot, her fear grew and her trembling increased. Aeryn's breath was short and ragged by the time they stopped, lined up level with her on the open field.

"Whose charge is this?"

"Mine, sir," Ryder responded.

Aeryn's head whirled around to where the voice had come from, but Ryder was nowhere to be seen.

"Front and center, soldier."

"Yes, sir!" Ryder snapped to attention, his rigid, firm stance the mark of a finely-tuned machine. With perfect rhythm, he marched forward, each foot in time with the other.

Aeryn's eyes continued to scan the horizon. She could hear him, but not see him. He had to be invisible. No, there - wow!

Ryder's shiny silver metal gear had changed to green and brown camouflage. He so perfectly blended in with the tree line behind him that he was impossible to see until he moved; he and all the others just like him. There were hundreds of soldiers all dressed in camouflage. Even his helmet had changed, like a chameleon. Ryder marched straight up to Aeryn's side and stopped.

"At ease," the sergeant commanded.

"How did you do that?" she whispered.

"Quiet!" the commander barked, stepping up to Aeryn's face. "You will train your recruit in the appropriate manner, Corporal. Is that clear?"

"Yes, sir!" Ryder's response was immediate and firm.

Aeryn's trembling burst out from inside her, and was clearly visible now to all who looked at her. No one moved. Not even her so-called protector standing just inches from her. "Excuse me," she managed to squeak out. "There must be some mistake."

"And what is that, missy?" The sergeant stood toe-to-toe, nose-to-nose with her.

Aeryn bristled. She hated that name. Her mother had called her that for years when she was younger. Tears came to her eyes.

"Awww, look everyone," he stepped back. "The new recruit misses her mommy."

Aeryn stared straight ahead. How could he possibly know that?

"Oh, we know everything." He smiled at her, frightening her even more.

Stunned surprise slammed her heart again. She looked at Ryder, standing right next to her. Sharp, rigid, eyes front, with just the twinkle of a tear brimming at the corner of his eye. He made no move to help her.

"I want to leave," she heard herself blurt out. It was like she was outside her body, watching a movie now. She had no control over what she had just said. "I'm not a recruit. There must be some mistake."

"Are you Aeryn Lyn Welch, of Summer City, California?"

Her eyes widened.

"Did you lose your father, Morgan, brother, Hunter, and friend, Ian, down here when you fell through an earthquake?"

All she could do now was nod.

"And do you wish to find them again, missy?"

Another nod.

"Then you, miss, *are* a recruit."

"But I didn't volunteer."

"Very few of us ever volunteer for the circumstances we find ourselves in, but we still have to deal with them. Ryder!" he barked. "Didn't you orient little Miss Princess?"

"Not yet, sir."

"Ah. Probably because she wouldn't be quiet long enough, no doubt." The sergeant marched back and forth in front of the troops. "Step forward, missy."

Aeryn was fully terrified now. She tried to move her feet, but they would not move. They felt like they were stuck in cement.

"Now!"

Aeryn felt a gentle push at her back. Ryder was next to her, coaxing her. With hands on her shoulders, he guided her forward to stand next to the sergeant, then gently turned her to face the crowd. She gasped. There before her were thousands of other soldiers and creatures, lined up in perfect rows. The green arrows that had rescued her earlier made up row after row. Their long, angular, legs unfolded; allowing them to stand at their full height. The light went on inside her eyes as recognition finally set in. They had rescued her, too.

"Yes, dear," the sergeant said. "Praying Mantises. The 'bugs' you so easily kill in the world above, but which were truly put here for your own good. Who do you think they pray to?"

Aeryn swallowed hard. Tens of thousands of tiny multi-faceted eyes were on her. "They have special communication abilities, Aeryn. They are the messengers of our world. It is not wise to randomly take a life, unless you know what you are taking. Do you understand?"

She nodded. Tears now running down her face, she kept her jaws clenched tightly to hold in the sobs.

"And over there," he pointed. "Those are birds."

"The trees?" she managed to whisper, a slight sob escaping her throat.

"No, but they just look like trees. It's all part of our Maker's camouflage. Things aren't always what they seem. No, Aeryn. Those trees are living, breathing, flying creatures that have hidden and protected you from the enemy."

"There's an enemy?"

The sergeant sighed and turned his head. "I knew you were sheltered at home, princess, but I guess I never realized how much. No worries love, that's my own fault for over-estimating you. Ryder will deal with that. Right now your job is to trust your guard and learn everything you can from him."

Aeryn shook her head. "I can't stay here. I have to find my brother."

The sergeant looked at Ryder, shaking his head. "She's a stubborn one. Good luck to you, man."

Ryder said nothing, his hands still gently resting on Aeryn's shoulders.

"There's only one way to leave here, princess, and that's to fly. You can fly, can't you, missy?"

Aeryn swallowed hard. She stood tall, shoulders back, head high, and looked the sergeant straight in the eye. "Of course I can."

"Of course you can," he mocked. "Ten-hut!" he barked. The entire assembly snapped to attention. "Wing men, right and left!"

Two winged mantises appeared from behind and flanked her. "Now!" the sergeant barked.

The creatures lurched forward and grabbed her clothing. Aeryn screamed, but it could not be heard above of the cheers and chants of the soldier assembly below. The creatures flew with her, straight up above the treetops to a platform high in the clouds. There they deposited her and flew away.

Aeryn was alone. All she could see around her were white puffy clouds and the platform beneath her feet. Without warning, the platform disappeared. Aeryn screamed. Falling, hurtling, end-over-end in space, she plummeted toward the ground. Racing faster and faster, the ground moving closer and closer, she hurtled through time.

"HELP ME!"

Two more green arrows shot out of the tree line and grabbed her. One held her right arm, and the other the bottom pant leg of her left side. They flew her back down to the crowd and dumped her in front of Ryder and the sergeant on her butt.

"Ryder!"

"Yes, sir."

"Orient your charge." He turned and walked away.

"Yes, sir," Ryder answered, looking down at Aeryn sprawled on the ground.

She was weeping.

Sinclair, 2014, 2016

Chapter 32: Cell
Cell [sel] *noun*
a small room, as in a convent or prison; a small group
acting as a unit within a larger organization

Aeryn slid from Ryder's arms into the bed. "This is your barracks," he said. "It will be your home as long as you are with us." Aeryn continued to sob softly, unable to look him in the eye. "Aeryn," Ryder whispered, "I know it is difficult at first, but you will get stronger."

"You didn't even try to help me. Why?" Her pleading eyes bore holes through his armor and into his soul. "You just stood there and let me fall. Why?"

"Because you wouldn't have accepted it—" He reached down to slide the shoes from her feet, setting them together at the foot of her bed. "I can't teach you to do something you are convinced you already know how to do. You need to understand what your limits are."

"Why do I have to have limits?"

"A good soldier knows what he can and can't do. He surrounds himself with others who complement his own strengths and weaknesses. No one is good at everything.

We are not here on earth to be alone, or to be perfect. We all need each other." He pulled the covers down for her to slide under. "You don't have to be able to do everything, Aeryn. Just make sure you are around others who can. You will pair their weaknesses with your strengths, as well."

She rolled toward the wall, refusing to look at him any longer.

"One day you'll trust me. I just hope it's not too late. The choice is yours." The light switch clicked, the door closed, and the room was doused in darkness.

The night dragged on without a wink of sleep. Aeryn's mind raced.

How did I get here?

Where is my family?

Why won't Ryder help me?

The more she tried to contemplate the answer to one question, a dozen more bombarded her mind. She was aware of everything around her. Through the tiny window next to her bed, she could see the sentry guards watching over her barrack's door.

Off in the distance, Aeryn could see an odd sight. Rows and rows of the green arrows lined up in formation. Only this time, it was not a traditional military formation. They were all huddled together in more of a circle than a line. It appeared as though the Praying Mantis-like creatures were communicating somehow. Aeryn climbed up onto her knees to see better.

The largest one was in the middle. The way he was sitting, the sharp jutting angles of his legs and arms, he looked like he was on his knees. Arm appendages were aimed skyward in an odd pointing manner. Surrounding this creature were all of the others, their arms all reaching out and touching the big one in the middle. With each additional touch, the one in the middle seemed to grow bigger and stronger, arms reaching higher and higher. The smaller mantises would move and circle, ensuring that each one had a chance to touch the leader and give him whatever strength or support he could glean from them. The circular motion that danced around outside her dorm window was like a well-oiled, well-practiced machine. There was no pushing or jockeying for position. Each one had a purpose and a time. When their time was up, that mantis would move and let another slide into its place, all the while the leader grew bigger and stronger before her eyes. She stood now, no longer trying to hide behind the wall or the window.

The stars twinkled above, brighter than any she had ever seen at home. Watching them through her window, it seemed as though they were circling her. It was hard to tell, but as one would disappear behind the roofline of her building, another would come out from the opposite side. Faster and faster they moved, forcing Aeryn to close her eyes to keep from getting dizzy. When she opened them again, the stars were spinning tightly in the sky like a top, leaving a long silver trail behind them. Spinning tighter and tighter, weaving the trails into a fine silver thread, the star formation now descended to the group of Praying Mantises in the middle of her compound.

The first touch was electrifying. Sparks shot from the tips of the leader's arms, landing on those surrounding him, causing them to all glow. The leader took on an electric blue color, fiery lightning bolts shooting out to all the others in the group. Held together by the glowing blue arc, they were one unit, one being with whatever was up in the sky.

The sound began very low. Buzzing. Hissing. Spitting and crackling. The sound grew louder and louder as the glow of the creatures increased. As the silver thread danced and swayed with the creatures below, so did their response. Their clacking mandibles could be heard above the increased frenzy in the compound.

They are messengers, Ryder had said. Whomever they were messengers for, it sure seemed like they were communicating with them now. The sound grew and grew, forcing Aeryn to cover her ears, but still daring not to take her eyes from the frenzied dance before her. Eyes wide, ears plugged, totally entranced, when—

SNAP.

The silver line burst into thousands of tiny shards of glass, raining down flaming sparks on the crew below. Each member was frozen in time at the split second the connection broke. With a uniformity only achieved in highly trained troops, hundreds of praying mantis heads all followed their leader and turned to look directly at Aeryn's tiny window. Thousands of miniscule glistening glass eyes glared at her, then uniformly looked back skyward and nodded their assent. Panic seized Aeryn's heart like a vise stopping it. When it started again, the beats thundered in her chest, neck, and head. Aeryn could feel the veins popping out on her temples with each throbbing pulse. She broke out in an instant sweat. Sliding down the wall, she dropped back down on her bed, buckled knees and wobbly legs unable to hold her weight.

One final star exploded above, and the world again went pitch black.

The silence was as deafening as the darkness that surrounded her. Aeryn's ears rang and her mind soared with what she had seen. Explosions. Spinning stars. And those messengers— they were communicating with someone, or something. But who, or what? What was that silver rope-thing she had seen? Over and over again, the scene replayed itself in her mind. All reference to time was gone. The night stretched on and on, with the same movie playing again and again, each time as vivid and frightening as the time before.

Both time and darkness seemed without end, but slowly Aeryn's mind finally cleared and the world settled back down around her. The spinning spots that had plagued her vision disappeared, and a little at a time, the normal everyday sounds of the world came creeping back into her senses. The one thing that she could not squelch was those eyes— tens of thousands of tiny glass facets, all staring at her. Then they all nodded in unison. She shivered involuntarily, though it was not cold.

Sinclair, 2014, 2016

The wind whispered ever so slightly through the tree feathers. The wildlife of the forest hooted and scurried around, foraging for food. The guards at the compound again marched in ranks outside the barracks, keeping watch against the night. Inside the safety of her dorm, curled up on her bed, Aeryn sat wide awake, unable to put the day's events out of her mind. The rhythm of the night was somehow comforting though.

Marching.

Swaying.

Marching.

Clawing.

Scratching.

Clawing?

Aeryn sat up straight. She listened for the sound again.

There it was. Inside the room. She scooted to the edge of the bed and looked down.

More clawing. Was it under the bed?

Scratch, scratch.

Nope.

There—across the room.

Gathering her courage, Aeryn sprang from the bed and landed in the center of the room. She ran to the wall and hit the light switch.

The floor scattered. Tiny creatures shot from view to the hidden areas beneath beds and under dressers. As fast as cockroaches, their tiny legs scratched and clawed against the hardwood flooring for traction. Aeryn was about to scream when she noticed one single creature remained in the center of the floor, staring at her.

Eight tiny legs and two big red eyes glared at her from under a sea shell. The creature sized her up, shell tilting to one side and then the other as it regarded her from the middle of the floor.

"Hi. Umm. Hi."

Aeryn's jaw dropped. It took a minute to find her voice again. "You can speak."

Click, clack, click, clack, click... It clawed its way a few steps closer to her.

"Are you a hermit crab?"

"Yeah, yeah. Crab. Uh huh, crab."

"What are you doing here?"

"Came to get you out."

"Me? Out of here? Can you help me find my dad?"

"Yeah, yeah. Take you to your dad."

Sinclair, 2014, 2016

Chapter 33: Follower
fol·low·er :[fol-oh-er] *noun*
a person or thing that follows; a person who follows
another in regard to his or her ideas or belief; disciple or
adherent; a person who imitates, copies, or takes as a
model or ideal

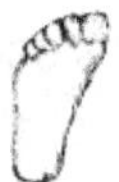

"I can't see where I'm going." Aeryn stumbled behind the clicking and clacking of the crabs' claws against the floor.

"No need to see. Yeah, yeah. Just follow."

"But, how do I know I'm going the right direction?" Aeryn turned her head all directions but could see nothing. She had felt her way out of her dorm room following the crab sounds. Now she was in a hallway of some kind. Trying to remember which way she had come in with Ryder, Aeryn stopped. "Wait," she said. "I think I came in from over th- - -"

"Shhhh! Must be quiet. Come this way," the command came through the darkness. "Yeah, yeah. This way." The scratching continued moving away from her. Aeryn followed.

She felt her way along the walls to the end of the corridor. There she reached the door — the door to outside. "Do I open it?"

"Shhhh. Must be quiet. Down here. Yeah, yeah. Down here."

A small ray of moonlight shone in from the base of the door. Kneeling, Aeryn noticed a vent to the outside. Crabs of all shapes and sizes scurried through the opening around her. Putting her face down close to the vent, she whispered to the leader. "This is how I am supposed to get out?"

"Yeah, yeah. Come on."

"But I can't fit."

"Take the cover off, stupid."

Aeryn couldn't believe her ears. "I am not stupid!" she blurted.

"Shhhhhh. Must - Be - Quiet! Want to see your father again?"

"Yes." She was whispering again.

"Must crawl, like a sp—, ummm, a crab. Yeah, yeah. Crawl like a crab."

"Ok. Ok. I'll crawl." Aeryn grabbed the vent grate with both hands. She tugged one direction and then another. She pushed and pulled. "It's stuck. I can't get it off," she whispered through the vents.

"Leaving." Clicking began.

"No! Wait."

"Too dangerous to wait. Girl does not wish to help her father. Must go now."

"No, please." Fighting tears, Aeryn called out again. "I'm coming." With one mighty jerk, she ripped the grate from the wall, leaned way down onto all fours, and squeezed through the hole. Halfway out, she turned and looked at the place where she and Ryder had last stood together.

I can't help you. His voice resounded in her head. *You have to learn your limits. You can't do everything, Aeryn.*

"I'll show *you*, Iron Ryder." She put her head down and finished crawling through the small space.

They were getting—well, not louder exactly. More like—just more. There were more tiny feet hitting the ground around her. The sound was much more intense than before. Still too dark to see, she followed the scratching and clacking. Through the feather trees and into a clearing, more moonlight filtered through the thick brush and on to the ground. Aeryn looked down. The ground scattered. She rubbed her eyes and tried to focus hard. Yes, the ground was moving. Black blobs were scattering from the clearing and lining up at the edge of the tree line. In front of her remained the crabs.

"What's going on?" she asked. "What are all those things?" She pointed to the rolling black blobs.

"You don't remember?" the big crab asked.

"Yeah, yeah. She don't remember."

Clicking and clacking, with another sound, surrounded her. The shells of the hermit crabs were twitching. Not quite shudders, but like laughter—suppressed laughter.

"He-he-he-he-he-he.   Ha-ha-ha-ha-ha-ha."   The snickers surrounded her. They started low, and rose up behind her as the hairs on her neck stiffened.

"Are you—laughing at me?"

"Yeah. Yeah. Laughing! Stupid girl." The crab shell shook harder.

"Hey, that's not nice." Aeryn turned around to leave, but the black blobs had grown into a black wall behind her. Legs stuck out at odd angles, linking together forming chains between the pillars of blobs. As she stared at them, red glowing eyes opened. Recognition hit a split second too late. She spun back around to the crabs.

"He-he-he-he-he-he-he-he. I think she remembers now." The crab hunched over, and the shell popped off his back, shooting up into the air. Underneath was a jet-black Spatz.

Shells shot up all around her. At her feet, spider-bats first circled then took flight with the bat-like wings peeling up from each angular leg. They circled her, slapping at her head and arms, just like earlier in the day when she'd first landed here. Aeryn screamed, dropped to the ground and curled into a tight ball. The wall of black spider-bats closed in, creating a living jail cell, bars locked into place with the interlocking legs.

Aeryn wept.

"Don't think those tears will have any effect on us, missy. You came here of your own free will. It was your choice." A big spider circled her, still prone on the ground.

"You lied," she managed to spit out.

"Lie? Me? That's not possible." Giggling from the black walls shook the ground. "What did I lie to you about?"

"You said you would take me to my father."

"And so I shall. "

Aeryn froze. Afraid to move, and afraid to ask any more questions, she sat still, barely breathing.

"You will be with your father very soon. Would you like to see him now?"

She sat up, wiping the tears from her face. A nod was the only answer she could muster.

"Very well, call to him."

"What?"

"Call to your father. He will answer and he will come. Trust me."

"Daddy?" Aeryn ventured, but dared not move too much. "Daddy?"

"Louder," her captor commanded.

"Daddy!" she called louder. "Daddy?"

"Aeryn! Run!" His voice came on the wind.

"Daddy, I can't run. They have me! I need help."

"Run, Aeryn! Don't come here!" His voice grew louder with each word. "Stay away! Run!"

The ground began to shake. The violent jolts were spaced out, rhythmic footsteps.

"Daddy! Save me!" Her screams became more insistent.

"Aeryn! Get away, baby. Run away!"

She slumped to the ground, shaking from the sobs that racked her body and her soul. "I can't, Daddy. They have me trapped."

Sinclair, 2014, 2016

The trees shook as the footsteps came closer. The feathered branches in front of her separated, allowing a giant black spider through. Taller than the trees they were surrounded by, the enormous arachnid poised itself over her prison cell. Huge mandibles clacking and dripping saliva, the giant red eyes glared down at her from high above.

"Aeryn!" Her father's voice was frantic now, causing the giant spider to laugh, shaking the ground beneath her. "Aeryn!" His voice came from right in front of her, but the only thing in front of her was the spider. Terror gripped her along with realization this spider was the source of him calling. It leaned in closer, bending its jointed legs down low. One giant red eye hovered over her. From the edge of the lower lid, a hand grabbed from the inside and tried to pull up. "Aeryn!" The hand emerged from the glowing eyeball, grasping at the air. On the third finger she saw her father's wedding ring.

"Daddy!" A wave of hysteria tackled her. Her breath came ragged and short. Crying, choking, screaming, the world closed in on her.

"Run, baby! Ruuuuunnnnnnnnnn!"

Dizziness engulfed her. Her cries turned to whimpers as the choking sobs cut off her oxygen. The giant spider swirled above her as the world went dark around her. The only light she saw was the glistening of her father's wedding ring.

The world, again, went dark.

Sinclair, 2014, 2016

Chapter 34: Web
Web [web] noun
something formed by or as if by weaving or interweaving;
a thin, silken material spun by spiders and the larvae of
some insects, as the webworms and tent caterpillars

Day 2
Aeryn's eyes fluttered open. *What a nightmare.* She blinked the morning light away, and sighed. *I have to get out of here. Home. I need to go home.* A huge yawn captured her lower jaw, stretching her face and filling her lungs with chilly morning air. Aeryn tried to shake away the cobwebs from her sleepy brain but her hair was caught on something. She raised her hand to check it out. At least she tried to raise her hand. It seemed to be caught on something, too. The glare of the sun was so bright against the morning dew she couldn't see anything. Aeryn tried to move, but couldn't. She rolled one way, and then another. Nothing worked. She was caught. Panic flashed back into her being as she recalled the details of her nightmare. Only it wasn't a nightmare anymore. It was real again.

Aeryn fought against the restraints that held her down. Once again she felt the ground shudder and shake as giant footfalls sounded louder and louder. Clacking mandibles— that's what she heard. Never again would she forget that sound. Ever so slowly, a giant clacking black orb slid down a slick web string and eclipsed the blinding sun. Only then did she see why she couldn't move. She was spun into a giant glistening web.

"Good morning, child," the spider greeted.

"Let me go!"

"But of course we can't do that. We have an agreement."

"What agreement?"

"My emissaries offered to take you to your father, and you agreed. That constitutes a verbal agreement— a contract of sorts. You are now bound to it."

"I don't want your help anymore." She squirmed and wriggled, but the web tightened on her.

"I am confused. Don't you want to see your father again?"

"Of course, but not like this." She fought against the restraints holding her down.

"I don't recall there being any choices given to you in the matter." Aeryn froze and stared at the giant salivating arachnid.

Sinclair, 2014, 2016

"You see, child," it continued, "my minions told you they would take you to see your father. You agreed. There was no mention of any circumstances beyond that."

Behind the big leader, she heard clacking— clacking that almost sounded like laughter to her, and then screaming. The thundering on the ground increased.

"You will be brought to your father soon enough, but not as a visitor. You will now be his fellow prisoner."

"What's that sound?" she demanded.

"Sound?" The black head turned one way, and then another, all eight of its eyes circling the surroundings. Another scream tore through the morning light. It was the sound of pure terror.

"That sound," she snapped. "That was a scream."

"Ahhh, yes. One of our less cooperative guests."

Aeryn's mind raced. Panic seized her senses. *Was it Hunter or Ian? Could it be her father?* She screamed. "Let me go! Daddy! Hunter!"

"Now, now, child. Is that any way to treat your gracious hosts?" The spider moved away, releasing the blinding sun against her tear streaked face. Her eyes closed to protect them. In the distance, the screaming weakened, and then stopped.

"What's happening?" she sobbed. "Why did it stop?"

The spider clicked as it moved away. Click, clack, clack, clack, click. Tsk. Tsk. Tsk. "Not to worry child. She is, as you say, breakfast." Reaching the edge of the clearing, he twisted several eyes backward. "Guard her!" was the last command barked at the camouflaged hermit crabs lining the perimeter of the web.

It wouldn't stop. She tried. Oh, how she tried. But they just kept coming in waves. Her violent trembles shook not only her mind and body, but also the web she was chained to. The strings were impossible to break. She watched the web strands quiver in the air, as though a steady wind blew through, but it didn't. The movement was that of sheer terror and she was completely helpless.

The girl's scream echoed over and over again in her mind. Aeryn tried to slow the sound, but couldn't. She wished that her hands were free so she could cover her ears and try to make this sound go away, but she was locked in place. She had long since given up her struggle against the web; it only made her chains tighter the more she fought. She had run out of tears, and hope. Aeryn hung in time and space, waiting to die.

Sinclair, 2014, 2016

That's when it hit her.

'She.' The spider had said 'she' was breakfast. Aeryn was the only girl in their group. That meant that Hunter, Ian, and her father were still alive. Sadness at the unknown girl's fate surfaced, but at the same time a glimmer of hope dared to swell inside of her. She opened her eyes. The guards were still there. She counted fifteen hermit crabs with spindly legs in a circle at the base of the web. There were probably more behind her, but what did it matter. There was no way she could escape. Even if she did manage to get out of the web, the guards would snatch her in an instant.

The crabs began to circle their prey. Aeryn tensed, as much as she could within the confines of her coffin-like cocoon. Moving with a military precision, the crabs crawled around her in rows. The only thing missing was the clacking. Faster and faster they circled, reaching out and touching one another as they passed.

Why does everything dance in circles around here? These look just like— the thought jolted Aeryn like a bolt of lightning. She remembered the scene from last night, yet so long ago. They gathered their strength from something above. Something or someone up there communicated with them— about her. Aeryn looked up. Her fingers and toes began to tingle. Whether from lack of blood circulation or something else, she didn't know. But she did know that her terror was subsiding and her courage was seeping back into her soul.

"Please," she started. "I don't know who or what you are, but I know you know I'm here. And I think you know I'm in trouble."

The forest took on a glow. Not an eerie one. This was more of a bright shadow. The presence of something was moving toward her. Aeryn began to cry. *Not the spiders again.*

"Please," she started again. "I messed up, bad, and I need help. I have to find my dad and my brother. I can't do it all by myself. I tried but it didn't work."

The light grew brighter. Shades of purples, oranges, reds, and blues moved toward her. It looked as though a rainbow walked through the forest toward her, a calming rainbow. No fear or shame came with it. Just peace.

At the base of a nearby tree, a single silver thread from under her web began to spiral upwards, dancing toward the sky. The tip swayed to and fro, but always staying within the glow of the rainbow. It almost looked like the web strands that held her captive, except this one was different. The spider's web was a glistening silver thread, but the tree thread, while glistening and silver, glowed with the rainbow that it danced within. The spider web did not. The rainbow overtook her position, but she wasn't afraid.

"Please, set me free," she asked. Upon her request, the silver thread lowered, touched her cocoon. The chains fell away. Aeryn was freed.

Pop. Pop. Pop.

Crab shells shot up all around her, revealing crouching mantises underneath.

"Psssst. This way."

Aeryn jerked her head around to see Ryder crouching on the ground behind her.

"Quickly; the spiders will be back soon."

Aeryn slid from the web, now immune to its sticky trapping qualities. She ran toward Ryder.

"No," he commanded. "On your belly. We have to crawl."

Aeryn followed the order without question, dropping to the ground and half-crawling, half-sliding to her rescuer. The mantises followed suit, sliding around them in a protective circle.

"I'm so glad to see you, Ryder. I didn't think—"

"No, you didn't think, did you?" he whisper-barked back at her. "Look around. These guardians all risked their own lives to come here and protect you."

Aeryn shrank back.

Sinclair, 2014, 2016

"It's time for you to grow up, Aeryn. This is no joke." He turned to crawl through the brush. "Hurry; when the spiders get back they'll be angry. We may not survive next time."

Aeryn broke into tears again. Ryder turned back. "If you want to rescue your father, then let me help you. Take the time to learn what you need to. Sharpen your skills. Be a soldier. If you run off blindly, then you will not only get yourself killed, but also the rest of the soldiers with you. We lost one this morning."

She wiped her tears away. Frozen in time, unable to move, she whimpered. Then the shaking returned.

"Look back, Aeryn." She turned to see the rainbow still in the clearing behind her. "That will never let you go. Don't you let go, either. Learn to trust."

She nodded.

"Soldier!" he whisper-barked again. "Attention!"

Aeryn turned front, wiped her face, and for the first time, she faced her fears.

"Follow me!" Ryder turned and slid away. She followed.

The mantises took up the rear, scraping away their trail in the dirt as they crawled.

Sinclair, 2014, 2016

Chapter 35: Train

Train - *verb (used with object)* to develop or form the habits, thoughts, or behavior of a person by discipline and instruction: *to train an army.*

"You are the sorriest group of recruits I have ever seen!" The commander paced back and forth in front of their line, head shaking. "No discipline. No direction. Everybody wants something but nobody wants to work for it. Am I supposed to just hand life to you?" He scanned the group in front of him. "WELL, AM I?" he screamed.

"No, sir," a few grumbled.

"You call that an answer?"

"NO, SIR!" they yelled back.

"Back straight! Chest out!" he ordered. "Head high! How do you slacking, sorry group of misfits ever expect to accomplish the impossible, if you don't believe you can do it?"

The group glanced around at each other.

"WELL?"

"Yes, sir!"

Sinclair, 2014, 2016

"Yes, sir, what?" The colonel stopped right in front of them, polished armor glistening in the morning light blinding Aeryn. "Yes, you don't believe you can?" he barked in Aeryn's face.

"No, sir," she shot back.

"No, you can't do it?"

"No, sir. I mean… Yes, sir, no…" she hesitated a split second too long.

"What exactly do you mean, Recruit Welch?"

"I can do it, sir." Her heart raced and her palms sweat.

"You can do what, Recruit Welch? Tell the group, if you please."

"I need to save my—"

"I didn't ask you what you *need* to do, Recruit. I asked you what you *can* do. So, tell me again, Recruit Welch. What *can* you do?"

Aeryn wanted to cry. She could see Ryder standing in a line of soldiers behind the commander. Her rag-tag collection of misfit recruits was lined up in front of him, with the commander alone pacing between the two groups. She looked at those around her for help. They dared not move their eyes to even look at her, that is, if they even had eyes. She saw what looked like a small Bigfoot, assorted enormous insect-like creatures, could be a lizard next to her, and possibly another human, all looking beaten down and dejected just like her. She opened her mouth to speak but nothing came out.

"Would you like some help, Princess?"

She nodded, the words not able to form in her throat.

"Nothing. You can do nothing, Princess. And would you like to know why?"

Again she nodded.

"Because you think you can do it on your own. You trust no one, receive help from no one, and you help no one else. Is that about right?"

Another nod.

"So tell me then, how did you get free from the Spatz?"

Aeryn jerked her head up and stared into his eyes.

"How did the web release you? Hmmm?"

"I don't know," she whispered.

"Did you do it?"

"No, sir."

"Then can we agree that you can't do everything?"

"Yes, sir," she whispered.

"And you absolutely can't do the impossible, correct?"

She lowered her head and nodded. The commander moved down the line, stopping at the Bigfoot. "And you— can *you* do the impossible?"

The hairy brown creature made a low rumbling growl.

"No, I didn't think so." The commander stopped pacing and stood tall. "One thing you failures need to get through your thick skulls right now is that you are never alone in this life, and we do nothing alone. There are highly trained and dedicated souls here for no other reason than to see you to safety. If you are to succeed in your respective quests of saving your homeland from deforestation— he gave a nod to the Bigfoot; wiping the planet free from Spatz— now nodding at the giant insects; and saving your father from certain death— he winked at Aeryn; then you must learn to depend on each other. The One who put us all here never meant for us to fight our battles alone. Like it or not, we need each other, so get used to it!"

"How are push-ups going to get my father released from prison?"

"Stop asking questions, Aeryn. Just focus." Ryder squatted at her head, bent low.

"I don't see— "

"You don't have to see," he snapped. "Just trust that the commander knows what he's doing. Is that so hard for you? This is about discipline and trust," Ryder cautioned. "You must be trained in the proper way to do things, so that when things get hard, you won't depart from what is right. Understand?"

"Up. Fifteen. Down. Up. Sixteen. Down. Up. Seventeen. Down. Up. Eighteen. Down. Up. Nineteen. Down. Up..." The drill sergeant's monotonous voice never faltered.

"I'll do push-ups if you answer some questions."

"Fine, Aeryn, whatever it takes. But you have to do them while I answer. If you stop, I stop. Deal?"

"Deal." She propped back up on her hands and toes, ready.

"Down," Ryder started.

"How did I get free from the web?" She went down.

"A friend."

She came back up. "What friend?"

"Down. The one you called."

She came back up. "I never called anybody."

"Down. Yes, you did. I heard you."

She came back up. "No, Mr. Ryder, I did no such thing."

"Down. Do you remember saying 'please help me'?." Aeryn stopped. "Down," Ryder barked, "or I stop." She went down and pumped back up.

"Yeah, I said that, but not to anyone. I just—said it."

"Down. Well, He heard you, and He came to help you."

"Who?" She rose, her arms shaking and muscles burning.

"The One who put us all here. Down."

"You mean like a Commander or something?"

"You could say that."

"I did say that, genius," she shot back. "How 'bout you answer me."

"Look, missy; you have no idea how much trouble you're in right now. I am here *trying* to help you. I'm fighting for you, so why don't you start behaving?" Ryder stood and stomped away.

"Wait!"

He stopped.

Aeryn wrestled with her thoughts for a moment. "The girl who was killed—the one who was screaming— did you know her?"

Ryder nodded without turning around. "She was from your world."

"Why didn't someone rescue her?"

"She wasn't mine. Besides, you can only rescue those who wish to be rescued, Aeryn. That one was headstrong and stubborn. Never felt as though she needed help from anyone. She ran off on her own to do everything by herself, and she paid the price. She never learned to truly fly on her own. Not everyone survives down here, Aeryn. It's my job to try to teach you—to save you, but I can't teach you if you refuse to learn."

"That's not fair."

"What's not fair, Aeryn? Life? No, it's not. You think I want to sit down here and listen to you scream for your life like that? I won't be able to help you then. You're my recruit. You've been assigned to me. I don't think you understand that."

"I understand."

"No, you don't. You don't seem to understand at all that I am here to help you, but I can't if you keep refusing."

"I never actually refused." She grinned. "And, besides, I was just testing you."

"Testing me?" Ryder's jaw dropped.

"Yes. I was testing your loyalty."

"Uh huh. And?"

"And what?" She smiled.

"Did I pass the test?" Clearly annoyed, Ryder just stared at her.

"For now," she smirked. "We'll see more when the flying lessons begin. Right now I have to do stupid, useless, push-ups because my angry mentor told me to. Don't actually understand why I need a mentor at all, but since I'm stuck with one, I might as well try to help him." She propped back up on her elbows, then dropped back down. "Wait," she said. "Tell me again why I need to do push-ups."

Ryder dropped his head and let out a deep mournful sigh. "Why me, Sir? Why me?"

Sinclair, 2014, 2016

Chapter 36: Fear

Fear: *noun* a distressing emotion aroused by impending danger, evil, pain, etc., whether the threat is real or imagined; the feeling or condition of being afraid

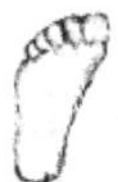

Day 3

"When can I fly, Ryder? Huh? Huh? When can I? It's time, isn't it? I can fly now, right? I did the push-ups. What do I have to do first?"

"Calm down, Aeryn."

"I can't. I'm too excited. It's already been two days. Today is my last day, so we have to fly now so I can move on. I only have today to find my dad. Is it time? Is it?"

"We have to wait for the others first."

"Why, Ryder? Why do we need to wait for them? You said I need to solo. That means I need to fly all by myself. I don't need anybody else. I can't solo with anyone else around. That means I have to fly by myself, then I can leave. When can I leave? Why do I have to wait? What are we waiting for again?"

"Aeryn, stop." Ryder felt himself losing patience. He squared his shoulders and looked her straight in the eye. A tiny tear quivered at the inside corner of her left eye. He wiped it with his thumb. "We're not ready yet. Certain things have to be done to ensure your safety. Just be patient a few minutes longer. Please?"

She nodded.

"I know it has been three days. Believe me, I know this well. There is still time. But trust me, and let me get things covered for you. Okay?"

She nodded again.

"Trust me?"

Another nod.

"Just sit down over there for a few minutes and be quiet."

"Okay, I'll sit down and wait for you. I do trust you, Ryder. I know you're here just trying to help me. I know now that you only want what is best for me. When we were working out, and you made me do endless push-ups, and run laps, I know that you were just trying to—"

"Aye, yi-yi."

Higher and higher the two ascended, Aeryn in the rear, and Ryder taking the lead, as usual. Through the treetops and up into the clouds, a single vine carried them skyward. Aeryn clung to the long feathery leaf, afraid to look down, while Ryder continued to climb as the vine grew at an accelerated rate. Aeryn could watch it sprouting new vegetation as each second passed. She held on in wonder. *Jack and the Beanstalk…*she giggled.

"Why were we waiting for people when there's no one here but me?"

"Everyone flies in their own way and time, Aeryn. Just because you don't see it, doesn't mean that it isn't happening. The fact that you don't see others around you, protecting you, doesn't mean they're not there." Ryder stopped climbing. Positioning himself against the main stalk of the vine, he glanced back down at his charge. "What's wrong?"

"Nothing."

"Why aren't you climbing?" Ryder scooted back down to where Aeryn was hanging on. "Are you afraid to fly?"

"No," she said. "It's not the flying that bothers me; it's the crashing."

"You don't have to crash. Just believe in yourself and the rest of us."

"Us? Who is 'us', Ryder?"

"Your support group, Aeryn. We are the people who believe in you and support you."

Sinclair, 2014, 2016

"And torture me," she quipped.

"Life is all about perception, Princess."

"Don't call me that." She pulled herself closer to the vine. "I just want to get this over with and find my dad."

"I know."

"Then why don't you help me, Ryder? If I'm your 'charge', then why don't you help?"

"I am helping."

"Oh yeah? How?"

"By teaching you how to fly on your own. My doing everything for you is not teaching you; it's rescuing you."

"Nothin' wrong with being rescued."

"Not until you become used to it. Some people use being rescued as a crutch. They feel as though they don't have to do anything because they know someone will come along and do it for them. They see themselves as victims and forget how to try." Ryder's gloved hand reached out and lifted Aeryn's chin, forcing her to look into his eyes. "I won't let that happen to you. You are not helpless and you are no victim. Now climb." He turned back skyward and began his ascent again.

Aeryn had scarcely moved a few feather-leaves when she heard Ryder announce they were there. Looking out from her perch, she saw nothing but billowy white clouds so thick her vision could not break through them. Above her was a floating platform. It took her only a split second to recognize it. She had been here before, when she first arrived. This was where Aeryn had been taken when she had lied and told the drill sergeant she already knew how to fly. Now here she was again, right back where she had started from. She had done nothing but come full circle.

Ryder took hold of her from above, hoisting her up on to the platform by the back of her shirt. She was unceremoniously dumped on her behind, and wrapped with some sort of string.

"What is this?" She fingered the fine silver string now loosely tied around her waist.

"Safety harness." He continued making his preparations for her first flight.

"It doesn't look like any safety harness I've ever seen." She tugged on the single thread, but it refused to let go of her. "Shouldn't there be more to it? I mean, like more straps, or something?"

"Don't need anything else. Think of this like your lifeline."

"Lifeline to who?"

"Our Commander."

"Why to him? Why not to you, or to the platform here, or something else? Something I can see and touch? Why can't I see the ground from here? Is this really more training, or a trick? Ryder, I'm not sure any more about this. Maybe I need more push-ups. Why don't we stop and—"

"Aeryn, be quiet and listen."

She stilled.

"Do you remember everything I taught you?"

She nodded.

"Good," he said, and shoved her off the platform.

Aeryn screamed, or at least she thought she did. She couldn't hear anything. With the speed of her fall and the wind whistling in her ears, all she could hear was a loud shrill. Panic gripped her. Aeryn flailed against the rushing wind, grabbing for anything, no matter how far; tree branches, leaves, stalks, Ryder.

"Ryder!"

How could he do this to her? How could he just dump her off like that?

"When I see you again, Iron Ryder, I'm gonna..."

"You're gonna what?"

Her head jerked sideways. Ryder was there, pacing her all the way down. She reached for him, but he ducked, gliding sideways away from her.

"Put your arms out. It'll slow the fall."

Aeryn thrashed and flailed more, trying to get over to Ryder. "Help me!" Over and over again she screamed. "Ryder!"

"Aeryn, let go of your fears! Don't panic."

Don't panic, she told herself. *Don't panic. Stretch your arms out. Learn how to soar.* Reaching outward, Aeryn stretched her arms as far as they could go. Opening her hands, she let the wind whip through her fingers. For a moment, she slowed. Panic struck again when the ground sped into view. With each inch she fell, Aeryn flailed again, screaming Ryder's name. Ducking again sideways, he soared toward her and reached out his hand. Aeryn grabbed and jerked him toward her. Drowning in sheer panic and speed, she clung to him, preventing him from being able to maneuver. He jerked back, forcing her grip to release, and shoved her back.

"Stop! You'll kill us both!" he screamed.

Aeryn tumbled end-over-end, barreling toward the ground. Righting herself, her body slowed slightly seconds before impact.

She slammed into the ground. Dust shot up around her like exhaust from a rocket, then settled again on her motionless body.

Sinclair, 2014, 2016

Chapter 37: Overcome

Overcome: o·ver·come, [oh-ver-kuhm] *verb,* o·ver·came, o·ver·come, o·ver·com·ing.
to get the better of in a struggle or conflict; conquer; defeat: *to overcome the enemy;* to prevail over (opposition, a debility, temptations, etc.); surmount: *to overcome one's weaknesses*

Tears came in racking sobs once she caught her breath. Aeryn was choking herself trying to suck in air to breathe, and cry out in anguish at the same time. Curling herself into a tight ball, she hugged her knees tight and sobbed.

Nothing around her made sense anymore. She was hurt and broken. Ryder had pushed her too far. Her heart ached. Her lungs burned. Her stomach churned. Bile rose in the back of her throat. She tried to choke it down, but could not. Her fight was gone. She turned her head and vomited.

Wiping her disgusting mouth with her sleeve, Aeryn pushed herself up. On the ground in front of her was a pair of iron boots.

"No." she cried. "I can't."

"Let's get you cleaned up." Ryder's familiar voice no longer carried its usual comfort.

Aeryn didn't want to go with him, but had no energy left to fight. He could do whatever he wanted. She didn't care anymore.

"I'm a failure."

"Why do you say that?"

"I can't fly."

"It's not that you can't fly; you just haven't learned yet."

"Haven't you been paying attention? She screamed, her patience and all self-control gone, Aeryn lashed out at the man in front of her. "I just fell from way up there and almost killed myself, in case you weren't paying attention."

"You were never in danger, Aeryn."

"Never in any danger! Are you insane? Didn't you see me? I failed, Ryder. I can't do it. I will never find my brother or my father. I will never get out of here. I will never see my mother again. I can't do it. I can't—" she slumped back down and wept.

"Ok, you're right. You can't, and you never will." He turned to walk away. "I give up on you."

"Why are you hurting me?" Her sobs stopped Ryder.

He turned back to his charge. "Close your eyes."

"What?"

"See what I see. Close your eyes." Ryder's gloved hands touched her temples.

Electricity shot through her veins from her head to her toes, washing away all of her hurt and pain. Aeryn felt clean. She looked down at her arms. No more dirt and vomit stains. No more bruising and blood. She was spotless, almost glowing; pure white if that was even possible. Aeryn looked up into Ryder's face. He was smiling through his helmet. For the first time, she saw the man inside the suit.

"Close your eyes," he whispered.

She did.

Aeryn was jerked up, feet firmly planted on the ground and watched herself fall from the sky, replaying the terror from minutes ago. Yet this time there was no fear, no panic. It was like watching a movie play out on a screen in front of her; a screen of her life.

Aeryn's body fell from the platform with the others.

There were others? Aeryn had never seen them before. She had been so caught up in herself that she'd never noticed anyone else.

One by one, their arms unfolded and wings appeared. They all, one at a time, caught the current of the wind and began to soar. One after another was swept away on the wings of the wind. All except her. Aeryn now stood firmly on the ground and watched herself falling, screaming, flailing, speed increasing, trying desperately to grab on to anything to save herself.

There was no emotion or fear in her now. The current of electricity still pulsed through her veins while she watched herself. Within feet of crashing into the ground, the mantises appeared. Three of them shot out from the tree line, hidden from view, and softened her crash. The one directly underneath her took the brunt of her weight from the fall. It lay mangled and broken beneath her. The other two quickly scooped it up and shot back to the trees, disappearing before she came back to her senses.

"I thought you said they were messengers."

"Messengers, protectors; call them what you will. Their mission is to keep you from all harm."

Her arm began to itch, followed by a sharp pain. She looked down and saw a single feather sprout. Not a big beautiful feather, but a straggly, thin, wisp of a thing. More fluff than feather, it blew lightly in the breeze.

"This is how you learn to fly, sweet Aeryn."

She looked at him, confused.

"Only when realize you are proud and unyielding, can you be made whole again. But you won't be re-made the way you were. Things will never be the same again. You will be made into a whole new creature, filled with a knowledge and belief in yourself that you never had before. That trust comes not from inside of you, as you tried to cling to before, but from something greater than ourselves. Close your eyes again."

Aeryn closed her eyes and saw herself back on the ground, but it was not ground. It changed. She was looking at the floor of her bedroom. Again, she was broken down and crying. Her mother was standing in the doorway. "One day you will see that this is for your own good. I'm sorry that I have to punish you, Aeryn, but what you did was wrong. You cannot take things that do not belong to you."

Aeryn scratched her arm, another sharp pain and another feather. This one was bigger than the last, but not fluffy. This was torn and mangled. It could never fly. Who could be proud of a feather like that?

"Not all memories are pleasant, Aeryn, and not all feathers are perfect. Some will reflect the pain and the misery that we have experienced in life. But it is those experiences that shape who and what we are inside." Ryder's thumb gently touched her eyes, and they closed.

Sinclair, 2014, 2016

She was at school. Aeryn took the certificate from her teacher, beaming with pride. "And congratulations to our study buddy team, Aeryn and Jessica, for the best class project this year! Working together, they were able to draw on each other's strengths to create a cohesive and coordinated report with stunning visual aids." The applause faded as she opened her eyes.

"Ouch!" There, on the back of her hand was a beautiful, fully colored feather. It fluttered in the wind, each delicate hair-like strand catching the breeze, lifting her hand slightly.

She closed her eyes. Memory after memory flooded back. Her arms, shoulders and hands itched and ached with an intensity she had never known. Scratching while she watched, her upper body transformed into a beautiful flying machine, each feather a memory and a lesson learned.

"What do you see, Aeryn?"

"The good memories are pretty feathers."

"And the bad ones?"

"Broken feathers."

"What do you know about the broken feathers?"

"They are bigger and stronger than the others."

"And what is in common with the bad memories?"

"They are all things I won't let anyone help me with, or things I did wrong."

"What are the good ones? The pretty ones?"

"Times when I let others help me."

Ryder smiled. "Accepting help from others is not a bad thing. It does not make you weak. You aren't perfect, Aeryn. You don't have to be good at everything. It's okay not to be perfect, and it's okay to accept help from others. It makes us stronger. We need all of our feathers; the strong, the broken, the tender, and the weak in order to truly fly."

"Why didn't you just tell me this, instead of making me go through this ordeal?"

"You had to learn it on your own. You would never have believed me. Besides, I had to show you the way. It is entirely up to you to whether you choose to follow. I can't make you go. Good leaders stand out front and lead; they do not stand behind and push. You had to come along on your own."

Aeryn nodded; finally understanding on a deeper, personal level.

"Now, spread your wings and fly. People are waiting for you."

Aeryn fluttered her wingtips while she descended through the floating feathery trees. She touched down lightly on the ground, the tips of her toes landing first, then settling back onto her heels. Her feathers ruffled in the light morning breeze, and lay down flat against her skin, sightless to the human eye. She looked around. In some ways she had come so far, yet here she was, right back where she started—alone in the woods, on a journey to find her family.

Aeryn took a few steps. The floating trees moved with her. No matter how many steps she took, or which direction, her view never changed. "So, Ryder, this is what you meant. I'll always be protected."

The breeze rustled the trees ever so slightly and whistled through the underbrush. "Yeeeeessssssssssssssssss," it sounded. She smiled. For the first time in her life Aeryn realized that she was not alone, and it felt good. She would never be alone again.

"Ryder, is that you?" Life around her was calm and peaceful. "Is this—my new friend?"

"Yeeeeessssssssssssssssss," the wind answered.

"Which way should we go?" Aeryn looked left. She saw nothing, and felt nothing. To her right, through a dark valley, sat the volcano, and beyond that, glistening clear water and open sky. She took one step to get a better look at some odd movement that direction. "Is this—?"

"Yeeeeessssssssssssssss."

A dark feeling of foreboding came over her. When she looked at the valley before her, she felt death. The shadows moved by themselves, and the trees were all dead. There was no foliage and no covering. It was a valley of pure darkness. A shadow of death. "Are you sure?"

"Yeeeeessssssssssssssss."

The trees turned with her. The wind rustled her long brown hair. She took a step. The trees fluttered and floated forward. "So I guess this is the way. Let's go then." Aeryn squared her shoulders and marched on, floating trees and slight breeze surrounding her every move.

Chapter 38: Reunite

re·u·nite [ree-yoo-nahyt] *verb (used with object)*, *verb
(used without object), re·u·nit·ed, re·u·nit·ing;* to unite
again, as after separation

The forest refused to move any more. Aeryn stood
on the precipice, looking down at the dark valley below.
Black rocks skittered across the valley floor by themselves.

Spatz. She shook her head. *Not again.*

Further beyond the rocks, leafless dead trees
uprooted and walked. As if they could see her, a number
of them turned toward her and replanted their roots. They
were glaring at her. Menacing knot holes in the dead wood
glowed red, daring her to set foot into their forbidden
realm. The creek at their base flowed thick black sludge.

Aeryn shuddered. The wind gently rustled the trees
behind her. She knew her friend was there. She still
trusted that she would never be alone, but it did not mean
that her senses weren't sharp, her nerves raw, and her
mind alert. Still, her feet refused to move. As if they had a
mind of her own, Aeryn willed them to take the first step,
but they did not, choosing instead to remain fully planted

at the top of the cliff overlooking the living death below her.

Behind her, a piercing shriek cut through the air. Black vultures, giants for their kind, launched from the deadened tree limbs and dove toward her. She dove for cover.

"Aaaaawwwwwww!!!!!"

The scream wasn't hers. Aeryn hit the ground, hiding beneath the branches of her guardian tree friends behind her. Her eyes darted for the source of the scream.

"Stop, ya mangy creature! STOPPPP!"

Scanning the forests, both living and dead, Aeryn's eyes settled on a wave of water rushing toward her. Hoof beats shook the ground, as if a herd of wild horses were upon her. Aeryn hung low, watching the waves, and a red-headed young man riding them.

"Ian!"

"Aeryn! Stay back! It's not safe."

The waves rushed forward, sloshing to a stop at the edge of a cliff. Aeryn watched as the water churned inside the crystal clear shape of a horse.

"What is it?" she asked.

"It's a water horse. Stay back! It's dangerous."

"Get off then!" The answer seemed so simple to her. The giant head turned toward her, waves raging inside its skull, menacing red glowing eyes staring her down. Nostrils flaring, the thing huffed, spewing heated breath, fighting for air against the darkening skyline.

"I can't. I had to dive off before the thing smelled any water. Now it's too late. I'm its prisoner forever." The horse turned back toward the dark valley ahead, reared up, neighing into the darkness, and landed back on all fours. Furious waves crashed against its insides.

"Run, Aeryn! Run for your life!" Ian fought against the raging tide holding him captive on the water horse. Unable to move his legs, hands glued to the thing's wet mane, he pulled and fought against the rising tide of panic.

"Ian," she called, "maybe I can —"

"No, Aeryn! Run!" Sheer panic erupted in his voice. "You can't touch it, or you'll be its prisoner, too. Save yourself! Get to your dad before it's too late."

The horse turned toward the valley below. Rearing up one final time, it neighed at the darkness. The giant vultures answered back, welcoming them to the darkness. The horse came down, stomped its front feet, testing the cliff side, and took its first step down.

A loud whistle shook the floating leaves from behind. The rock shot from the tree cover like a bullet, striking the horse on the butt. The horse's crystal casing cracked, circling like a spider's web from the point of impact, but did not release its fluid insides. It backed up from the cliff side, turned to face the attack head on, snorting and neighing again. This time, it was not a typical horse sound. This was a battle cry. The eyes raged red with hatred. Nostrils flaring, the war horse stomped and prepared itself for battle. Facing the trees head-on, the horse lowered, Ian still holding on for dear life, and charged the forest.

One single rock struck squarely between the eyes, and the creature fell. Its crystal exterior exploded releasing his rider in a rushing wave of seawater. Ian flopped around like a stranded fish. Finding his hands and feet, he scampered toward Aeryn, covering her, protecting her as best he could.

"Relax guys. It's just me." Hunter stepped into the open, and smiled at his sister and friend.

Each step was chosen with precision and strategy. There was nothing random about the placement of their feet.

"Why are the rocks moving?"

"They're not rocks," Aeryn said.

Sinclair, 2014, 2016

"What are they?" Ian asked, "and why can't we touch them?"

"Long story," she whispered. "Just keep putting your feet exactly where mine were so we can get through this. Touch ONLY the real rocks, nothing else, or we all die."

Ian followed her, eyes darting ahead at the moving shadows. He turned back to Hunter, bringing up the rear of the group. "Why are the trees moving?"

"They're not trees." His hand balled in a fist, he clenched a rock. Eyes following the movement of the shadows, he carefully trailed his sister and friend, stone doubling as a weapon at the ready. His strike would be instant and deadly. "Hey," he looked at Ian, "what was that thing you were riding anyway."

"A water horse."

"Where'd you find it?"

"Long story. Where'd you learn to hunt like that, man? That was awesome."

"Long story," Hunter whispered back, eyes still darting every direction. "Very long story."

"So," Ian's flat, dry voice asked, "What now?"

The three stood on the outer edge of the dead forest. They had descended the cliff, and crossed the blackened creek. Now, all that awaited them was the black forest. Hunter's eyes never stopped moving.

Sinclair, 2014, 2016

Aeryn scanned the blackened forest. "One wrong move and we're toast, just like those trees," she whispered.

"Too late." The first rock struck with deadly accuracy, taking down the enemy. Hunter's hand found another, and another, lobbing them toward the towering trees.

"Those aren't branches," Ian said, voice trembling slightly. "They look like - - "

"Antlers," Hunter said, eyeing his next target. "The one thing I used to fear most."

"Used to?" Ian swallowed hard. "That's good. I guess."

Deep, glowing red eyes blinked through the darkness. "What now?"

"Strike the leader and the rest will scatter."

"Okay, so which one is the leader?"

"He'll be a giant,"

Ian's voice quaked again. "B-b-b-big-g-g-ger than them?" A single trembling finger reached forward.

"This feels like death." Aeryn's gaze never moved. Her eyes remained locked on the black mountain in the background, until it, too, started to move. "Hunter."

"I see it."

The ground shook as the mountain took its first step. "Hunter."

Rising to full height, eyes glistening red, fangs bared and dripping, enormous antlers scratched the sky as the mammoth head swung back and forth against the dark horizon. The tips of the antlers crackled and buzzed, a blue arc of electricity shooting back and forth between them.

"Don't panic." Hunter's hand was steady and his gaze locked.

Saliva dripped from its mouth as giant silver fangs emerged.

"Hunter!"

"Trust me, Aeryn."

She froze. Ian took her hand gently, pulling her back out of firing range.

"When I say 'run', head straight through the middle of those trees."

"The trees that aren't trees? Is that what you mean? The tree-monsters?"

"Yes. If we get separated, meet me at the mouth of the volcano."

"You want us to run there?" Again, Ian squeaked a little.

"Yes. Right through the middle."

"What are they, Hunter?" Aeryn whispered.

"My worst nightmare, Aeryn. That's the monster my fear has created, and now I must defeat it." Hunter clenched the rock harder. "If I can do this, I can do anything."

Ian squeezed Aeryn's hand harder. Her feathers ruffled, fear creeping over them.

"Don't be afraid," Hunter warned. "Keep your wits about you. Be ready."

The earth shook in waves with each step. Hunter could feel the snorting breath now, rancid stench, warm and revolting. He wanted to wretch, but dared not take his eyes from his prey. Closer and closer the fear monger came, growing in size with each thundering step.

"Hunter."

"Wait."

"Hunter."

"Wait."

"Hunter!"

The rock shot like a bullet from his hand. "Now!" he screamed.

All three took off like a shot, never looking back.

The tree line tore open, each manifestation of evil turning toward their fallen leader, clearing a narrow path for escape. The ground rumbled beneath them. No longer watching their steps, they ran over Spatz after Spatz, causing a black cloud of frenzied flight over their heads.

Aeryn ran in the lead, Ian following, with Hunter bringing up the rear. Single file, they darted through the trees, antlers, or whatever these things were. Something very similar to branches slapped and grabbed at them, but the split second lead they had was enough to escape the enemy's grasp. Bursting through the other side, all three slammed face-first into the base of the volcano.

Aeryn was the first back up on her feet. Getting her bearings again, she scanned the volcano for danger, and froze. Shock set in. Tears filled her eyes as her legs gave way beneath her. Hunter and Ian kept her from collapsing.

"What's wrong?" Hunter tried to sit her up again. "What is it, Aeryn?"

A small shaking finger pointed. "Dad."

Puppet pup·pet: Spelled [puhp-it] *noun*
an artificial figure representing a human being or an
animal, manipulated by the hand,
rods, wires, etc., as on a miniature stage

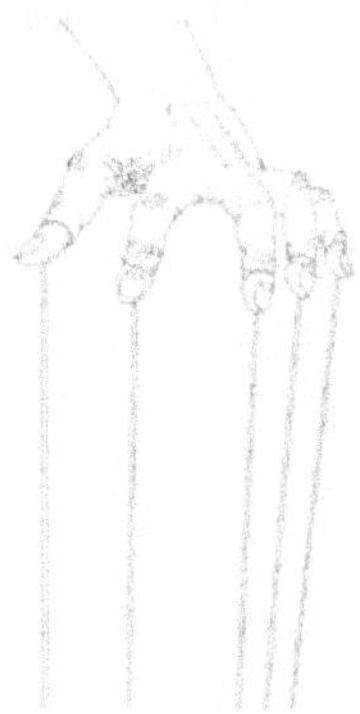

Sinclair, 2014, 2016

Chapter 39: Castle
cas·tle [kas-*uh* l, kah-*suh* l] *noun, verb,* cas·tled,
a strongly fortified, permanently garrisoned stronghold

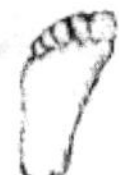

The crack of a whip sliced through the air like a knife. The snap so jarring, all three flinched.

"Shhhh." Ian stepped forward, in between Aeryn and the scene unfolding in front of them.

"Dad," she called again. "Is that you?"

Ian's hand clamped down over her mouth. "Shhh. Not now."

The whip cracked again, followed by an eerie laugh. At the rear of the crowd loomed a serpent. Not just any serpent. It was the razor-toothed monster that had taken their father what seemed so long ago. It hovered over the crowd below, dripping saliva from its enormous jaws, tongue whipping out and snapping at the prisoners below.

Chained beneath were rows of sheep. Not ordinary sheep, though. Each had a human head. Sheeple. They blindly followed, one after the other, wherever the smaller serpents at the front of the line led them. One of the smaller serpents seemed to take extra pleasure leading the group astray. It zig-zagged this way and that, as the sheeple blindly followed its lead. When the followers ran into one dead end after another, a tree or a cliff, the monster would exude a deep belly laugh, then turn the group another useless direction. All the while, the other serpent guards applauded and watched, snickers plastered across their hideous faces.

When the group turned toward the children, the sheep with Morgan's head swung their direction and saw them. "Ruu-uu-uu-uun," he managed to bleat out.

"Daddy!" Aeryn screamed out, but little sound barely cut through Ian's tightly clamped hand.

"Get baa-aa-aa-ck. It's daa-aa-aan-gerous."

"Pleaa-aa-aa-aase," one of the other sheeple begged a guard. "It's ho-o-o-ot. Can we haa-aa-aa-ve some waa-aa-aa-aa-ter?"

"You want water?" The whip cracked again from the giant serpent's tongue. Here's your water." Gills on the side of its head flared out, making the thing look like a giant cobra. Small appendages raised outward and the thing howled, head thrown back toward the darkened sky, flames bursting out of its snout. The darkness tore open with red jagged lightning and the rain poured down, soaking the sheeples' thick woolen coats. They trudged on aimlessly, bumping into one obstacle after another, now weighed down heavily. Again, the giant serpent laughed. A winter chill swept over the group, and the sheeple began to shiver, frost from their breath filling the air. "Noo-oo-oo-oo," they all begged.

Aeryn started to cry.

"So what— Now you want the rain to stop?" The serpent shook his giant head in disbelief.

"Plee-ee-ee-ee-ase," they begged again.

"I gave you what you asked for, you lousy ungrateful, stupid creatures. Fine!" it growled. "You want heat, here it comes!"

Again howling at the sky, gills spread, the creature snarled, and set fire to the rain. "Careful what you ask for. Now move!" Every ounce of moisture burst into flame.

Aeryn's tears stung her eyes and burned her face.

Hunter reached out and extinguished the flames from his sister's cheeks. He clenched a rock. "I can take the big one," he told Ian. "Move so I can get a clean shot."

"No," Ian blocked the way. "Not now."

"I can take him," Hunter ground out between clenched teeth.

"And then what?" Ian fought to keep his voice a whisper. "What about the others? You can't take them all." Ian refused to move. "Wait till the time is right. Then we strike."

"I need to get my dad. I can save him."

"No. You can't. Not like this. You can't save them all now. Wait," he cautioned Hunter again, "till the time is right. Don't let your anger drive you."

"Welcome to your new home," the smaller serpent at the front snarled.

"Moat!" he snapped toward the sky.

The earth shook and the sky flashed. Again, the fiery rain poured down, spewing flames from the top of the volcano, heavier this time. It rumbled and roared, glowing brightly in the sky. The mountain groaned and split the earth in front of them, tearing a ring around itself. The ground beneath them gave way. All three slid down the side of the crater circling the spewing mountain. The thick black liquid that had run through the black valley behind them, now flaming, diverted its path and turned to fill the moat. All three were trapped in the trench.

"We gotta get out." Ian's panic was evident. "Now!" He scrambled up the side ahead of the other two. Bracing himself against the top, he grabbed a branch from the ground and extended it back down to the other two. Aeryn grabbed it, and pulled herself up alongside Ian. The branch went back down. The thick black sludge continued to fill the ditch, black mounds and rocks spilling over the edge with the flaming rain. Hunter scrambled to keep his feet from becoming submerged.

"Don't let it touch you!" Ian called.

"Drawbridge," they heard the serpents command. Obeying the order, three dead trees fell from one side of the moat, laying perfectly in line with one another over the expanse of the flaming moat, forming a footbridge for the sheeple to cross.

"Hunter!" Ian's voice was near frantic. "Grab it!"

Hunter turned back from the bridge to the extended tree limb. He took hold and pulled himself up, just as the jaws of a giant croc pierced the flaming black sludge and snapped down where his ankle had been.

Ian hoisted him to safety and the three sat, backs to the volcano, watching the lost, helpless souls cross over the bridge.

"Castle!" Earth moved and sky flared. The volcano transformed before their eyes into a beautifully lit palace. The entrance was wide and accommodating. "See," the serpent leader smiled, fangs glistening in the radiating glow. "I promised you a large home, filled with many others just like yourself. I am the prince of this dark world, and all princes live in castles. You will live here forever now, too. All you had to do was follow me." When he laughed, the world shook.

Hunter, Aeryn, and Ian all watched as Morgan was led, chained to the others, into the castle. The snarling giant was the last to cross the bridge. Reaching the other side, he turned to the three children, huddled on the side of the moat and winked. A cruel smile spread across his horrid jowls, sliding across jagged glistening fangs.

"Close" he commanded, disappearing into the castle.

The dead trees rose back up again, re-rooting themselves on the other side of the moat. The entrance to the castle dimmed and closed. Again the earth shook, the sky rained fire, and the castle disappeared in a flash. The three were huddled against the side of the cold, dark volcano.

Chapter 40: Fortress
for·tress *noun:* a large fortified place; a fort or group of
forts, often including a town; any place of exceptional
security; stronghold

The tips of his fingers and toes barely clung to the
rocks, yet still Hunter climbed. Higher and higher, burning
and bleeding, he clung tightly to both the razor sharp rocks
of the volcano, and to hope. Methodically, he scanned the
black lava mountain looming above them.

"Tell me again why we're climbing up the side of an
active volcano." Ian struggled to keep up with his friend.

"Because my father's inside."

"Hey, where'd you learn to climb like that, anyway?"

"I already told you," Hunter said, stopping to scan for
his next move, "from the Indians."

"Oh, yeah. Right. You just happened to run into a
band of indigenous people who took you in, taught you
how to hunt, fight, apparently climb, and then they sent
you on your way. Does that about cover it?"

"Yup." Hunter stretched and grabbed another thin ledge. Pulling himself up, he paused and smiled. Pleased with their progress, he scanned for his next move.

"Slow down, man," Ian snapped. "I can't do this." A gust of wind burst around him. Ian clung to the thin rocks at his fingertips.

"You wouldn't have to," Aeryn fluttered behind him, "if you would just trust me."

"Oh right! I forgot. You," he tried to point at her and nearly lost his footing. Ian snapped back to the mountain and the tiny ledge. "You were with some paramilitary boot camp who taught you how to sprout wings and fly."

She danced on the air, twirling, flapping her wings, and laughing at the two struggling boys in front of her. "I can help you, if you just let me."

"Help us where?" Ian snapped. "Up to the top where the lava is boiling? No, thank you. I'll take my chances behind the Lone Ranger up there."

"What do you say, Hunter?" Aeryn asked her brother. "Let me help you?"

"I have to find the best way first. We need a good defensive fortress."

"Why?"

"The best defense is against the rocks."

"Why do we need a defense?" Again, Ian stopped. "I can't go any more. I'm not strong enough."

"I'm sorry?" Hunter turned back. "What did you just say? Where's the Ian who used to get mad and bully his way through everything."

"Choose your battles wisely," Ian shot back. "Fight only those you can win."

"So, tell us then," Aeryn probed, "where were you for the last three days?" She floated down to the ground, settling at the base just a few feet below.

"With the pirates."

"Pirates?" Her eyebrows rose.

"Hey, they saved my life."

The siblings nodded, and turned back to the looming mountain in front of them. All three stared, motionless and speechless.

"Sure is big," Aeryn whispered.

"Big, and impossible," Ian said back.

"Not impossible," Hunter said.

"Look," Ian pointed up to the top, "we need a better plan. We can't climb up to the top and slide down inside with the lava. It's enormous." He pointed up to the top. "Look how jagged it is. Our hands will be shredded by all these sharp rocks. It's like a giant cheese grater. There are no landings to rest on. We'll be here for days."

"Well, right now there aren't any better options. We have to get inside. Besides," Hunter said, "there have to be some landings somewhere." He tried to settle back, but couldn't rest, hanging from the rocks. "You're right," he conceded, "we do need a better plan." Hunter took a deep breath. "Aeryn, help me down."

She flew up to her brother, hovering behind him. "Piggy-back," she said. Hunter climbed on, wrapping his arms around her neck, legs around her waist. She fluttered a little, zig-zagging her way down. Hunter laughed. For the first time in three days, Hunter laughed. Aeryn landed at the base of the volcano. He released his grip and slid down to the ground.

"Hey, how 'bout me?" Ian still clung tightly to the ledge.

"Jump," Hunter laughed again. "You're only three feet up."

"Really?" Ian turned his head. Looking down, he laughed. "Sure seemed like a lot more." He released the rock and jumped back.

"Definitely have to find another way inside," Hunter whispered to Aeryn.

"So what now?" she asked.

"We check the volcano for alternate access."

"And just what," Ian asked, "does alternate access look like?"

"When I find it," Hunter winked at him, "I'll let you know."

"Hey, look," Aeryn blurted out. "That looks like a face up there." She pointed halfway up at the rock formations in the side of the volcano. "See, there's the nose, two eyes, and a mouth." Her finger pointed nearly straight up.

"Yeah, it does."

"Sure does," Hunter mused. "The eyes look almost real from here."

The eye closest to the trio glimmered, and winked at them.

"Whoa! Did you see that?" Ian jumped back and tripped over some rocks.

"Careful!" Hunter snapped. "You'll fall back in the moat!"

"It winked. It winked. Did you see that?" Aeryn fluttered off the ground, voice giddy. "It winked at us. The volcano winked at us."

"So, what does that mean?" Ian stood up and rejoined the group. "Does it like us?"

The lava mountain winked again.

"There! There! It did it again!" Aeryn could barely contain her excitement. "What now?"

"What are you askin' me for?" Ian looked at his two companions. "I've never had a mountain wink at me before. I don't know. Let's wink back."

"Maybe we should just talk to it." Aeryn looked back up at the smiling face.

"Talk to a pile of rocks? Are you insane?"

"Yes, Ian. After three days down here and all of the stuff that we've been through, I would have to say I'm pretty close to insane right now." She was losing her patience. "But we still have to get inside and get to my father."

"Go ahead," Hunter said. "Give it a try."

Aeryn stuck her arms out. She shivered, fluffing her feathers, and floated a few feet off the ground. Looking up, she spoke loud and clear. "Please, can we get inside?"

The face nodded, dislodging some of the smaller rocks beneath it, the boys deftly dodging them as they tumbled down. When the head moved, Aeryn noticed a prickly circle around the forehead area, almost resembling a crown, but not really— more thorny. It circled the forehead, as far as she could see. She looked at the boys for help. Two shrugs answered her. She looked up again, and flew a bit higher. "How?"

The face smiled at her. She felt at ease for a moment, until the face wrinkled, gritted its teeth, squeezed its eyes shut, and shook. Rocks loosened and raced down the slope, forcing Hunter and Ian to again dive for cover. Tons of black, hardened lava bounced from one mountain ledge to the other, finally crashing at the base, throwing dirt and mud up into the air.

Aeryn raced down like the wind. "Hunter! Ian!"

"We're okay." Ian was the first to emerge from their hiding place behind some boulders. "That wasn't exactly what I'd call a success."

"Maybe you'd like to try, smart-aleck."

"Maybe I should." Ian stood tall. "At least I could manage not to get us buried by an avalanche of rock."

"Hey, what's that?" Hunter pointed toward the rocks at the volcano base. As the dust cleared a door emerged. The three stared at it. In unison looked back up at the face. It winked.

"A door? No way." Hunter shook his head. "It can't be that simple." The other two stared, dumbfounded.

"Knock," Ian said. Hunter shot him a nasty glare, but didn't move. "No, really. Trust *me* now. Just knock."

Hunter stepped up to the door, reached out, tentatively trying the handle. Locked. Gathering his resolve, he tapped lightly on the massive wooden door.

The lock clicked. The handle turned. The door opened.

Chapter 41: Game

game [geym] *noun*; a competitive activity involving skill, chance, or endurance of two or more persons who play according to a set of rules.

The three crept through the open door. It slammed shut behind them. Aeryn, Hunter, and Ian all stood huddled close to one another. The blackness spoke.

"Do you want to see some magic?"

SCREEEEECHHHHHHH.

A high-pitched squeal like nails scraping down a chalkboard pierced the darkness. A quick whiff of sulfur wafted by, and the darkness sprang to life. At the end of a long stone hallway dangled a puppet holding a long matchstick.

"Let there be light," it laughed, in a mocking tone. It extended a jointed wooden arm toward the three still huddled by the door, the match head pointed directly at them like a microphone. "Come in," the puppet beckoned. "Welcome to your new home." His arm swirled above his head like a flaming halo, flinging sparks as it swirled. Those sparks each splattered against the dark walls, bringing to light even more puppets holding matchsticks. There were dozens of them.

Aeryn recoiled against the two boys. Round wooden heads, brightly painted with glowering eyes and wicked smiles, stared down at them from every angle of the cave. Each one held out a long wooden blazing match head from a jointed wooden arm, legs dangling beneath them, a plethora of knotted strings holding each one in its unnatural hanging pose.

"Come in," the main puppet urged again. "I am so pleased you have finally made it. We have been waiting for you."

"Waiting for us?" Hunter asked.

"Why, yes, of course."

"Who are you?"

"Where are my manners? I do apologize. I am the proprietor of this establishment. These are my 'friends'," he said, pointing at the other puppets adorning the walls.

"What's your name?" Hunter ventured again.

"Umm. Well, that's a bit complicated," the puppet replied. "I have many names. You can just call me, 'Sir'."

"Sir," Hunter took a slight step forward, "we saw some others being brought in here earlier, and I was wondering—"

Sinclair, 2014, 2016

"Oh yes, yes! Yes!" The gangly creature leapt from the wall, leaving behind its strings. It moved under its own power now, toward the trio at the door. The shrill laughter had a sharp giddy edge to it, and the painted face illuminated its sheer delight through the dancing flames. "They, too, are my guests, although they didn't wander in so easily. We helped them along, so to speak."

"Please," Aeryn spoke up. "One of them is our father. We need to see him."

"And so you shall, little Princess. And so you shall. There are just a few housekeeping items we need to attend to first."

"Housekeeping?" Ian asked.

"You could say so." The puppet danced with excitement, inching closer to the three. "It's just a formality, really. Nothing to worry about."

"What kind of formality?" Hunter's tone grew sharp. His keen senses began to sniff danger. The little hairs on the back of his neck stood on end and his nerves turned sharp.

"Let's call it, sort of registration. Like when you begin a new school year— except there is no more school in here. From now on, life will be nothing but fun and games."

Sinclair, 2014, 2016

"Fun and games?" Hunter's arm instinctively pushed his sister behind him.

A bright, white, wooden, toothy smile glittered at them. "Uh, huh. Forever and ever. I promise."

Ian stepped up, shoulder-to-shoulder with Hunter, shielding Aeryn behind them with their bodies. "What's the catch?"

"Catch?" The puppet feigned a hurtful expression, but quickly replaced it with the toothy smile. "More like some fine print, for sure, but let's not dawdle. We have lots to do. Come," he turned and walked down the long hallway and around the corner. "Come, come now. Lots of business to take care of before all of the festivities later tonight."

"Festivities?" Aeryn whispered.

The toothy smile shot back around the corner. "Yes, yes. Tonight we're having an— ummm— well, initiation, I guess. Yes, that's it. An initiation into our very own private club. Very exclusive. Coveted, in fact. If we hurry, you can all join with Morgan, too. Kind of a family affair. Yes, yes. Come. NOW!"

The puppet disappeared again, leaving the three to follow.

"Come. Come, children. We don't have a lifetime—or do we? Ha-ha-ha-ha-ha-ha-ha-ha-ha…"

The puppets hanging against the walls clattered and shook. They looked as though they were trying to laugh, but no sound came out. Their stares, however, followed the three young friends into a great cavernous room. It, too, was lined with burning puppets on all sides. Their leader stood in the middle.

I've got them now. All three are mine, just like their useless father.

"Where are we?" Hunter's eyes took in his surroundings. In the middle of the rock room was a well spring. Circular stones built up thick sides about three feet tall, keeping the bubbling warm water contained. Around the sides of the room were four doors, with a darkened hallway at the far end. Scattered around the room was everything from pebbles to boulders. Dense black onyx, silver ore, and glistening opaque quartz gems littered the floor. Hunter scanned the room from one side to the other. "Where do the doors lead?"

"Oh, come now," the puppet laughed. "Surely you've played this game before. You choose the right answer and you get what you want. Choose wrong, and— well, let's just say, I win."

"What kind of game are you playing here?" Ian barked.

"Where's my father?" Aeryn demanded.

The puppet master clacked around the rocks and stood in the center of the room. "I guess you could call this the game of 'Life'," he giggled through wooden teeth and cherry painted cheeks. "But one question at a time, young friends. This," the puppet said, grinning and spreading his stick figure wide, "is Zin."

"Zin?" Hunter asked. "What is a Zin?"

"Zin is not a thing, young Hunter. It is a place."

"Looks like cave to me."

"Ahhh, yes, Master Ian. To the untrained eye, that would be so. But you must look deeper to see what is here."

"So, what kind of place is it?" Ian reached down to pick up a black rock, but it skittered across the cave floor away from him, untouched.

"It is a place of great fantasy and wonder, and a place of nothingness. It is neither here, nor there. It is something, yet it is nothing. A place of transition. Here is where you will decide your future."

"Huh?" Ian scratched his head.

"Zin is whatever you want it to be. Think of it like a custom-made playground. You choose what you want, where you will go, and it will be given to you. And to question number two, Mistress Aeryn, your father is here. He has chosen to stay with us." The puppet gritted its wooden teeth together. "Forever."

"What?" It was nearly a shriek.

"Well, almost. His time to make his choice is close." Seeing her distress, he smiled. "Fear not, young child. You can follow in his footsteps, as well. We can all be together forever, one big happy family. And now to the games—"

"What if I don't want to play?" Ian glanced around the room for a reaction from the smaller puppets, but there was none.

"Then I win by default, young man. Because, you see, you have already entered my domain. The only way out is if I allow it. So right now, you all belong to me."

Aeryn inched closer to the other two.

"Now I am a sporting man, of sorts. I will allow you an opportunity to see your father. You can even try to 'rescue' him, if you like. But first, a simple test."

"What kind of test?" Hunter asked.

"To see if you are worthy to stay in my little kingdom. It's simple, really. Around you are four doors. Do not concern yourselves with the one directly behind you. It is merely a storage closet for supplies. It will be of no consequence to you. The other three are your test. Choose the right way out, and I will let you *and* your father go free. But choose wrong, and you will all be my prisoners, forever. You see, life is all about choices."

Before the puppet master had finished the last words, chains began to rattle and bang against the cave's walls. The three looked around. No longer were there puppets lighting the way. Now, the walls were lined with prisoners— people chained to the walls, hanging in misery, their weeping eyes a testament to the suffering that filled them on the inside. Aeryn gasped, clutching the first arm that was handy.

"Yes, it is a sad thing," the puppet master said. "They did not choose well. Let this be a warning to you. You have but one chance, and one chance only. Use it well." He laughed again, a high-pitched, shrill laugh that sent palpable shivers down their spines. Then he spun on his wooden heels and disappeared, dousing the room in a choking, thick blackness.

They're mine!

Chapter 42: Deceive
de·ceive: [dih-seev] *verb,*
to mislead by a false appearance or statement; delude; to
be unfaithful to another.

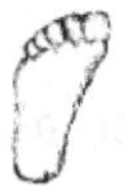

SCREEEEEECCCCCHHHHH
Sulfur wafted through the drafty air again, and the
room erupted in a hazy glow. Above the first door, a lone
hanging prisoner dangled, holding a long, burning,
matchstick. The door beneath him creaked open. Aeryn
gasped.

"Don't move." Hunter blocked the entrance. His keen
senses on edge, nerves raw, they peered through the
doorway and into a dense forest.

"Dad's in there. I can feel it." She was pleading.

"No. It's a trick. Wait here." Hunter turned and ran to
the door behind them— the storeroom door. Flinging it
open, he disappeared inside.

"What does he think he's doing in there?" Ian shook
his head and turned back to the open door at hand.

"Help!" The word flew at them from the thick wood.
"Ian! Aeryn! Is that you?"

Sinclair, 2014, 2016

"Yes, Dad." Aeryn lunged forward, but Ian threw out his arms to block her.

"Wait."

"But he's in there, Ian. We have to rescue him."

"Hunter said it might be a trick. We should wait for him."

Through the trees, a small rustle began.

"What's that smell?" Aeryn recoiled at the odor. "It's like mucky, wet dog."

The rustle turned into a crash. There stood Morgan.

"Dad!" Aeryn's voice neared a frantic level. "I'm coming."

"Hurry," Morgan plead. "Something's after me."

"HAAAAAA!"

Aeryn and Ian jumped at the sound behind them. Hunter leapt from the darkened storage closet. Stripped down to his under shorts, giant mask on his head, he was painted like an Indian warrior. Wooden sticks protruded from his head like the antlers of a deer. "Don't move," he ordered. "Danger is near." Hunter stepped back in front of the door, in front of the other two.

"Hunter," Morgan called. "I can see you, son. You're the only one who can save me from the predator."

Hunter eyed the surroundings, spotting areas that were rustling.

Sinclair, 2014, 2016

"Hunter. I need you. Come now."

Moving leaves parted and three rabid-looking deer emerged. Lips snarling, saliva foaming, and nostrils flaring, they all circled Morgan in the woods.

"Hunter!"

Ian wrapped his arms around Aeryn, holding her tight. Hunter raised his clenched fist, and waited.

The predators circled. Morgan shook, spinning around, trying to keep an eye on them, never letting one get behind him. His eyes teared, and a sob escaped.

Hunter remained stone-like, arm poised, senses sharp.

Morgan turned again, pleading red eyes boring into Hunter's soul.

The arm swung, releasing the stone. It whistled through the air, hitting its mark with deadly accuracy. Striking right between the eyes, Morgan fell to the ground with a blood-curdling scream.

"Daddy!" Aeryn tried to wrench herself from Ian's grip, but he held tight.

The human heap slumped on the ground giggled. It shook with laughter, dissolving into the ground. The room went dark.

Sinclair, 2014, 2016

"Well done, young Hunter," the puppet master's voice boomed from the darkness behind them. "Perhaps this was not the right choice for you."

Scraping and scratching sounds surrounded them. "Where're your clothes, man?" Ian asked.

"In the storeroom."

"Well, put 'em back on, dude. This is a little weird."

"Ok, as soon as I can see again."

SCCCRRREEEEECCCHHHH

Another waft of sulfur, and a second match lit, followed by a second open door.

Cheers and jeers escaped from the second door and bellowed out into the great room outside. Ian was the first to the door jamb. There, inside the room was a half circle of cheering, jeering men, egging on a fight in the middle. Two men slugged it out, pummeling each other to a bloody pulp for the entertainment of the crowd. The half circle surrounding them threw down money, placing bets on who would win, or even survive the match.

They were on what appeared to be a ship. Water separated the three in the doorway from the men on the ship's deck. One fighter was obviously winning, and one losing. The losing man was on his knees, back to the door. He tried, over and over again, to rise to his feet, but time and time again he was pummeled back down. The crowd refused to help, cheering instead for his opponent.

"I'll give 500-to-1 odds that Morgan Welch will battle back and win! Who's a taker here?"

Another blow spun the man on the ground around to face the door. There the kids all looked into the black and blue, bloodied face of Morgan Welch.

"Dad!" Hunter dove for the door, but stopped when he saw the water separating them from the ship's deck.

"No!" Ian jumped in. "It's a trick."

"They're beating him up," Aeryn sobbed. "We have to do something."

"Help him!" Hunter screamed

"No!" Ian still blocked the door.

"You're a coward!" Hunter shoved Ian toward the door. Ian grasped the door jamb and held on tight.

"That's not your dad! It's a trick!" he screamed back. "It's a trick." The slight pause in Hunter's anger was all Ian needed. "This is not a battle we can win. They're trying to divide us. The only way we can get your dad out is if we all stick together. We have to stay calm and keep a level head. Don't let your anger get the best of you. We should only fight the battles we can win. Please, Hunter," Ian pleaded.

The ship and water both disappeared in an angry flash. The room was again doused in darkness.

SCCCRRREEEEECCCCHHHHH

The room flared into bright light again and the third door was already open.

"Aeryn? Hunter? Ian? Where are you? I came to take you home." It was a soft, sweet, woman's voice this time. A familiar voice.

"Mom?" Aeryn's feathers ruffled. She half-ran, half-flew to the last open door. Inside, was the smiling image of her mother, just the way Aeryn had remembered her these long nights here in this strange underworld. She was wearing Aeryn's favorite red dress, and had her hair pulled back into a pony tail, like she always did on the days she worked around the house. Tears sprang to Aeryn's eyes, and she choked back a sob. Until this very minute, she hadn't realized how much she'd missed her mother since this whole ordeal had begun.

A loving maternal hand reached toward the children. "Come. I will help you find your dad. Then we can all go home together."

"I can't do that, Momma."

"Yes, you can, sweetheart."

"No, I can't." She was openly weeping now.

"Why ever not, my sweet baby? Don't you trust your own mother?"

"Yes, absolutely I do." Her resolve strengthened now. Swallowing hard and wiping the tears away from her eyes, Aeryn looked back into the room. "But you're not her."

The picture of love took on a ghostly appearance. The face scrunched up into an angry snarl. "Come here right now!" it barked, echoing off the cave walls. "I mean it. Don't make me come over there, or you'll all be sorry!"

Aeryn turned to the two boys, all standing with their mouths open. "This is not the right room. We can't trust her. She's not our mom."

"NNNNNOOOOOOOOOOOO!" The ear-piercing scream shattered the darkness. The three threw their hands up and covered their ears. The walls shook and the floor rumbled beneath their feet. Boulders shifted and pebbles shot from one end of the room to the other. The darkness flashed with bolts of brilliance, and the puppet master dropped back into the middle of the dimly-lit room.

Around them, the puppet-like humans hung from the walls, holding their burning match-sticks.

"You - must - choose - one," he said pointedly, enunciating each and every word, trying to contain his rising anger.

"No," Hunter said. "That was never the rule. You said we must choose wisely." He swallowed hard. "We choose none."

Rage glared from the puppet master's painted wooden eyes. His anger bored into them and seared on their minds. "Then you shall pay the price for your indecision." The wooden arms clattered, flinging wide. "Seize them!" he commanded.

Sinclair, 2014, 2016

Chapter 43: Temptation

temp·ta·tion [temp-tey-sh*uh* n] *noun;* the act of tempting; enticement or allurement; the fact or state of being tempted, especially to evil

"Where are my manners?" the puppet master gloated. "Release them."

Hunter, Ian, and Aeryn were thrown unceremoniously to the ground. Three puppet guards clacked around them and stood at attention, back against the rock wall at the outskirts of the room.

"Perhaps violence isn't really necessary. We're all intelligent souls, right?" He ambled around the well in the center of the room, to the side where the three were sprawled on the hard volcanic floor. He squatted, peering into their eyes. "You're scared. That's good." Seating himself next to them, he smiled. "I can teach you."

"Teach us what?" Hunter asked.

"Everything!" He doodled on the ground with his wooden finger. "I can teach you how to do magic."

"Magic?" Hunter asked.

Sinclair, 2014, 2016

The puppet nodded. "You see, I know you had help getting here. I know each one of you failed on your own." He looked at Hunter, Ian, and Aeryn, one by one, and went on. "How would you like to never have to depend on anyone ever again? You could be as great as me. You don't need anybody or anything. Why, just think of it! The possibilities are endless!" He laughed that shrill laugh again. "No parents telling you what to do. No 'helpers' making you go through endless tests. Oh, yes," his wooden eyes glistened. "I know all about those weaklings. They didn't help you at all did they? Noooo. But I can."

"How?" Ian scooted a little closer.

"Simple." The word came out as a simple whisper. "Just promise the rest of your life to me."

"What?" Hunter leapt to his feet.

"Now, now. It's not as bad as it sounds, Master Hunter." Puppet scooted over nose-to-nose with him. "The only catch is— and it's so minor it's hardly worth mentioning— but when I call upon you, you must respond. That's all. The rest of your time in all eternity belongs to you. You can do whatever you want, to whomever you want. There are no more rules." Clacking wooden arms spread wide. "You will share all of the same powers that I do. You can 'lead' your own band of misfits and miscreants. You have the brains to do it, too. You three are the smartest pris—, ah, guests I've had in a long, long time. Whaddya say?"

"We say no!" Aeryn was on her feet now. "We didn't have to promise anything to anybody out there, and the Commander helped me, just because He loves me. All I had to do was call out to Him. No strings attached. He did it all. You are a liar, and a cheat. You are not to be trusted and we won't promise anything to you!"

Hunter and Ian joined her, toe-to-toe with the wooden creature.

A nod was his only response. They were seized again from behind by the puppet guards. Forced to the ground for a second time, they were again powerless.

"Now I've got you." The giant puppet's voice echoed from the dark walls of the oubliette and laughed. "You have *not* chosen wisely."

"You can't win," Hunter snapped, his anger rising once again.

"Oh, I can't win?" The puppet laughed a haunting shrill that chilled the three to their very core. "I can't win?" he said again. A disjointed puppet arm flew from its body, striking Hunter squarely across the face and knocking him to the ground. Aeryn screamed and stepped back, only to be thrust forward and over the top of her brother piled on the floor, skinning her hands. She began to cry. Ian, grabbed by the hair, was dragged across the room and forced to his knees in front of the open well, head dangling dangerously over the side, teetering on the edge of the dark abyss.

"I *CAN* win!" the puppet screamed, contorted face changing into the head of the snarling deer that had pursued Hunter in his journey. "And I *WILL* win!" this time twisting into the face of a sea serpent. "Because I *NEVER* lose!" screamed the giant Spatz. Laughter again settled the puppet back to his jointed wooden being. "You see, I have been with you every single step of the way. I know what you have. I know what you know. And, most importantly, I know what you *don't* know." The puppet sauntered over to the children cowering on the floor, pausing at Ian's side. He calmed slightly. "Okay, let's be honest here. Yes, this great Commander, or Great Spirit— whatever you want to call Him— has great powers, even rivaling that of my own." A snarl forced its way onto his crudely painted lips. "And I guess you could say that He loves you, in His own way. Ways that you and I will never understand. But why yoke yourself to another for all eternity? I mean, if He wants you to call on Him in order to be saved from yourself, what fun is that? Here I am giving you all the power for yourself. No middle man! Just think of it, young friends. Every ounce of power coming from within you, whenever you need it, and to do whatever you want. Pure magic. Whaddya say?"

The three remained silent.

"Nothing?" Red eyes glared at Ian. "You can be great, like me."

"You don't have a chance," Ian ground out from between gritted teeth.

"And what you don't know," the puppet snapped back, "is that you cannot possibly win against me." He laughed again. "Oh, it's not your fault. I'm just too—," he hesitated a second admiring his reflection in the water of the well, "—great. Do you believe me, boy?" He winked at his reflection in the water and then smiled at himself. The reflection smiling back was that of a red diamond head, horned, with razor-sharp teeth.

"No." The second the words left Hunter's mouth, a giant wooden foot slammed into his mid-section.

"You will!" the puppet screeched with the shrill of the Spatz. "YOU WILL!"

Hunter was in agony, rolling on the floor holding his stomach, coughing and retching. Aeryn tried to wrap her arms around him to try to protect him, but she couldn't reach. The wooden foot recoiled to strike again. Before it could hit its mark, a huge hairy brown flash from behind knocked the giant puppet guard to the floor. It realigned its appendages and stood, turning to face an angry Bigfoot, snarling and growling with a ferocity that stunned the room. A single blinding blow sent Mikey hurtling into the cold stone walls, landing with an ear-piercing yelp and thud. He slid down the wall leaving a trail of blood behind his head, landing in a motionless heap on the floor. The puppet again rounded on its prey, one step closer to the children, but then froze.

The growl started low. From behind, they could hear the snarling once more. The room looked back to see Mikey begin to stand from a bloodied heap on the cold stone floor. The guttural growl now took on an unearthly tone—deep gnarling thunder reverberated off the stone walls and shook the room. Bigfoot slowly stood to a height twice what he previously had been. Elongated snout, fangs bared and sharpened claws out, he hunched over, hair raised down to the tip of his spine. Nerves raw and senses sharp, he opened his mouth and barked with a force that knocked every living thing to the ground. He continued to grow to an unimaginable height, and from behind, a set of shimmering sterling silver wings unfurled and flapped themselves free, releasing a long glistening sword, engraved with a single word. JUSTICE.

"Michael, my old friend," the puppet said. "Sorry I didn't recognize you sooner. You've changed."

Another ear shattering bark was the reply, knocking the room to the ground a second time. Michael the Warrior began to circle the room. Deep purple eyes, narrowed and glaring, held a tension so intense the room could feel it.

"I really wish you wouldn't do that," the puppet said, laughing as he tried to untangle his arms and legs to stand again. "At my age, it isn't always so easy to get up."

Mikey rounded on him and barked again, blowing back the hair glued to the puppet's painted wooden head.

"And might you be Raphael?" Puppet looked up at the Iron Ranger now hovering over the heads of the hostages. A nod was his only answer. He grew in both color and size, morphing into a creature both frightening and dazzling at the same time. Covered in shining armor from head to toe, iron wings flapping, he descended to the floor next to Aeryn. Electricity sparked and crackled around him, charging the room. Across his glistening chest he bore a single engraved word. HEALING.

"Ryder?" Aeryn whispered. A nod was her answer.

"And where is my old friend, Gabriel?" the puppet asked, unfazed, looking back at Michael. "I don't often expect to see one without the other."

Ian, still dangling precariously over the edge of the well, screamed and jerked back against the force holding his head down. He slid down the outside of the well skinning the side of his face, jerking back when the floor exploded out from under where he had just been. Up through the cavernous hole flew Nestor, but not Nestor. Like Michael, he had transformed into a fierce warrior. Towering over Michael and the others, Gabriel's massive and muscular frame could barely be contained under the ceiling of the dungeonous room. An elongated snout bared the scissor-like teeth of a carnivore, dripping with saliva. His long tail, nine jagged barbs on the tips, whipped around and slammed into the stone wall, ripping down bricks and mortar with the talon-like tips. He, too, hunched over, revealing an equally blazing set of sterling silver wings and glowering royal purple eyes. On his sword as well, a single word; TRUTH. Gabriel circled the room the opposite way from where Michael was, cornering their prey in the dungeon opposite the children. Rearing back, he inhaled so deep he nearly sucked the room into a vacuum with his enormous lung capacity. Extending his neck out flat and head low to the ground, Gabriel let out an earth-shattering roar, unrivaled by that of any dinosaur that had ever walked before. From his mouth blew searing flames, scorching everything in its path. Raphael covered the children with his metal wings.

Puppet, flaming head and hair burned to a crisp, giggled again. "Let the games begin."

"Run!" Out the last door and up the darkened stairway, Raphael led the children now under his sole protection. Flying overhead, toward the battle raging on behind them, flew a multitude of winged creatures from every species, known and unknown. The floor rumbled and shook beneath their feet, the force causing the walls to disintegrate. Raphael's iron wings again shot out, protecting his charges from the crumbling walls. Rocks and wooden beams bounced from his solid metal frame.

"Earthquake!" Ian yelled.

"That's not an earthquake," Raphael shot back over his shoulder as they ran through the dark, dank stairwell. "It's a battle for your souls."

Sinclair, 2014, 2016

Chapter 44: Destiny

des·ti·ny [des-t*uh*-nee] *noun*
something that is to happen or has happened to a
particular person or thing; lot or fortune; the
predetermined, usually inevitable or irresistible, course of
events.

"WAIT! WAIT! WAIT! Everybody just stop!" Ian panted, trying to catch his breath. "What was that?" He paced the landing on the stairwell like a caged animal, his anger boiling over. "What was that? Huh! What? What?" he screamed at Ryder. "That? What! That!"

"Calm yourself, Ian." Ryder checked the stairs, up and down, from their position. Once their safety was ensured, he turned to face the three charges.

"Calm myself? Are you serious? After what I just saw?"

Aeryn took Ian's arm. "Ian, it's okay. He's okay."

"Okay, Aeryn? There's nothing okay about where we are and what just happened!" Ian turned back to Ryder. "And how do you know me? How do you know me? And what was that?"

"That," Ryder stepped in close to Ian, "was a battle you could not possibly have won. That was an enemy far greater than you could ever possibly imagine." He stepped in, nose-to-nose with Ian. "That was your life being saved."

"Who are you?" Ian calmed enough to stop screaming.

"I'm Aeryn's angel."

"Aeryn's what?"

"I'm Aeryn's guardian angel." The battle still raging below them, angry screams and painful groans assailed their senses. "Your angels are still battling back there." A finger pointed downward. "We don't have all day. We need to move."

"I have an angel?" Ian looked dumbfounded.

"Yes, Ian. Nestor is your angel. And Hunter," Ryder looked at him, "Mikey is yours. We are assigned by the Great Commander to keep you safe and battle for you when you cannot battle for yourselves."

"I am not alone?" Hunter asked.

"Sometimes you see us. Most of the time you don't, but we're always here."

"How did I get you?" Ian's mind was working overtime. Ryder could see his scrunched brows and tilted head. "I don't understand."

"When you accept that there is a power greater than yourselves ruling this place we call home, you are assigned a protector, a guardian angel who is willing to give his life to keep you safe from the enemy. You don't have to be perfect, Ian. You don't need to carry the burdens of this life by yourself. You are not alone here. You have friends you never even knew about here to help you. Lean on us or, at the very least, stay out of our way so we can do our jobs."

"What about my dad?" Aeryn's plea pierced Ryder's heart. "Where's his angel?"

"He has not yet accepted this truth, Aeryn. We need to get to him before it's too late. His angel awaits. Time is short. The end is coming for him."

Ian jumped, throwing his arms in the air. "Then what are we waiting for! Let's move." He looked forward and then back. "Which way?" Hearing the sounds of the battle wafting toward them again, he shrank back behind Ryder. "You can lead."

At the top of the dark, dank staircase sat an equally dark, imposing door.

A closed door.

Ian was the first to reach it. Grasping the knob, he wrenched with all his might.

Nothing.

"Open it." Hunter was on his heels.

"It won't turn, man. I'm trying."

"Let me see." Hunter grabbed the knob and cranked.

Nothing.

"It's hot." He jerked his hand back, rubbing it on his jeans.

"This is the top of the volcano." Ryder's voice came from behind, "the place of no return. This is the entrance to the gates of misery and pain."

The three stared at him tucking his silver wings back, yet still holding his glistening silver sword.

"Listen to me, and listen well, for this is the time when you must stand up for yourselves. The choices you make now will determine where, and if, the rest of your life will go on." Ryder choked back a thick sob. Ear-piercing screams and the rumble of rock battled away beneath them.

How can I make them understand?

"Where's my dad?" Aeryn's pleading look stung his tearing eyes.

Sinclair, 2014, 2016

"Listen to me carefully, all of you. Morgan is on the other side of that door. You will need to draw on everything you have learned to make him turn from this evil."

"How can we save him?"

"You cannot save him, only he can save himself. You can lead him the right way, but the choice must be his and his alone. The time is right. His heart is open, but you must lead him away. It is a job that only you three can do. Others would fail. This is your time, and your destiny. It is what you were called for."

"How do we save ourselves?"

Again Ryder's heartstrings tugged at the look in her pleading eyes.

"You know the way, Aeryn. Trust your instincts. Step out in faith." Ryder squeezed Hunter's shoulder. "The enemy is a fierce hunter, ready to strike. Strike back when you need to. Do not be afraid." He placed a strong arm around Ian's shoulder. "Do not let anger cloud your judgment and your senses. Lean on one another, and when the time is right, let go and fly."

A fierce, snarling growl echoed up from the stairwell. Clashing metal and searing flames burst up through the darkness towards them.

"Go," Ryder urged.

"That's Mikey!" Hunter turned back from the group. "I need to help him."

"Michael is a trained warrior. He is fulfilling his destiny, as you must now fulfill yours." Muscular arms raised overhead, Ryder struck the door with his sword. It blew from its hinges, flying through the air, barreling end over end, and splashing into the bubbling molten lava, bursting into flames and disappearing in a brilliant flash.

"GO!" Ryder ordered. "NOW!"

Towering silver wings shot outward striking the volcanic walls. Rocks and ash fell to the ground under the sheer force of the blow. Ryder turned back, and raced toward the battle raging below.

Chapter 45: Freedom
Free·dom [free-d*uh* m] *noun*
the state of being **free** or at **liberty** rather than in
confinement or under physical restraint; the power to
determine action without restraint.

"What do we do now?" Ian shied back from the lava boiling through the open doorway.

"I don't know, but Dad's in there," Hunter said. "We have to get him out."

"We've come so far. We can't stop now." Aeryn wiped at the tears erupting from her beautiful brown eyes.

"We can never survive the volcano, Aeryn." Hunter tried to reason with his sister. "Dad can't, either. He may already be dead."

"No!" she screamed. "He's not!" She backed away from the two boys. "That's a lie!"

Ian stepped in now. "Aeryn, we don't have the resources to do this on our own. Ryder deserted us up here. We're all alone."

"No, he would never do that," she insisted. "We can do this."

"That's boiling lava. It's like nine billion degrees. Did you see what happened to the door?"

She backed up from Ian even further. "No, we can do this."

"We don't have any help. They're gone. They're all gone. We can't do this alone." Ian still tried to reason with her.

"'Step out in faith', Ryder said." She looked at the door. "Things are not always what they seem." As she reflected inwardly on her thoughts, her feathers popped out, one at a time. "'Step out in faith', he told me. So here goes, Ryder."

She bolted for the door and launched herself from the edge, disappearing into the steam and smoke rising from the glowing red bubbling rock.

"No!" Hunter screamed and bolted after his sister, grabbing Ian's arm on the way.

"Oh, no!" were Ian's last words before hurtling through the doorway toward their torturous death.

THUD.
THUD.

Sinclair, 2014, 2016

"AAAYYYIIIEEE NNNOOOOO!"

Hunter and Ian slammed down onto a rocky formation just under the doorway.

"What was that?" Ian demanded. "Are you trying to kill me?"

"No, you idiot, I'm trying to save you." Hunter turned to face Ian on the rocky outcropping.

"St-o-o-o-o-o-o-p." Morgan spied the boys. "You have to le-e-e-a-a-ve this pla-a-a-ce. Not sa-a-a-a-fe." He tried to move their direction, but was still chained to his fellow sheeple. One by one, they were being led over the brink and falling into the volcano's flaming pit. "Where is A-a-a-a-a-e-ryn?"

"AAAYYYIIIEEEE!" The scream came from above. Morgan and the boys looked up to see her wildly flapping her wings, flipping over and over in the heated updraft from the pit's liquid heat.

"Hu-u-u-u-u-nter. Do-o-o-o-o so-o-o-o-o-meth-i-i-i-i-ing." Morgan's eyes teared as he stood on the rocks, inching closer and closer to the hell pit below.

"There's nothing that can be done," a wicked voice snapped.

The serpent's head and long neck rose from the liquid center of the volcano. Droopy lips drew back in a wicked smile, revealing the razor-sharp teeth within.

"You see," the serpent said, "humans are easy prey. You are my targets." It smiled, looking more like a snarl. "Once I set my sights on you, there's nothing you can do. Your free will is gone. There is no more freedom of choice. You are mine, and there isn't a blasted thing on this planet that you can do about it." It laughed. Deep and guttural, the growling sound pleased its owner. "Leap," he commanded, and the first sheep with its human head teetered off the volcanic ledge and into the flames below. The line moved forward. "See." he said. "Helpless."

The sky began to rumble above. Sinister dark clouds formed, hovering directly overhead.

"Useless." Another sheeple fell off, and the line stepped forward.

Lightning ripped across the sky. The following roar of thunder shook the lava ledge they were perched on.

"Weak." One more sheeple disappeared. Morgan stepped up. "Stupid."

"No!" Hunter screamed.

Lightning struck the mountaintop. Thunder clapped. Morgan teetered on the edge of the ledge, unbalanced and falling forward.

Aeryn dove, fighting the thermal air pockets to get to her father. An updraft caught her, sending her flapping off away from him. At the last second before he fell, Morgan turned, locked eyes with the boys, and disappeared over the edge.

"Dad!" Hunter screamed, diving toward the edge, grabbing Ian on the way.

"No!" Ian screamed.

"He-e-e-e-lp   me-e-e-e.   Ple-e-e-e-a-a-ase!" Morgan screamed.

A blinding flash of lightning tore open the sky one more time, and the thunderous roar of the earth crying out followed.

And then, the whole world went black.

Again.

Lightning slashed through the darkness, lighting up the night sky in its blazing fury. The electric blue arc crackled and buzzed, splitting into five separate jagged bolts, still attached at one end. The bolts raced toward the falling four, plunging high speed toward their certain death. Passing them, the bolts expanded in yet another blinding flash, to form a giant hand. Grabbing the four, it slowed their descent, cradling them gently, protectively, until settling them safe on the ground. One final brilliant flash tore open the darkened sky, and the hand from above retracted, then disappeared.

Morgan, Ian, Aeryn, and Hunter all sat quiet, staring at one another, no one able to trust their legs or find their voices.

"He has many names," a voice from behind said. "Great One, Master, Healer, Father. He cares not what you call Him. His favorite is Father, or Dad, if you will."

The group looked around. Morgan was on his feet— two of them, the sheep's body now gone. He spun around, seeking the source of the voice. Seeing it, he froze.

Out from the shadows, stepped a magnificent, perfect, eight-point buck with deep, royal purple eyes. It spoke again. "He wants you to know that He loves you, and will protect you when you call upon Him. You are His, and He is yours—forever."

"How—, wha—" Morgan broke off.

Hunter stepped forward. Reaching out, he nudged the snout of the giant creature. It reciprocated the affection, turning its giant head toward the young man. "You have come far, young Hunter. You have overcome your fears and learned to face your enemy without flinching. You are a great warrior, but you are only great because you know that you cannot do this alone. He is

Sinclair, 2014, 2016

very proud of you. You have learned much, about yourself and about others." The buck turned to the others.

"Miss Aeryn, you have learned to let go and truly soar. There are no limits for you now. Be proud. The Great One sees you, and He likes what He sees. Did you know you smile when you fly?"

She beamed, blushing.

"Master Ian, master of adventure, master of your own anger. You have done well. It pleases Him to see you step back and think your way out of things, rather than fight. You have used your brain well. Do not stop now. There is much yet to do."

"And Master Morgan," he said. "You, sir, are forgiven for all wrongs and shortcomings. You have shown your sorrow and shame. Your ransom has been paid. You are free to go." He blinked back at the others. "You must all go back to your world above and tell them. Tell them you are not alone. Tell them there are helpers here to fight for you every single day of your lives. They will not rest until they know you are safe. There is evil in this world, but that evil cannot prevail. You must tell them. Make haste. Time is growing short."

"How will we get there—home, I mean?" Morgan looked skyward, to the rock ceiling above. "And how will we know our helpers can actually help us?" Morgan asked.

Aeryn took her father's hand. "You have to trust them, Dad. They won't let you down."

"Nothing is impossible for those who believe," the buck said. "Your helpers will bring you home. It has been a long journey, but the journey is just beginning. It will not be enough just to get home. Home is where the real work will begin."

"Thank you." Hunter nodded toward the buck.

"Just remember," the final warning came. "We are everywhere. Look carefully. What you think you see, and what you actually see are, at times, two different things. Perception is the difference. Learn to discern." The buck winked a purple eye at the group and turned back toward the shadows.

"Wait." Aeryn stepped forward. "Will I ever see you again?"

The buck nodded, giant antler rack lowering almost as if in a formal bow. "We are a forever family now. Nothing can separate us for the remainder of all time."

"Tell Him, thank you," Morgan asked the buck, "please. Umm. Father, I mean."

"He hears you, Master Morgan. Just speak as though He was standing right next to you, for in actual fact, He truly is... for all time.

"Therefore go and make disciples of all nations, baptizing them in the name of the Father and of the Son and of the Holy Spirit †, and teaching them to obey everything I have commanded you. And surely I am with you always, to the very end of the age."

~ Jesus of Nazareth,
The Holy Bible, Matthew 28:19-20 NIV

Epilogue

"I thought he said that our helpers would guide us." Morgan looked around, a bit nervous still.

"They are." Aeryn was in the lead.

"Where?" Ian shot forward. "I don't see anything but green leaves."

"Look closer." She stopped. Youngest of the group, but by far the most confident now, she winked his direction.

"I'm sorry. What was that?" Ian demanded.

"What?" She smiled.

Hunter and Morgan caught up with them.

"Why did you do that? Why?"

"What's wrong?" Hunter asked, looking back and forth between his little sister and his best friend.

"She winked at me. Your kid sister winked. At me!"

"Did not." Aeryn smiled.

"Did, too."

"Did not. "

The leaves rustled behind them, slightly at first, but then a little louder. "She, in fact, did not, sir. She winked at me."

The group turned and faced a large Praying Mantis resting on a low hanging branch of a giant redwood-type feathery tree.

Ian's hand flew out to smash it. Aeryn screamed, and a dozen more even larger insects converged on the scene. An even larger mantis addressed the group. "I wouldn't do that. Not if you want continued protection up in the world."

"You- You're, a, a-" Morgan's mouth hung open. "Helper?"

"Some of us are, sir, but not all."

"Wow." Ian withdrew his hand. "Sorry. I should have known better."

"Yes, Master Ian, you certainly should have. You, of all three young ones, embraced your life down here. You did not fight against it as the others did."

He smiled, and nodded.

"You truly loved your pirate friends, did you not?"

Another nod.

"And one should love their friends as they love themselves. It is the right way."

A little green flash trailing hysterical laughter dashed by in front of them. "I found it. It's mine! Mine, I sayz. Alls mine!"

The mantis heads all turned to follow Alistair's little leprechaun body toward the end of the rainbow that still hung over their heads, their multi-faceted eyes reflecting his little running body in the sunlight.

"GGGGOOOOLLLLLLDDDDDDDDDD!!!!!!!!!" The scream wafted back on the wind.

The bushes rustled again, and there was the buck, purple eyes glistening, just the hint of a smile on his face. "Take our friends safely home, please. Daylight grows short, and the darkness will bring danger."

"Danger?" Morgan's face grew weary, eyes darting, hands clenched.

"Worry not, Master Morgan, for you have seen the light. This does not mean that you will be free from troubles in your life, but you will have others to call upon during times of crisis. Never forget this. And never," the buck turned to Ian, "forget your friends."

"Be we together, or be we apart," Ian whispered.

"None kin tear ye and yer brothers apart!" The chorus drifted down from above. Ian jerked his head up to see the Wayfarer floating in the clouds above, every pirate hanging over the side, yelling and cheering at their friend below. He leapt into the air, waving frantically at his friends on high. "I telled ye ye's could comes back iffin ye did weel, laddie." A rope dropped from the sky. "Man overboard! Drop the sails and hold the riggins. Get ye yungun up here's so's we kin get! Thar's sailin' to be's done!"

Ian leapt at the opportunity, never looking back. Hoisted up into the clouds, the ship disappeared into the dusky sky, leaving no trace behind.

"He has made his choice." The buck turned back to the group. "Take great care returning home, my friends. There will be many questions. Hold tight to what you know is the truth. Do not be afraid to let your light shine."

Morgan stepped forward. "That day, in the forest, when I first saw you—"

The deer nodded.

"I was going to—"

The deer swallowed.

"I'm sorry."

"Fear not, Master Morgan. I will still be with you for all time. I am now your helper. Let's go home.

Hebrews 13:2, NIV
Do not forget to show hospitality to strangers,
for in doing so,
some have shown hospitality to angels
without knowing it.

...Angels walk this world with us.
Where is yours?

See Life Differently
Re-Invent the Impossible.

Join *The Impossibilities Blog*, at
http://www.sinclairinkspot.com/the-impossibilities-
blog.html

Coming Soon: Book 2

<u>*Darkness RiZing*</u>

Justice [juhs-tis] **noun**
The administering of deserved punishment or reward; the maintenance or administration of what is just by law, as by judicial or other proceedings.

Bang.

The gavel slammed onto the tall oak desk at the front of the courtroom.

"All Rise. Court is now in session. The Honorable James Williams, presiding."

"Be seated," the judge ordered, whisking his way into the room and up onto the platform that set him above all others in the room. "Bailiff, are all parties present?"

"All parties are present and accounted for, your honor. They have been sworn in."

"Very well; Morgan Welch, please rise. Bailiff, read the charges."

The officer of the court stood tall, facing the defense table and cleared his throat. "You are hereby charged with Involuntary Manslaughter in the negligent death of Ian Murray, a minor child in your custody at the time of his disappearance and subsequent death."

"Thank you, Bailiff." Judge Williams turned to face Morgan and his defense team. "How do you plead?"

"Not guilty," Morgan's attorney stated.

"He's not dead, sir," Morgan blurted out. Morgan's attorney placed her hand on his shoulder, trying to calm him. "This is all a terrible mistake."

Ian's family was on their feet. "You're a liar!" Mr. Murray, Sr. shouted. "You left him out there to die all alone!"

Ian's mother broke down and sobbed.

BANG. BANG. BANG.

"Order in this court!" Judge Williams was on his feet. "You will hold your tongue, Mr. Murray! Is that clear?"

Ian Murray, Sr. nodded, unable to trust his own temper.

"Anyone who cannot maintain their composure will be escorted from this courtroom. Now, sir, I ask you again; guilty or not guilty, Mr. Welch?"

"Not guilty," Morgan got out.

There was a low grumble in the back of the room, but no single voice was loud enough to be made out.

BANG. BANG.

Morgan glanced back over his shoulder at his family seated directly behind the defense table. Wife, Mary; son, Hunter; and daughter, Aeryn, all smiled, holding hands and trying to be as encouraging as they could.

"Very well, are there any motions from counsel?"

"Meagan Moore, counsel for the defendant, Your Honor. We would like to ask that the defendant be released on his own recognizance at this time."

Again the room erupted into disarray. Mr. Murray, Sr. was on his feet in an instant. "No, you don't! He killed my son, and you want him to walk away with no bail?"

BANG. BANG. BANG.

"Sir, this is an outrage," Mr. Murray pleaded with the judge. "He was my only child, and now—, " His emotion got the best of him and his voice cracked. "I'll never see him again."

Mrs. Murray was still sobbing into her handkerchief, inconsolable.

BANG. BANG. BANG.

"Look, Mr. and Mrs. Murray, I understand the position that you are in, but it is my job to make sure that due process is followed. He is not guilty until proven so by a jury. I promise you that a trial will happen. But for now, if I have to speak to you again, you will be banished from my courtroom for the remainder of these proceedings. DO YOU UNDERSTAND?"

Again, two nods were the only answer.

"Opposing counsel. Motions?"

"Your Honor, Jacob Pike, County Prosecutor. We oppose release without bail for a number of reasons," the man in black said with no emotion whatsoever. "Primarily, Mr. Welch poses a flight risk. He is a trained hunter and outdoorsman who knows how to escape without being seen." He wiped tiny beads of sweat from his brow and cleared his throat to continue. "Moreover, we believe that his life is in danger should he be released."

"What?" This time it was Morgan who was on his feet.

"Ms. Moore, control your client, please." Judge Williams held the gavel tightly in his hand, at the ready for another outburst.

She grabbed Morgan's arm, dragging him back down to his seat. "Shhhh!" she warned.

"Explain," the judge ordered.

"Certainly, Your Honor. Not only," counsel explained, "is there the threat from the outraged community and the victim's family, should these parties be unfortunate enough to meet, but there is also the matter of Mr. Welch's mental state."

"My what?" Morgan turned to his red-headed attorney. "Is he kidding?"

Jerked back quiet again, Ms. Moore glared a severe warning at him.

"If I may continue, Your Honor?" the chubby, black-suited attorney asked politely.

"Please do."

"When Mr. Welch and the Welch children first returned from being lost in the wilderness for days, Mr. Welch told a bizarre story of being kidnapped by a sea serpent, becoming — a sheep of all things, and leaping into an active volcano."

The courtroom erupted in laughter, encouraging the opposing counsel, while Morgan turned a rosy shade of pink.

"If I've got it right, Your Honor, there was a tree that was not a tree but a vending machine, pirates, a paramilitary boot camp, Indians, and gnomes."

"No," Morgan blurted. "No gnomes; he was a leprechaun."

Now the courtroom lost complete control.

BANG. BANG. BANG.

"Order! Order in my court!"

BANG. BANG. BANG.

"Order! Bailiff, clear the room."

Once settled, Judge Williams took his chair again.

"Well, we certainly have a unique situation here, don't we?" He sighed. "For the first time in my career I am at a loss." He turned to Morgan. "Please rise, Mr. Welch."

Morgan rose, as did his family behind him, and his counsel. "I happen to agree with the Prosecutor. For your own safety, and for the safety of your family and this community, I order you to be held without bail until trial."

"No," Hunter's mom collapsed back into her seat, both kids flanking her on either side for support.

"Furthermore, I order you to undergo a full psychiatric evaluation to determine your mental state prior to trial."

"Sir," Morgan pleaded, "Ian's not dead."

"Can you take me to him?" the judge asked.

"Ummm. Well, not exactly; he's under the ground, in that other world."

BANG.

"So ordered. Bailiff, take Mr. Welch into custody and remand him to the psychiatric ward of the County Jail until further notice. Court adjourned."

BANG.

Judge Williams stood and whisked out of the room.

Morgan pulled back against the grip of the police on either side of him. "No, please!" he begged. "Let me say goodbye to my family."

They nodded. "You have one minute."

"Mary, it will be all right. Just give me some time to figure this out."

She was still sobbing, unable to look her husband in the eye.

"Hunter; you have to save me, Son."

"How, Dad? How can I save you?"

"Go back and bring Ian home. It's the only way. You are the only one who can do it. You are the man of the house now that I'm in here. I need you."

Hunter said nothing, soaking in the true meaning of the request, he stared blankly into his father's face.

"Go, Hunter. Go find the others. Get the helpers and bring Ian home. It's the only way."

"Sir, let's go." The police officers pushed Morgan toward the side door which led back to the holding cells. Morgan continued to yell while being led away.

"It's the only way, Hunter. You're the only one who can do this! It's all up to you, Son! Go! Bring Ian home!"

The door slammed behind him, leaving Hunter, Aeryn, and Mary all alone in the courtroom.

Hunter was stunned, and Mary in shock. Aeryn leaned over and whispered to her big brother. "Can I come, please?"

Check for the Official Release Date
For *Darkness RiZing* at:

www.SinclairInkSpot.com
or
www.thePriZinofZin.com

Loretta Sinclair
Re-Inventing the Impossible
http://www.sinclairinkspot.com/the-impossibilities-blog

~There's no friend like God!

All Bible verses are from the NIV version
©Zondervan Press

All Dictionary quotes are from ©Miriam Webster's
Online Dictionary, or ©Dictionary.com

Used under United States Copyright Code
Under Title 17 of the U.S. Code
Fair Use Rule